A REIMAGINED FAITH

BOOK 1 • FAITH REIMAGINED SERIES

J. A. BOUMA

PROLOGUE

THEY CALL it the soul's dark night, that gauntlet of spiritual doubt, frustration, and crisis on one's journey toward full union with God.

Saint John of the Cross wrote the book on it. Therese of Lisieux was plunged headlong into its icy darkness. Even Mother Theresa, that shimmering example of Christian faithfulness, experienced its wet-blanket suffocation for nearly fifty years.

Apparently I was in good company.

It was comforting to know that I wasn't alone as I traveled through the angsty ravine of faith deconstruction and reconstruction the likes of which I'd never experienced before. I was comforted that others had traversed its rocky paths ahead of me, charting a course and serving as trusted guides and kindred spirits for my own exploration of the outer reaches of faith.

For I was wholly ill-equipped for that leg of my spiritual journey.

Questioning the Bible and faith and God were never allowed in my neck of the Christian woods. I was bred the kind of Christian who accepted faith at face value. We all were. Generations deep.

"God said it, that settles it, I believe it!" was the foundation upon which my beliefs bloomed from seedling to petaled daffodil.

Yet, when the winds blew, the rain came, and the waters rose, that foundation couldn't hold my faith's rickety structure. I discovered, as much to my family's surprise as my own, that it was a facade assembled with duct tape and bailing wire.

I've realized there comes a time in the pilgrimage of every Christian through this life when they reach a crisis moment. Storytellers have a word for this kind of thing. *Inciting incident* they call it. A catalyst, a fork in the road, a blue-red-pill moment when you're beckoned, wooed, shoved face forward and summoned to decide the fate of your own faith—for yourself.

For some, that moment comes through the fiery furnace of political oppression, where the summoning happens in a dark, dank cell; staring down the barrel of a shotgun; or dangling from the end of a slipknot.

For others, it's less dramatic yet just as petrifying. Social oppression might force the choice between family blood or Christ's blood. Professional oppression might force the choice between remaining closeted or coming out, so to speak.

Regardless of the *how*, the *what* is always the same.

The day of reckoning for me, Peter Daniel Young, came through the most unlikeliest of places.

Religious vocation.

Which made sense the more I thought about it. Because it's when we are most required to give a reason for the hope we have in Christ that we are also required to own that reason. To own the scaffolding of reasons that have been assembled over the years to support the elements of that faith. Whether for others or for one's self.

For over twenty-five years on this rock-of-a-planet, I had cobbled together an assortment of planks and beams to construct my faith. Come to find out, they weren't as stable as I once assumed. One by one, I found them disconnecting and tumbling all around me as I helped mentor college students, walking with them through life and their own spiritual journey. The Lord seemed to be dismantling the Christian structure I had carefully pieced together over the years.

And that was all at once frightening and exhilarating!

I didn't have a clue where the path cutting through the valley of death's dark shadow would lead me. Whether I would survive my deconstruction and evolve into a new state of faith through my reconstruction efforts. Or whether it would destroy me and my faith.

All I knew was this:

I couldn't go back to where I was. Yet I didn't have a clue where I was going.

This is the story of my faith's death and rebirth.

This is my story reimagining the Christian faith.

CHAPTER 1

"LORD, we come to you this morning praying for the field you've given us to harvest, believing that you will help us bring in the bountiful sheaves of converts this day!"

Roger always started our Monday morning ministry team meeting this way, praying as if the people we were trying to reach were a field of collard greens or radishes waiting to be plucked for a dinner salad. I knew Jesus used that language himself, but wasn't there a better way—a modern way—of talking about what we did? Of coming alongside people as guides on the side through their journeys, rather than sages on a stage dispensing super-secret spiritual insight as if we had it all figured out?

Because we didn't. At least I didn't anymore. At all.

"We ask that your Word would go forth and convict the students of their sins. Lord, save the students whom you've chosen and whom you've entrusted to our care. And we pray that you would just produce a bountiful harvest through our efforts at Georgetown University."

There's that language again: Sinner. Save. Harvest. Although that *chosen* bit was new, though not surprising coming from hyper-conservative Roger MacArthur.

"We pray that the enemy would be bound and prevented from disrupting our work, so that you would reign on that campus. In Jesus' name we pray. Amen."

Amen, we echoed dutifully.

"Good morning team!" Roger exclaimed as if under the influence of a gallon of coffee. "Are you ready to save some pagans today?"

You'd think I was exaggerating with that "pagans" comment. Nope. That's Roger: us vs. them all the way.

"So who wants to go first?"

Each morning at Campus Ministry, the college group where I worked, we began the week with a team meeting of the ministry leaders and office staff, all huddled up on faux Victorian couches in a cramped meeting room straight out of a '90s issue of Better Homes and Gardens, with its gaudy green flower-pattern wallpaper and the hovering scent of way too much potpourri. My immediate boss, Bernard Walsh, sat to my right, but everyone called him Bernie. Across from him was Ainsley Jones, an underling ministry leader like me and our resident Southern Belle. Next to her sat her boss Peggy Smith. Tabitha Washington to my left, a sweet woman who was a cross between Calpurnia from *To Kill a Mockingbird* and my mom, Maggie, managed the office. And then there was Roger, our fearless Executive Director sitting at the head who was a cross between Andy Griffith and Ned Flanders: meant well and was the kind of guy you'd want stopping to help change your tire in the dead of night, but his dutiful Christian demeanor was a cartoon caricature of Christianity. He was nice enough, treating me like the son he never had, but lately I had grown annoyed by his bumper-sticker Christianity.

"Peter?" I heard Roger say.

I looked up and noticed the rest of the room eyeballing me. Apparently, I had zoned out.

"Yes?" I quickly said.

"Would you like to start us off with a ministry update?"

Sure thing. Why not.

"Sure. So this week I'm launching a study using Dan Brown's book *The Da Vinci Code*."

"Now, by study you mean *Bible* study, isn't that right?" Roger questioned, the caterpillars chilling above his eyes wiggling with suspicion.

"Well, it's not really a Bible study, per se," I responded, trying to rein in my irritation. "More of a book study with a side of Bible."

I chuckled, thinking they would appreciate my wit. All I got was a room full of blank faces.

"Now, Peter, we talked about this. We want to get our students in the Word. Because, as the book of Hebrews says, it is *alive* and *active*. It's what's sharper than any double-edged sword, penetrating even to dividing soul and spirit, joints and marrow. The *Bible* is what judges the thoughts and attitudes of the heart. Not Dan Brown's *The Da Vinci Code*."

I stifled a sigh and dropped my head slightly. It wasn't even nine and I was already ready for a stiff one.

I said, "I get that, but I'm trying to meet my students where they're at. They're the ones who wanted to do this thing. They suggested it. And my goal with the study is to point them to Scripture along the way. Point out the problems with Brown's book and then relate it to what's real about the Christian faith."

"Sounds good, Pete," Roger said, his white, gleaming teeth shining bright and strong. "But maybe next time you could do a study on, say, Romans. Give them a good dose of the gospel!"

Sure thing. Why not.

"Thanks, Roger. I'll take that under consideration."

I moved on before I burst a blood vessel, talking about my new student visits and other mentoring relationships. This seemed to mollify the chief for the time being.

"Thanks for your report, Pete. Oh, before I forget, we're sending you and Ainsley to Dallas for evangelism training."

"Evangelism training?" I asked, brows raised in obvious suspicion.

"Yes, our *Everyday Evangelism* training program. You're gonna just love it, Pete! Dr. Harrison is teaching this session. What a treat that will be."

I bet.

"You leave in a month so make sure you both block off the end of the week. So how about Peggy?" Again, the over-caffeinated exclaiming. "Did you get in touch with Alfred Morris's people?"

Alfred Morris? As in the *Creation Studies Institute* Alfred Morris? I felt my brow involuntarily wrinkling, my eyes narrowing, my lips pursing.

"Yes, Roger, I did!" Peggy said with as much over-caffeinated hype. "And he's agreed to come do a seminar."

"Thank you, Jesus! That's wonderful."

"Excuse me," I interrupted, "but what are we talking about?"

"Pete, you're gonna just love it. Peggy and Bernie and I were dreaming about ways to reach our young people with Christianity. So we thought, what better way than with a seminar on science?"

"A seminar on science?" I said, my face falling as I looked from Roger to Bernie to Peggy and back to Roger again.

"We all know the primary way secular society destroys what little faith our students have is through the science curriculum. So, we've invited Alfred Morris to come and set them straight. We're planning on using his visit as a major outreach event."

For real? They thought Freddy Morris was going to reach my students? And set them straight on science?

Are you kidding me?

"That sounds great," I heard myself saying, smiling and nodding on cue.

The rest of the staff shared updates from their past week and outlined their next week ahead. I sat stewing over the backwardness of my ministry.

Did they not realize we were swimming in an entirely different culture than generations past? It's so cliché, so overused, but also so true: we're not in Kansas anymore, Toto!

"Alright, gang," I heard Roger say as I continued stewing. "That's a wrap." He clapped his hands together and jumped up, like he usually did, saying what he usually said:

"Onward Christian soldiers!"

We said what we usually said:

"With the cross of Jesus going on before!"

It's funny, because growing up in my little country church in Coopersville, Michigan, I loved that old hymn. Sang it with all the gusto of a West Point cadet in training.

Now...not so much.

I shuffled back to my desk to retrieve my laptop and Bible, a new NIV I started using a few months ago. If Roger ever found out I was using the "gender inclusive" translation, he'd blow a KJV-only gasket. Whatever. It's what my students resonated with. It's what *I* resonated with.

"Hey, Peter," Peggy said, popping her head into my cubicle.

"Mornin'. What's up?"

"I wondered if you had time to pass some of these flyers out this afternoon?" She gave me a stack of paper advertising the Freddy Morris event.

"Pegs..." I moaned. "You know I hate handing these sorts of

things out. I feel like some New York merchant peddling counterfeit purses."

"I know, but we need to get the word out, Pete. At the very least, can you hand them to your students? Maybe hang a few up on the bulletin boards in the student center?"

I sighed, thinking my students were the last people I wanted coming to this, quote, *science seminar,* unquote. But I caved.

"Sure." I snatched the flyers from her and stuffed them in my bag. "Gotta run, Pegs."

"Thanks, Pete," she said, side-hugging me. "You're the best."

"Don't mention it," I mumbled as I headed out into my day.

CHAPTER 2

WHAT A WAY TO start the morning. Reminded me of everything I had been struggling with the past few months, with the faith I'd been handed and all of its backwardness and anti-scienceness and disconnect from real, modern life.

And now I'm stuck with this version of Christianity, even paid to stuff it down the throats of my college friends...

I lumbered down the stairs, head down and sighing in frustration as a growing sense of unease about my future blossomed into an ache in the middle of my forehead. I reached the bottom and went to massage the bridge of my nose when my phone vibrated. I pulled it out to find a text message from one of my guys, Clint.

We need to talk, it simply read.

I stopped short of the door exiting our office. My pulse quickened as I texted him back, wondering what was going on, trying to glean more information. He gave me nothing in response, other than a time and place to meet: 9:30 at Saxbys, the neighborhood coffee shop and our watering hole for meeting up.

I pushed my shirt cuff back to check the time. That was in

eight minutes. I texted him back and told him to sit tight, I was on my way.

Before I stepped outside, I said a quick prayer for guidance. Then I grabbed my umbrella at the front door and unfurled it as I stepped out of our row house onto soggy O Street. Sitting two blocks over from campus had its advantages, especially on stormy days like today that brought the full fury of fall to bear on our neighborhood street.

Orange and brown leaves stuck to my shoes as I sloshed down the street in the direction of Georgetown University to grab coffee with my friend Clint Winslow. Clint was a junior double-major in neurobiology and philosophy. Smart as whip, for sure. And way above my pay grade. We struck up a friendship after he attended one of our on-campus lecture seminars we used to connect with new students. We brought in British bioethicist Nigel Cameron, who, unlike Freddy Morris, gave an intellectually stimulating discussion about the ethics of taking, making, and faking human life from a Christian perspective. Clint was struck by Nigel's sound, sturdy arguments and took an interest in the rest of our ministry offerings.

We hit it off instantly, connecting over a shared love of tea, jazz, and backpacking. We also resonated because of our shared Christian stories: we both grew up in small Midwest towns and even smaller conservative fundamentalist churches. Lately, though, many of our conversations about faith and life had turned negative. Clint began to have serious questions and doubts about Christianity. Or at least the version of the faith handed to him as a child. I totally understood his angst, having begun to question the version of Christianity I'd known for two decades myself.

I threw open the grayish-blue door to our favorite stomping ground to find relief from the relentless rain, overcome with the force of brewing coffee, baking blueberry muffins, and the rumble of conversations. The red-brick space anchoring the corner of

35th and O Street since the eighteenth century was packed with students grabbing a caffeine and sugar fix before class. Offering a dose of cheer that fall-drenched morning was a display of orange flowers sitting on top of cases filled with cookies and breads and bagels and scones, greeting and tempting patrons waiting in line. Grey plastic tables and chairs lined the walls and filled small alcoves in the back and across from the register, all brimming with folks putting last-minute touches on papers or cramming for tests, or both.

I folded my umbrella and scanned the space searching for Clint. There he was; I should have known better.

Clint had already settled into our favorite spot, sitting in a high back chair in the bay window with a large coffee and chocolate croissant, his favorite.

"Brother," I said, unzipping my jacket and setting my bag on the chair across from him.

"Thanks for coming, Pete," he said with tired eyes uncharacteristic of him.

"You OK? You look like someone died."

"In a manner of speaking...yeah, *something* has died."

Lord Jesus, give me strength and give me words...

"Alright, man, alright. Let me get a coffee and something to eat."

I matched Clint's large coffee but traded the chocolate croissant for a blueberry scone. I settled into my chair, thunder rumbling in the near distance. The fall morning storm continued its assault on the bay windows, large drops slapping the panes with purpose and furnishing a foreboding backdrop to our conversation.

I sipped my coffee, noticing Clint's well-worn Bible resting on the small table between our chairs, bent page markers peeking out at odd angles from wrinkled, red-stained pages after years of use.

"So, buddy, why the four-alarm text?"

He brought his gaze from somewhere off in the distance to me, and then to his Bible and back again.

"I'm through, Pete." He took a sip of his own coffee, then shook his head and said it again: "I'm through."

"Through?" I questioned with a mouthful of blueberry scone. "Through with what?"

"This." He tossed his childhood Bible at me. It bounced off my lap and flopped to the floor, its pages unfurling to reveal hand-scrawled reflections and multi-florescent highlights. I stared at it as my heart began to pick up pace, even as my stomach sank to the floor with dread. I repeated my prayer:

Lord Jesus, give me strength and give me words!

I ducked dramatically, and said, "Dude, watch it! There's a lightning bolt with your name on it after that stunt."

I was trying to lighten the mood, but it was obvious that Clint wasn't playing. He was serious, penetrating me with those icy-blue eyes of his. He was withdrawn, he was downcast. It seemed something had died, and I feared probing for the *what* to that equation.

"So, what, you're dead to the Bible now? Or God? Faith?"

"Yes."

OK, all of the above.

I knew Clint had been struggling with issues of faith for some time. It started the first semester of his sophomore year. It made sense that he'd begun to struggle under the weight of two semesters of science and philosophy. And considering his mother died of cervical cancer last year, it made even more sense. But after a year of walking through Scripture together and talking about the basics of the Christian faith, I thought we had made progress. And even when things began to shift a month ago after the semester started, I thought he was managing to sit in the tension of our modern world and faith in Jesus.

I guess I was wrong. I hadn't known he was on the verge of chucking his faith in the gutter.

I picked up his Bible and set it back on his side table.

"No, keep it," Clint said.

I smiled. "Wow, so dramatic! OK, buddy, break it down for me. What's going on?"

He sighed heavily and raked his hand through his shaggy dirty-blond hair. "I just can't see how this old-time religion connects anymore to our modern world. It's so stogy, so *irrelevant*! And I'm sick of how the Church holds on to these antiquated notions of the way things are supposed to be—the way things *are*."

"Like what? Dancing and playing cards?"

He cocked his head to the side with a look of less than amusement.

"I'm serious, Pete."

"OK, OK," I said, holding up my hands. "What do you mean? What things?"

"Like the human genome, for instance."

So we're reaching for the cookies on the highest shelf this morning!

I shifted in my seat and crossed a leg. "The what?"

"Oh, come on. Don't tell me you don't know what the human genome project is."

"Hey, be nice. I'm not some super-cool scientist like you." I broke a piece of scone and popped it into my mouth. "I mean, I know its like a map of the human body. Or something. Isn't it?"

"It's more than a map! It's the cypher to humanity. The entire code to human nature."

"Well, what about it? What's the deal?"

"The human genome project proves beyond a shadow of a doubt that there could be no Adam and Eve," Clint said, sweeping his hand from left to right. "The facts are in, Pete.

Our genetic human ancestry can't be traced to less than ten thousand people. Yet the first book of the Bible, the book of Genesis, says all of us came from just two people. And millions of Christians believe it, taking it as science. That's not even addressing the crazy idea that the universe is less than six thousand years old!"

My mind jumped to our ministry meeting earlier that morning, and Roger's brilliant idea to trot out the purveyor of all things creationist—the very definition of the backwards, anti-science thinking that was catapulting Clint over the edge.

I sighed and shook my head.

"Why are you shaking your head?"

"Huh?" I said, zoning back in.

"You shook your head? Are you dismissing me?"

"No, no! Not at all. I totally get where you're coming from, Clint. More than you know...So I hear you saying you're through with Christianity because of science, is that right? You're done with Jesus and the Church?"

"That's not all of it," he responded defensively.

"There's more?"

"Lots more!" He paused, taking a large swig of his coffee and chomping into his uneaten croissant.

Munching, Clint said, "I'm tired of the Church only caring about life after death with no regard for life *before* death. It's like we're just waiting to escape to some distant world *out there*," he said, pointing toward the ceiling, "with no regard to what's happening *here*. I mean, I want a faith that cares about extinct animals and oil spills. I want a faith that cares about human trafficking, and then does something about it! I want a faith that makes sense to my life, right *now*. And the Christian faith just doesn't offer it, Pete. It offers children fairytales and escapism. Narrow-mindedness and hypocrisy. It's as relevant to our life now as Aesop's fables and the Iliad!"

He stopped to catch a breath. I noticed a few patrons standing in line glancing our way. Then he started up again.

"And how about the bazillions of people on this planet who weren't chosen for the privileged birth in Western society? People like you and me, Pete. Let's face it: we were born into Christianity. It would have been almost impossible for us not to have been exposed to Jesus and the Church. But what about my roommate Hanish who grew up in India? He was born into Hinduism, so it was impossible for him to have heard about Jesus —until I made the mistake of telling him about him!"

That last comment caught me off guard.

"Mistake? How do you figure?" I asked.

"Think about it. If I never told Hanish about Jesus, how could he be responsible for believing in him? After all, how can he be held responsible for believing in something or someone he's never heard about? But now that he does know, doesn't that mean he'll go to hell if he doesn't believe? And then what about all of those *other* people back in his hometown who never heard of Jesus, who only knew about Krishna and the other gods? Aren't they faithfully following what little they know about the spiritual world? What, they're just gonna fry forever because they never heard the story of some guy who lived two thousand years ago?"

Again, that pained, exasperated expression.

"And what is belief, anyway? Is it about something you say? Is it about saying the right prayer or saying the right *abracadabra* words to somehow convince the Almighty of one's religious convictions? Or is it something you do? I find the religious rigor of Muslims to be way more spiritual than what most Christians commit to. We're spiritual wimps compared to them!"

Clint raked his hands through his hair again before taking a sip of his coffee. He set down his mug with a sigh and looked back out the window.

"So, yes, Pete, I'm done," he said softly. Then he looked at me, and said, "With the Church. With the Christian faith." He paused, as if considering something before continuing. "Not with Jesus. Because he's the only sane thinker in the whole movement."

He's finally boiled over. It had been a long time coming, really. The end of a long, tiring journey of questions, doubt, familial accusation, and self-flagellation in an attempt to make sense of a faith that was built on as shaky ground as my own.

Clint crossed his legs and sat back. He folded his hands on his lap, as if waiting for me to give my best shot at bringing him back into the fold.

Yet I had no shot. I had no move, because I didn't know what to do. I felt my brain trying to spin out a web of well-reasoned arguments and finely-tuned responses.

But they didn't come. I was numb. I had no answers.

Why don't I have any answers? I wondered with not a slight amount of panic. He was looking to me and I was just sitting there, slack-jawed and dopey-eyed. Some campus minister I was.

Perhaps it was because I felt the same way. Had for some time. Yet, between the two of us, he was the one who could admit it.

The one who had the *courage* to admit it.

"I understand what you're saying, Clint," I finally said. "Because I'm right there with you."

Did I just say that? Here I am, his spiritual mentor, and I'm admitting my own doubts?

"You do?" he asked, wrinkling his brow and cocking his head to the side.

I cleared my throat and shifted in my seat before continuing. "I mean, I don't have as much issue with the science side of the Christian faith, but I'm there with you about life before death. I totally get it. I wonder myself what on earth this whole Christian thing is about sometimes. I see us running around playing politics, trying to get our guy elected and get our laws passed—and I'm like, is *that* what it's about? And then there's the whole us-versus-them and in-and-out mentality you mentioned."

Clint nodded as I joined him in assessing the modern manifestation of the Christian faith.

I continued, "But I have to believe there's more to Christianity than what we've been led to believe. Than our *parents* and childhood church led us to believe."

"Like what? What's more than what we've known?"

Good question.

I leaned back in my chair. I sighed and shrugged. "I don't know, brother. I don't know. But how about we find out together? Maybe there's a way to reimagine the Christian faith for a new day."

My question seemed to bring some relief to our conversation. Clint had always been one for dialogue. He seemed to brighten at the idea of reimagining the Christian faith together.

"Reimagine..." Clint said, trailing off. "Yeah, I like that idea. I'm not sure why I didn't think of it myself."

"Because you're not the spiritual mentor rock star I am." I grinned as I finished my coffee.

Clint did the same. We walked outside and embraced before departing our separate ways, two fellow journeymen charting a new spiritual course for ourselves.

"Thanks for listening," he said before leaving. "And thanks for not answering my questions. I think I just needed to vent what's been bottled up for so long without getting an earful in return, you know?"

"I understand. But my not giving you an earful was more because I really don't know what to say. Honestly, Clint, I don't have many answers."

"That's OK, bro. That's OK. How about we discover them together?"

I liked that idea, but I chided myself for not knowing how to respond. That was my job, after all. Or at least what I had been trained to believe was my job—giving answers to everybody's spiritual questions.

Clint headed back to campus and I headed back to our ministry row house a few blocks over.

Why didn't I know how to respond? I questioned myself as I sloshed back through the leaf-covered sidewalk. *Why couldn't I help Clint navigate his questions? What are the answers to his pressing issues with the Christian faith?*

The questions kept coming, keeping pace in their assault with the frigid fall rain.

So what *is* the relationship between science and faith? *Does* science trump Scripture? Or can we hold both in tension? Can Clint embrace both science and faith as a Christian science student?

What about his roommate Hanish? Was he better off having never heard about Jesus than he was now after Clint evangelized him? Wasn't he onto something? How can someone be held responsible for believing something or someone they've never heard about?

And what is the nature of belief? Growing up, it was all about reciting the Sinners Prayer—confessing one's sinfulness and faith in Jesus as Savior. Once you invoked those magical words, you were considered *in*. But is *that* what God desires— what God *demands*?

I reached our building and hesitated before entering. I felt like a phony, like I had no right to enter. But I did, and I headed straight for my desk, slumping in my chair with the full weight of Clint's questions pressing in against me.

I was at a loss. I was also shaken. Clint's revelation and his questions had awoken something that had been percolating deep within. Something I had known to exist, and had secretly fed in bits, but hadn't fully allowed to manifest itself.

Is there still a way forward with the Christian faith in this crazy world—with evolution and our awareness of other religions, with the human genome project for crying out loud?

Is there still a way of being Christian for Clint?

For me?

CHAPTER 3

THE QUESTIONS KEPT COMING. And I was annoyed I didn't have answers.

No, scratch that: I was shaken to the core that I didn't have answers!

Of all the people in Clint's life, I should have been the one who could help him navigate his questions. Of all the people on the planet, I should have had answers to people's deep questions about faith and life, considering the kind of Christianity I grew up in.

I mean, I was like the apostle Paul: of the right religion; of the right *tribe* of the right religion. We weren't just Christians: we were *fundamentalist* Christians. We stood upon and stood for the fundamentals of the Christian faith. I knew my Bible backward and forward thanks to years on the Bible Quiz Team. I preached to prisoners in our jail ministry, even won second place in a youth preaching competition. Shoot, I even led backyard summer Bible school classes when I was a kid!

We were bred that way, after all.

And yet, there I was, at the threshold of Google's temple

seeking answers to the deep questions of life I should have known by heart.

I paused and sat back before rubbing the bottle for genie Google to come do my bidding. Because something struck me in that moment of self-flagellation: it wasn't that I didn't have any answers; I had plenty of those. The problem was that I had the *wrong* answers. Or, rather, the right answers to the wrong questions, the questions Clint and my other students weren't even asking.

Clint wasn't worried about going to Heaven when he died. He was wondering about life *before* life after death. He wasn't interested any more about the abstract answers to his theological questions. His questions were personal, because the abstract impacted an actual person living in his dorm room named Hanish.

"So where do I begin?" I mumbled as my fingers drifted back to the keyboard, the Google search field taunting me as I considered what to ask it.

Then a word came to mind: *Reimagine*. The one Clint and I had voiced.

On a whim I typed *reimagine the Christian faith*. Then I hit *Enter* and waited for Google to work its magic. Within seconds, it brought up a whole list of websites and books in response to my query. At the top of the list was www.prosurgent.org.

Prosurgent? Never heard of it.

The tagline next to the name read, "Reimagining the Christian faith for a new day."

"Well, that pretty much hits the nail on the head!" I exclaimed as I continued scanning the search results.

Underneath that search result was another as intriguing one. It was a link to a book, *A Reimagined Christian*, by someone named Bryan McLaughlin. I clicked on it and was brought to an Amazon purchase page. It looked like a fiction book that traced the journey of a pastor through the same kinds of questions Clint and I were asking. Looked exactly like what I had been looking for.

I went back to the Google results and clicked on the Prosurgent website, then I began scanning the page.

It felt like I had stumbled through the looking glass into a whole new world of high-definition color. Every sentence on the "About" page screamed of a group of people on the same journey as me, asking all the same questions about how Christianity connected to our twenty-first-century world. And apparently they had local chapters that met and discussed those questions. One even met right here in DC.

"Hi, Pete! What are you looking at?"

I jumped and almost hit *command-w* on instinct to close the window and hide my googling. Thankfully I didn't, because I would have drawn the scrutiny of Roger, who was now hovering over my left shoulder.

"Hey, Roger. Just looking up some information about a new Christian group I heard about in the city."

"Neato! What group is that?"

Great. How much should I reveal?

"Looks like they have similar passions as ours, desiring to share Christ with people and all."

It wasn't a lie, exactly. They did want to share Jesus' story. Just a slightly modified story than the one we were telling.

"Sounds great, Pete. Listen, I was stopping by quick to see if you got the flyers from Peggy for the Alfred Morris event."

Yes, I did. After my conversation with Clint I could almost feel them pulsating in my bag, a stack of kryptonite weakening my Christian resolve.

"Yep. I'll post them up later."

"Good. It's our most significant outreach event yet, and I really want it to be a success. Make sure you hand them out to your student contacts, like Clint. He's a science major, isn't he?"

"Yeah," I managed through barely parted lips, cringing inside at the mention of his name. He was the last person who needed this event.

"I think he'll find the conversation absolutely stimulating!"

He'll find it something, alright.

Roger slapped me on the back like one of his former high school football players and left me to my googling. I returned back to the Prosurgent website in search of more information on the local DC cohort. Apparently, they were meeting tonight at The Front Page in Dupont Circle, led by a one Darren Thomas.

Make room at your table for a visitor, Prosurgent DC.

I jotted down the time and location on a sticky note and stuck it in my wallet. I grabbed my bag, the Freddy Morris posters a leaden weight at the bottom, and headed back out into the rain.

Please, Lord, let the day end better than it began.

THE MORNING and afternoon storm had given way to a frigid fall evening, feeling more like the end of November than mid-October. Leaves blew down on me from above, fluttering like confetti as I made the long mile-high ascent from the subterranean DuPont Circle Metro subway station. As I reached the surface, a ping of anxiety began tracing a route from my head to my heart and on to my gut. My ticker started thumping on cue and gut twisting with apprehension as I realized I would be walking into a room full of unknown people, engaging a conversation that was as unknown. I was a naturally shy person, so I was surprised by my gumption, that I was about to walk into a room full of strangers to talk about a strange new conversation happening within Christianity.

Yet I was thirsty. Thirsty for answers. Thirsty for a common community asking the same questions I was asking. Thirsty for a way forward through the Christian faith.

That night, my thirst was carrying me through my anxiety and apprehension.

I made my way south along the roundabout circle and followed it toward New Hampshire Avenue, then took that to The Front Page. When I arrived at the restaurant, a few brave patrons were sitting outside, protesting the onslaught of fall in the chilly evening while smoking cigars and enjoying a drink. I breathed in the burnt spicy scent that mingled with dead leaves as I headed inside, all at once excited and apprehensive. I told the hostess I was here for a group meeting and she walked me to the back.

Several tables had been pushed together. Ten or twelve people were already gathered in the space, engaged in lively conversations no doubt fueled by both drink and mutual purpose.

A thirty-something man in the back made eye contact with me. He had shoulder-length blond hair drawn into a ponytail and was wearing a black turtleneck. He had that look of someone sitting around smoking a pipe and sipping bourbon in a Viennese café, while waxing theology with a group of similarly dressed progressives.

I imagined I looked petrified as I took in the room, a proverbial deer caught in headlights wondering what the heck I was doing. The man left his conversation and walked over to me.

"Are you here for the Prosurgent cohort meeting?" he asked in a thick Australian accent, which didn't surprise me considering how international my city was.

"Yes. I'm Peter Daniel Young. I found you all through the Prosurgent website." I stretched out my hand. He took it.

"Fantastic, mate. Good to have you on board! How long have you been part of the conversation?"

The conversation? The word had a cultish tinge to it.

"Oh, I'm not conversant. I just stumbled upon...the conversation, as you put it," I checked my watch, "about nine hours ago."

"Wow! You're diving straight into the deep end, aren't you? Again, good to have you on board. Please, come join me! I'm Darren, by the way. Darren Thomas. Have a seat. What'll you have to drink?"

"Do they have Dogfish Head here?" I asked, picking up the beer menu.

"Sure do. Billy," Darren shouted to a server across the room. "Get this guy the Dogfish Head IPA, on my tab."

"No, that's alright, you don't have to do that."

"Nonsense. Consider it your welcome goodie bag, minus the bag."

I smiled and laughed. "Some goodie bag. Love IPA, so thanks. Appreciate it."

"Sure thing, mate. So what brings you to the cohort meeting? You're not some fundie spy or anything sent to infiltrate the ranks, are you?"

"No, no. Not at all! Well, recovering, maybe."

"Nice. Did you hear that, Andrew?" Darren said to the guy next to him. "We've got another recovering fundamentalist!"

"I'm telling you, Darren," a burly man said next to the Aussie, "we're like a fly strip. We just keep attracting them."

"Andrew, here, is a fellow recoverer. Andrew, meet Peter."

The large man with a full, bushy, salt-and-pepper beard and wearing a tie-dyed *Grateful Dead* t-shirt nodded and raised his glass in salute.

"Hey, fellow recoverer. What branch of fundamentalism? Brethren? Baptist?"

"IFBC," I replied.

"IFBC?" Darren asked.

"Independent Fundamentalist Baptist Churches. Or as I like to say, *I Fight and Blast Christians*."

Andrew whistled. "Wowie. Them there legit fundamentalist creds!"

I laughed again. "Yes, yes they are."

"Where's the church you attend that's IFBC?"

"Not a church, a ministry. I'm with Campus Ministry at Georgetown University."

"Ahh, a collegiate colonialist," Andrew said. "Gotcha."

Collegiate colonialist?

"You'll have to excuse Andrew, mate. He's on a bit of an anti-conversionism kick of late. Sounds like interesting, rewarding work."

"It has been the past few years."

"But it isn't in the *present?*" Darren questioned with raised brow.

The server interrupted us, bearing my drink. I thanked him and took a long sip, considering my words.

"Well, it's sort of what brings me here tonight. Lately, I've been struggling with the questions my students are asking." I stopped and took another drink, then held my mug and stared at the froth sliding back down inside. "No, it's more than that. It's more about the answers to the questions my students are asking. Or at least my complete inability to give meaningful answers that connect to their deep questions."

Darren and Andrew both nodded with understanding, propelling me forward.

I was surprised by my openness, which was so unlike me in these kinds of foreign social situations. But I needed to share. And Prosurgent seemed to be the oasis of like-minded people I had needed to express myself.

"Actually, it's deeper. I feel like my whole life I've been trained to give answers to questions about faith and life that people aren't even asking."

"Preach it brother!" Andrew exclaimed as he slapped the

table, causing me to jump and send some of my beer sloshing over the sides of my glass and onto its surface. "Oh, crap! Sorry about that." He took a napkin to sop up the spillage.

"It fascinates me how out of touch and ignorant we Christians are of the spiritual journeys of the rest of the world," Darren said as Andrew finished cleaning the table. "Perhaps if we listened more before opening our big, fat yappers, we might have more insights into the deep, genuine questions of those around us."

"Totally understand you there," I said, "and I got a good dose of that this morning."

"Really? How so?"

"One of my students opened up about his recent rejection of the Christian faith."

I took a sip and set down my drink, the morning memory turning in my stomach along with the alcohol.

"This was a guy who was solid, man. Solid. Like me, he grew up in a conservative fundamentalist home. Was a dutiful youth group kid who memorized Scripture, prayed every day, went to church three times a week. When I met him last year, he was still committed, but he began asking some head scratchers."

I paused, my mind tracing its way back to Saxbys. Our server returned and the three of us ordered another round of drinks.

He left to fetch them, and I continued sharing. "This morning he was looking to me to help him navigate those questions, but I was totally unprepared. I had no answers. To make a long story short, that's how I found Prosurgent. I googled what I hoped could happen for both my friend and for me. That we could reimagine the Christian faith for a new day."

Darren smiled. "Well, mate, you've come to the right place for that. I'm not sure we have any of the answers you're looking for. In fact, we're really not all that interested in answers as much as the questions themselves. Because it's in the questions that we believe we are closest to God. God is *in* the questions. And it's in the questions that we believe the best version of the Christian faith can rise up out of the ashes of our ancestors' traditions in order to move us forward in following God in the way of Jesus."

A smile worked its way upward as I listened to him describe the Prosurgent movement. It sounded exactly like what I had been looking for: a way forward through and beyond the traditionalism of my youth to a new, better version of the Christian faith that connected to our modern world.

"Are you familiar with the ancient myth of the phoenix, Peter?" Darren asked.

"Vaguely. I know it's some sort of fire bird."

He laughed. "Sort of."

Our server returned with the drinks. Another Doghead IPA for me.

"Thanks, mate," Darren said to him. And then to us: "Cheers!" Andrew and I echoed him and promptly took long swigs of our brew.

He took a swig himself, and then continued. "Now, legend has it that the mythic desert bird cyclically regenerates itself from the ashes of its parents every few hundred years. It gains new life by arising from the ashes of its predecessor. Of course, the Church has been following in the footsteps of the phoenix since its birth two thousand years ago. There was the collapse of the Roman empire during the fifth century and the transition to monasticism and medievalism. Five hundred years later, there was the bitter division between the Eastern and Western churches, known as the Great Schism. And then, of course, brother Martin Luther launched the Great Reformation in the 1500s, giving rise to Protestant Christianity and all of its variations apart from Rome. And now, at the dawn of the twenty-first century, we believe the Church is rising once again out of the ashes of a disintegrated Western Church and postmodern, post-Christian world in order to shift Christianity forward."

Darren took a breath and a sip of his beer before continuing. He smacked his lips together and hummed with pleasure, then said, "So you see, Peter, this symbol best represents our hopes and dreams for a reimagined Church. Not only because of the cyclical nature of the Church itself—which seems to regenerate itself every few hundred years—but because early Christianity embraced the phoenix to represent the resurrection, the bringing of new life. It's a tangible icon to represent this forward-rising Church movement."

"Cool," I whispered, enchanted by the prospects of a true revolution in the Church that could propel it forward into the modern era.

I drained my beer and checked my watch for the time. It was getting late.

"I should go," I said, flagging down the server. I handed him a twenty to pay for my second drink and tip.

"Alright, mate," Darren said. "Good to meet you. Hope to see you around here more. And here's my contact information."

He handed me a business card. Apparently, he was an associate pastor of a church just north of DC. Dogwood Bluff Community Church. I stashed his card in my wallet, said my goodbyes, and headed back home, riding high off the fumes from the engaging conversation.

I hoped I myself could reimagine the Christian faith for a new day. Though I had no idea what that would ultimately mean.

CHAPTER 4

OVER THE COMING WEEKS, I dived deeper into this group of kindred spirits who were charting a new course for Christianity. Who were charting a new course for *my own* Christian faith.

I learned that Prosurgent formed out of a group of burned out and bummed out conservative pastors who dreamt of an alternative movement to connect the Christian faith to the changes taking place in the world. They were true revolutionaries as much as missionaries, seeking to help the Christian faith rise forward out from the ashes of the post-Christian modern world.

Hence the name *Prosurgent*, a mashup of two latin words, *pro-* for "forward" and the verb *surgere*, meaning "to rise." Their mission was to provoke the traditional Church to rise forward for the sake of the faith.

And I liked it!

Leading the charge was pastor and author Bryan McLaughlin, who was apparently the lead pastor of the church Darren Thomas worked at, Dogwood Bluff Community Church.

Pastor Bryan had become something of a grandfather figure to the Prosurgent movement after his book *A Reimagined Chris-*

tian sparked a broader conversation about Christianity at the turn of the millennium when it launched. He was seeking to better connect the Christian faith to the twenty-first-century world by reimagining and redefining what it meant to be a Christian in the first place. He was giving a new generation the permission to question the faith that had been handed to them, while charting a course forward into new Christian territory.

Shoot, he was giving *me* permission to question the version of Christianity handed to me! He was permitting me to ask the questions that had been percolating deep within me like a stew of molten lava underneath my surface for several months now, the ones that were bursting forth thanks to Clint's inciting incident.

It was Friday morning, but I wasn't feeling the ministry vibe. Since my calendar was empty of appointments, I popped off an email to Tabitha and Bernie letting them know I was feeling under the weather and would take a personal day. Which wasn't a lie entirely; I needed a mental health day.

After breakfast, I decided to drive over to the Georgetown Barnes & Noble to check out Bryan's book. I read online how the story followed the journey of one fictional pastor, Pastor Jack, out of conservative Christianity and into the lonely uncharted territory that Prosurgent Christians themselves were exploring, aided by a new friend, Nelson Edward O'Donnell.

After parking and making my way to the bookstore, I found Bryan's book nestled in the Religion & Spirituality section. I didn't buy it, too apprehensive. I felt like a teenager in a porno shop, clutching the book to my chest, looking over my shoulder as I stood in line to order a coffee, expecting Roger to walk in on my new literary pursuit. I paid for my coffee, then I found a spot to read and settled in for the long haul.

Ironically, the book was set in the DC-metro area just north of town in southern Maryland. Perhaps it was one of the reasons why I was drawn to it, because I devoured the first few chapters sitting in my perch overlooking M Street. It was like I was having a conversation with myself as I read about Pastor Jack's journey as a person in ministry who himself was having a crisis of faith.

"I'm losing my faith," the fictional man wrote in his journal after a long day of ministry. "I no longer have the confidence I once had about the answers I was trained to give."

Hear you, brother. Preach it, preacher!

Page after page, I found my own story writ large, as if Bryan McLaughlin had connected a USB cable to his laptop and uploaded my own hidden anxieties and apprehensions about faith in the modern world to his fictional script.

Jack wondered about how to read the Bible in this modern world. He'd seen how the Church has used and abused it over the years—from slavery to the environment. And yet he was conflicted, because he believed it was God's Word, that it meant something and had bearing on what we believe about God and the world and how we live in it.

Before long, my twin was meeting the next main character at his son's high school soccer game, Nelson Edward O'Donnell— though he insisted Jack call him by his nickname, Neo. Which I guess was an intentional way of introducing the new, reimagined kind of Christianity Nelson shared with his new friend.

Pastor Jack and Nelson formed an immediate bond out of necessity on Jack's part and compassion on Nelson's. They began meeting to chat about reimagining the Christian faith, not so much to help Jack chart a course forward in his ministry for his people's faith, but to help his own faith from fraying. They got breakfast together and drinks together; they took walks through the Billy Goat Trail along the Potomac River together; they traded emails together—all in the interest of helping Jack recover from his fundamentalism and emerge into a version of the faith that was more sustainable.

Bryan's book was opening up a whole new world to me. I felt

like Dorothy opening that rickety door into the Land of Oz after her house had landed in Munchkinland, leaping from a world of stale, staid black and white into one of full-on high-definition color. It was positively intoxicating.

And yet, as freeing and permissive as his book was, I still wondered...

I set the book down on the table and stared out at the people milling about below. I wondered whether there was a danger in swinging the pendulum too far by throwing out the fundamentals of the Christian faith in the interest of reimagining it.

Take creation: I got that Genesis was probably not to be viewed as a history lesson about how the universe was formed. Why would God need six literal days to set into motion his glorious creation? But did that mean he needed six billion years? Was evolution, even a God-directed evolution, the best alternative to a rigid reading of the creation narrative?

Same thing for sin. Lord knew I'd grown sick and tired of certain views of human nature that made us out to be so rebellious and so far gone that the Almighty was just waiting for an excuse to flick our little heinies into hell. But was the alternative an overly optimistic view of human nature, one that suggested we're able to do good on our own without Christ's saving power and the power of the Holy Spirit?

And what about other religions? I sympathized with Clint, wondering along with him whether Christianity had the corner market on religious belief. But then again, it really wasn't about religion, per se. It was about the person of Jesus, what he did and who he was. And if Jesus is who he said he was, if he did what the Bible said he did—dying for the sins of the world, rising again to new life to opening the way for rebirth—then didn't that mean other religions were false? But then what about Hanish's family and friends back home? Were they screwed, doomed to eternal destruction simply because they had never heard about Jesus?

An electric current of doubt walked its way up my spine, causing me to shiver with suspicion at the thoughts raging through my mind. I suddenly felt very alone sitting with this book and my questions, like an alcoholic with a bagged bottle of booze and a pocketful of worries.

I closed the book and walked it back to its shelf. I went back out into the brisk, sunny Friday, making my way back to my car parked a few blocks away. The sun felt good on my face, a balm for my burgeoning worries.

I can't do this alone, I thought as I continued walking back to my car. But where could I turn?

Not to Clint. I didn't think it was wise to be that vulnerable with him in his own state of disbelief and doubt.

Definitely not my ministry. They wouldn't understand and would write me off in an instant. Probably fire me, too.

Darren Thomas seemed like a safe person. But why would he sit down and chat with me, a stranger he met once a few weeks ago?

I slid into my car and started it up, the muffler offering an irritated rattle in response. I sat waiting for it to warm up before driving back to my row house apartment.

What's the harm in asking? He sure seemed nice enough.

I pecked out a text message to Darren and sent it off, hoping he was willing to come alongside me in my own spiritual journey.

Just like Nelson Edward O'Donnell did for Pastor Jack.

CHAPTER 5

I WOKE up the next morning to a text from Darren: *"Good to hear from you, mate. Thought we scared you off ;) Yes let's connect. Brunch today? Dean & Deluca? Happy to help however you need."*

I smiled as I texted him back, thanking the Lord for his provision. Perhaps it was a sign I was on the right track after all. Within fifteen minutes we had a date for brunch in an hour. I threw on a hoodie and jeans, and fifteen minutes later headed out the door. I managed to find a parking spot on M Street a few blocks from our rendezvous point, bumping both cars in front and behind as I tried to parallel park my aging, sagging Honda hatchback. I chided myself for still struggling with the gymnastics of urban parking after two years living in the city.

The autumn morning was crisp, cloudy, and muted. The air was laced with the heady scent of dead leaves and burning wood. It was the kind of morning I relished growing up back home in Coopersville when the long summer days gave way to family outings to the local apple orchard and piles of leaves waited for my brothers, James and Johnny, and me to rake.

On the way to Dean & Deluca, I passed Georgetown Tobacco. I stopped to peer in its window at the pipes on display, making a mental note to fill up on tobacco when I returned to my car. A sizable line had already formed at the popular Georgetown eatery when I arrived, so I secured us a table near the back inside the green-awning enclosure attached to the historic red-brick market building. Soon Darren arrived, and I flagged him over to our meeting spot.

"Brotha, Peter. Good to see you, again," Darren said, greeting me in his perfect Aussie accent.

"You, too, Darren," I replied in my perfect Midwestern drawl. "And thanks for hanging out with me, especially on a weekend."

"Nonsense! D&D is part of my Saturday ritual. Happy to share it with a new friend. Let's grab a bite to eat. I'm starved."

After negotiating the Saturday-morning queue, we both returned with oversized quiches. Darren got a deep-dish quiche Lorraine with applewood bacon and gruyere cheese. I went for a more adventurous Maryland crab and tarragon quiche. I sat and waited for Darren to finish doctoring up his coffee with too many creams and sugars for my taste—pure, unadulterated black coffee was the only way to go, in my book.

He returned and we both dived into our quiches. He stuffed a forkful in his mouth, and said, "So Peter, you said you've been reading through Bryan's *A Reimagined Christian* book. Is it rocking your world yet?" He smirked as he blew on his coffee.

"I only read the first few chapters at Barnes & Noble. But, yeah. Definitely feeling rocked!"

Darren laughed. "That's typically how people respond after having read or listened to Bryan."

"I'm sure you know that well, considering you work with him. I bet everyday you're uncovering more layers to this reimagined kind of Christian he speaks about."

"It certainly is a delight. And, yes, it's like Alice through the looking glass, but magnified a bazillion fold."

I smiled and nodded as I chewed a piece of my quiche, discovering a nice-sized lump of Maryland crab.

Darren wiped his mouth and took another sip of his coffee, then continued. "From what I remember from our first meet up a few weeks ago, you're a recovering fundamentalist working for a campus ministry at Georgetown University who's stumbled into our little heresy movement. That about right?"

I laughed and finished swallowing. I sipped some of my coffee before answering. I nodded. "About sums it up."

"I'm guessing there's more to the story, so care to fill in the details?"

"Yeah, lots more." I took a breath, then dived into my story. "So, I grew up in a small town in the middle of Nowheresville, Michigan. A small farming town called Coopersville. Mom's a teller at the local bank. Dad works for GM at a stamping plant. Or at least *has* been working there. Looks like that's about to change soon because of the recession."

"Sorry to hear that, mate," Darren responded with concern. "So he's getting sacked?"

"Yeah, they announced last month the plant is closing in the next year or two."

"How's he taking it?"

I paused and looked off, considering the question.

"I don't know, actually. We don't really talk much. Anyway, so I grew up in a pretty conservative town and church—"

"An *I Fight and Blast Christians* church, as you put it."

I smiled. "Right. Grew up with all the trappings of fundamentalism. KJV-only Bible. Hymns only, aided by a piano and organ. Fifty minute sermons that hammered home how sinful we are and how wicked the world is thanks to Budweiser and Disney."

Darren snorted as he sipped his coffee. "Disney. Nice one. Let me guess, no movies, no card games, no work on Sundays?"

"And no sex before marriage. Because, you know, sex could lead to dancing."

We both laughed with recognition at the exaggeration that wasn't too far off the mark, unfortunately.

I continued, "But, yeah, we basically avoided culture like the plague. Although that's how the rest of my church rolled. Our family was a bit rebellious. We watched plenty of movies and played our share of Gin Rummy. And Mom even let a curse word rip once in a while."

"What? Like shoot and heck?"

"And don't forget gosh darn it all."

We chuckled again at the legalism before we took bites of our quiches.

"So we've established you grew up in Fundieville," Darren said as he chewed. "Then what?"

"Then I got educated in Fundieville. Went to Freedom University out in York, Pennsylvania, and studied government before I moved out here to win back our nation for Christ."

"Oh, Lordie loo. Because that's *exactly* what America needs. To return to some dreamt up utopian theocratic era."

"Don't you know we were founded as a Christian nation, Darren? Oh, wait, you wouldn't, because you're an Aussie expat."

The man made a face and sputtered his lips in disgust. "I'm no expat! I've still got my citizenship papers safely stowed away for when people like you install some right-wing nut-job into office. Kidding, of course. Go on, go on!"

"So, anyway, I moved out here and landed a job with the Majority Leader's office in the House of Representatives. I did that for a year before getting pretty jaded at the whole Church and State thing. Couldn't stomach how the Church whores herself to both political parties, and how they willingly use her and abuse her for their own flights of orgasmic fancy."

"Cheeky picture you've painted there, mate," Darren groaned. "Thanks for that."

I winked. "No problem. But it's true. And, now that I think about it again, I think that's where all this began."

"Where all what began?" he asked, finishing his quiche and shoving his plate to the side.

"This whole journey out of fundamentalism and into...whatever it is I'm moving toward. This whole reimagining the Christian faith thing, I guess. Though, I gotta say, I'm a bit skeptical of it all."

"Great place to stop, because I need to relieve my pea-sized bladder and fill up on some more high-octane fuel. But I want to hear more, Peter. Sounds like you've had quite the ride the past several years."

Darren headed off, and I said a silent prayer of thanks for God bringing me a friend for this specific moment in my life.

He returned a few minutes later with another cup brimming with coffee—and more sugar and cream, no doubt. He sat and skimmed a sip off the surface. He hummed with pleasure, then said, "Before I unceremoniously left our conversation for the loo, you used the word *skeptical*. Tell me more about that. Skeptical in what way?"

I sighed, searching for the right words to express the tension I had felt reading Bryan's book and considering my own spiritual past. "I don't know. Maybe it's the ghosts of my fundamentalism haunting me, whispering caution in my ears and throwing up red flags."

Darren laughed. "Those pesky fundie poltergeists have a way of worming their way into our ears, don't they? What specifically is a red flag?"

"Like when Bryan talked about the Bible—or I guess Nelson

Edward O'Donnell did for him. He says we all interpret and read the Bible through a grid, which seems to suggest there's no right way to read it. That it's all just relative to individuals and the authority of the Bible is what we make of it."

"But isn't it?" Darren said, a wry smile curling upward as he pressed me.

I wrinkled my brow and sat back. "No! The Bible has one message. It's saying certain things about how to live and we need to figure it out. And God has given us his Spirit to help us do that."

"Agree. Somewhat. This is where I think postmodernism nails it. Are you familiar with postmodernity or postmodernism or the postmodern worldview?"

I tilted my head and narrowed my eyes, then I frowned and shook my head. "Not really. Other than hearing that it's as big of a threat to Christianity as secularism and liberalism."

He laughed again. "Some would say that, yes, all the while perfectly content to live in their *modern* worldview. So one of the things postmodernism has helped us realize is that no person or group interprets the world through crystal-clear lenses. We all come from a particular viewpoint. Like when we think about the economy, for instance. As a white, middle-class man from West Michigan, you're going to have a far different perspective on minimum wage laws than an African-American woman from Harlem. So who's right?"

Silence grew before I realized he was waiting for an answer.

"I'm not really committed either way to a particular view on the minimum wage," I said.

"Spoken like a true politician!" Darren roared.

"No, for real! But I guess I hear what you're saying. When I think about the people who are against minimum wage increases, it's usually people who have decent paying jobs. And those who are for the increase—well, not so much."

"Exactly. We all bring things to the table, whether our nationality or economic status or education—even our religion or denomination. And Bryan's point, or rather Neo's point, is that when we interpret the Bible, we're not reading this sacred text with crystal-clear lenses. Conservatives read it a certain way because of their grid of literalism. And, frankly, liberals read it their own way because of their own grid."

I considered this while Darren took a drink of his coffee.

He continued, "So when conservatives argue for the Bible's absolute authority, what they are *really* arguing is that their own traditional grid through which they read the Bible is absolutely authoritative. Superior, even."

"But doesn't that make the Bible fallible and unreliable?" I asked.

He sat up closer to the table. "Not at all. It means our *interpretations* are. Think about it this way," he said as he smacked his left hand on the table. "The authority of the Bible isn't embedded in the ink on the paper and in what I say that ink says it says." He pointed with his right hand to his left and scribbled on it, using his finger like a pen. "The authority is up here," Darren explained, now hovering his right hand above his left. "It lies in what *God* says the text says."

My mind was streaming a thousand different thoughts at once, feeling like Darren was opening the Bible up to more possibilities. Yet I also found it difficult to accept those possibilities. What Darren said sounded suspect and right all at once. Perhaps it was my traditional grid getting in the way, my conservative fundamentalist past barricading this new way of seeing the Bible for what it was.

"I can tell you're struggling to come to grips with what I'm saying, Peter. And that's OK. Here's what I'd challenge you with, and what I think Bryan is challenging all of us with as we reimagine what it means to be a Christian in our modern world.

If the real authority for faith and life doesn't reside in the ink on paper, in the Bible itself, but in the God who hovers above it, then we'd better scooch to the edge of our chairs, start praying more, listen to each other more, and read the Scriptures in fresh ways for all the wisdom that God wants to share with us for our day, right now."

Darren was getting animated now, moving his arms while wielding his cup of coffee to emphasize his points.

"You know," he continued, "people want the Bible to be some sort of answer book, a rule book and encyclopedia that answers all of our questions about science and good moral living. So they go to it and read it literally. There was a time when the Church read the Bible in such a way that validated and permitted slavery and the subjugation of women and marginalization of minorities and exploitation of the environment. But not anymore. That was then. And God gave us wisdom, and he wants to give us even more wisdom for our day. That's what happens when you let go of the Bible as an answer book and embrace it as something more."

"What's that?" I asked, sitting on the edge of my chair —literally.

"A family story of a God who is taking his people on journey, maturing them, evolving them from one state of existence into another."

He set down his coffee on the table with force, as if putting an exclamation point on his sermonette. He crossed his arms and sat back with a slight smile, squinting at me for a response.

I said, "I like, Darren, I like. The way you talk about the Bible sounds bigger than the way I've thought about it before. And weightier. I think I've been treating God's Word like a frog to be dissected. Rather than this...family story, as you put it—of people on journey with God. I think I remember Bryan talking about that part."

"Yes, he did. And I like your analogy. I think it's easy to think about the Bible that way, as some specimen to poke and prod and run through our systematic theologies, all the while failing to realize that each of those theologies impact how we read the text."

I glanced at my watch while Darren finished his coffee.

"It looks like you need to go," Darren said, "so I'll just say one more thing." He paused, leaned back in his chair, folded his arms, and looked at me square in the eyes. Then he said, "Don't be afraid, Peter."

"I'm not afraid," I quickly said, sitting up straight and shifting in my seat. And sounding way more defensive than I intended.

He raised an eyebrow knowingly.

"OK, maybe just a little," I admitted, settling back into my chair and folding my arms.

"Of course you would be. This is new, uncharted territory. And you've got parents and your ministry coworkers on each side of your shoulder whispering words of warning into your ear like Jiminy Cricket. Christianity has been reimagining itself ever since it was born two thousand years ago. The time is ripe to reimagine anew, so lean into that reimagining, Peter. And know that I'm here for you if you need anything."

I offered a weak smile, and said, "Thanks. And thanks for the little push to set sail. I don't know if I'm fully there yet, but it's good to know I've got some people in my corner should I choose to jump in with both feet."

We said our goodbyes and I headed back to my car, but not before I made a stop into Georgetown Tobacco to buy a pack of mild, pleasant-tasting Burley pipe tobacco.

I figured I was going to need it for the road ahead.

CHAPTER 6

"COME ON, Pete. We're going to be late!" I heard Ainsley shout outside through my closed apartment window as I finished stuffing my suitcase for our trip to Dallas.

Everyday Evangelism here we come.

Or if it was anything like I pictured it in my mind, more like Bible-Thumping Bonanza.

I came out of my row house apartment in Adam's Morgan to an irritated Ainsley and an almost as irritated cabbie—though he didn't have long blond hair that swayed in sync with his irritation.

"Sorry," I pleaded as I stowed my luggage in the taxi's opened trunk. "Let's roll!"

"Dude, if we miss our plane..." she warned with arms folded and face fixed forward.

"Relax, Ains. We'll be fine."

We were, with two minutes to spare until we wouldn't have been able to even get our tickets. After squeaking by security, we boarded our plane, found our seats, and settled in for what I imagined would be a very interesting trip. Especially considering what Bryan had been teaching me about evangelism.

Spiritual colonialism, is what he called it. Like the conquistadors and colonists of Old Europe who came to tame the wild lands and their inhabitants for New Europe. It wasn't that he thought we shouldn't share Jesus with the world. It was just that we shouldn't do so at the end of a spear—or a well-sharpened evangelism pamphlet.

I heard that. I'd felt the skepticism laser-beaming me in the face whenever I had chatted with students in Georgetown's cafeteria or on the quad. Not that I'd done what Roger did, mind you, just walking up to random strangers and assaulting them with questions about their spiritual life.

Now, that's spiritual colonialism if I've ever seen it!

Yet there I was, somewhere over America on my way to train to be a colonizer.

My gut twisted with a mixture of apprehension and anxiety —apprehension over our training and continued anxiety over these shifts occurring inside my soul. Shifts no one knew about but Darren. If I ever told the people who mattered to me—my parents, my ministry co-workers, even some of my students—I'd be questioned as some sort of liberal backslider.

Ainsley was sleeping next to me, mouth agape and nodding at random intervals. I decided to join her, hoping our training wasn't going to be as bad as I feared it would be.

Just shy of four hours later, we landed in the Friendship State and made our way to the megachurch owned and operated by our parent ministry. Everything is bigger in Texas, they say. Their Christianity was no exception.

We arrived to a swath of land just off the south side of I-20 that rivaled major European estates. The drive from the main street to church entrance was like something out of Vegas: fountains lined the center boulevard, each dancing to some pre-recorded gospel hymn that serenaded us on our way in; I counted twelve large fruit trees that shouldn't be able to grow in the otherwise arid Dallas soil, no doubt using their own reservoir to hydrate the landscape accented by basil-green grass and wild flowers; banners welcomed us in Jesus' name and announced the current teaching series; and two triple-decker parking garages flanked the over-sized church building that looked more like a shopping mall than a sacred tabernacle for worship.

I rolled my eyes at the spectacle as we parked between a Hummer H2 and Cadillac Escalade. We made our way into the church to commence our training as Navy SEALs for Jesus, gut twisting even more than it had on the tarmac back in DC. After picking up our welcome packets, we filed into the awaiting class-room and took our seats just as Dr. Harrison stood to begin the morning training session.

"Welcome, Christian soldiers!" the silver-haired man exclaimed in a well-honed baritone voice.

I guess Bryan wasn't too far off the mark with his spiritual colonialism charge.

"Through this training, we're going to train you to conquer people for Christ by convincing them of their need for Heaven and then telling them how Jesus paved their way for free."

As I sat listening to Harrison describe the process of converting people, something seemed off. It was as if Heaven was the point of God's good news and the Christian message, rather than Jesus and his story, and what both meant for life now. Then there was the whole "conquer people" bit—which I didn't even want to think about.

"Through this process, we will help you share your own story of conversion. People love stories. Stories are the books of the living. And if you're alive in Christ, you have a story to tell. Your story can help people find Heaven by helping them see and understand how Jesus makes a difference in their life."

Why on earth is my story the focus? I thought Jesus' story is what rescues people?

"In the end, our gospel sharing method will give you a simple, reproducible model you can use with anyone to show them how they, too, can get to Heaven when they die. The gospel is the beautiful truth that Heaven is a free gift. It is not earned nor deserved. This can be seen more clearly when we understand what the Bible says about people. The Bible says people are sinners and cannot save themselves. This comes into sharper focus when we look at what the Bible says about God. God is merciful, and therefore does not want to punish us. But he is also just, and therefore he must punish our sin. God solved this problem in the person of Jesus Christ. Christ is the infinite God-man. He died to pay for our sins and purchase a place for us in Heaven, which he offers as a gift. This gift is received by faith. Faith is not mere intellectual assent or temporal faith. It is trusting in Jesus Christ alone for our salvation. That's the gospel, folks. It's as simple as that!"

A few of the other participants dutifully said *Amen*, including Ainsley. I was conflicted.

Yes, at one level what he said was true. But at another level, I felt uncomfortable with how he framed the Christian message. That it was about getting to Heaven, rather than simply a relationship with Jesus—and all that his life and death and resurrection means for life, right now as much as later.

My mind jumped to Clint: *I wonder what he'd have to say about all of this?* Because this gospel, this *good news*, didn't even come close to connecting with his burning questions or the questions of any of my other students.

It didn't come close to connecting to mine, either.

"Alright, let's dive in, shall we? Open to page seven in your training manuals. We want to begin by outlining the two most important questions you'll ever ask someone. The two diagnostic questions, I call them."

I moaned, apparently loud enough so that Ainsley shot me an

irritated, furrowed-brow look. I looked away and tried to focus on page seven.

"Excuse me," Harrison said. "Excuse me, young man," he said again.

I looked up to find Mr. Silverhair three feet away, staring at me with his hands cupped behind him. I felt my face flush, heat rising at the back of my neck and blossoming in my cheeks.

"Umm, yes?" I said, putting my pen down and glancing around at the others staring back at me.

"Do you know for sure that you are going to be with God in Heaven when you die? Or is that something you're still working on?"

It hit me that Harrison was roleplaying, and I was his lucky dance partner. I also remembered back to times I had seen Roger use this tactic at Georgetown with students on the quad. Usually said students stared back with a mixture of surprise, violation, revulsion, and confusion. Some walked away in disgust. But others engaged him, taking him up on his offer to duel.

I played along, responding as the students usually had.

"I'm not sure. I'm still figuring that out."

He proceeded with the other question in his arsenal. "Well, suppose you were to die and stand before God and he were to ask you, 'Why should I let you into my Heaven?' What would you say?"

I'm not sure why, but I felt violated. It was like an SS officer had ripped open the front door to my row house and stormed inside to interrogate me, pressing me for intel on the whereabouts of societal undesirables or my political affiliation.

Perhaps this was how those students felt on the quad. My gut twisted with disgust, yet I stuffed my feelings away. I chose to give him what he wanted.

"You know, I think I'm a pretty good person. The good outweighs the bad."

"Most of my life I thought as you, young man," he intoned. "To get into Heaven required that I be a good person, that my good works outweigh my bad ones. Then someone shared with me the best news I have ever heard. I discovered the *good news* that Heaven is a free gift! And then off we go into the EE gospel outline." Harrison walked back to the front of the room. "Give our young man here a hand for his magisterial performance."

Magisterial performance? I thought as people clapped. Ainsley patted my arm and smiled. I smirked back and stared down at page seven in embarrassment.

Dr. Harrison spent the rest of the morning walking through the EE outline of the Christian message's good news. Heaven, of course, was the point of this good news. Apparently, life after death was God's loving gift—as if life *before* death was just window dressing, just dress rehearsal for the main act. And then there was the bit about humanity, that we're all sinners who cannot save ourselves. There was truth to his words, given what the Bible teaches. But I was surprised he didn't say we were totally depraved, which was unexpected coming from this hyper-conservative pastor. Perhaps he knew his audience of ministers were from mixed denominations and theological persuasions.

Harrison continued, walking us through the finer details of the EE outline regarding God and Jesus. As I listened, I couldn't help but think how non-contextual this whole good news was. From what history I remember of our fearless founder, Harrison forged his evangelism method through the fires of a thoroughly religious sector of his beloved southern city. After assuming his role as pastor of First Dallas Reformed Church, his dwindling numbers forced him to pound the pavement in search of church-goers. Day and night, he went door-to-door like one of those traveling Kirby vacuum salesman. What he first encountered was people who were desperate to understand how they could get to Heaven. The second thing he discovered was that those who thought they were going to get through the Pearly Gates did so based on how they lived, rather than what Jesus did on the cross through his sacrificial death for sins.

And so Heaven became the offer in his spiritual sales pitch, one we can't work for or earn.

Again, all true as far as what the Bible teaches, that eternal life is found in Jesus through his death and resurrection. But the more I thought about it, the more I realized people nowadays weren't all that concerned with going to Heaven. I didn't recall a single conversation with my college students that centered around fear of death or their eternal state. Their fears were entirely *this* worldly, not *other* worldly.

There were the existential questions: What is the point of my life? Why am I here? Where did we come from and where are we going?

And the personal: Will I find a job after graduation? Will I get married? Do I even want to get married? What even *is* marriage?

Then the deeper spiritual questions about faith: Is there a God and how can I know him? If God is so good, why is life so bad? How can I fill this nagging sense of unfulfilled desires, the ones that seem deeper than merely 'what's the meaning of life?'

The gift of Heaven, while nice at one level, was entirely unfulfilling and disconnected at another. It was like gifting a bookworm a set of skis and a trip to Copper Mountain in Colorado. Or giving your wife a Dyson vacuum cleaner for Christmas when what she really wanted was a set of diamond earrings.

Total disconnect between the offer and the desire.

Harrison ended this first training section like any good salesman: tactics for closing the deal.

"Faith is the key that unlocks the gift of Heaven," he said. It was what salespeople called the *call to action*. Any salesperson worth their salt would give their prospect instructions to provoke an immediate response, usually using an imperative verb—*Buy now!*—and with a sense of urgency—*While supplies last!*

Same with *Everyday Evangelism.* Buy now, before you get hit by a random bus and die and go to hell! Receive the gift of heaven now before Jesus comes back and it's too late!

I felt ill. Jesus had been reduced to a set of kitchen knives sans nifty accessories. And I was being called to sell him like this. To my students.

No way. There had to be a better way to share Jesus' magical, revolutionary story of rescue with my guys. With Clint.

I determined to find one.

CHAPTER 7

WHEN WE BROKE FOR LUNCH, I was disheartened and demoralized.

Is this what the message of Christianity is all about? A sales pitch to get people to Heaven? Is this what the Church is all about? A force of salespeople trying to meet sales goals and benchmarks—all in the name of Jesus?

"Pete, what's your problem?" Ainsley questioned as I sat stewing.

"What do you mean?" I said with a defensive edge. I closed my notebook and shoved it into my bag.

"The whole mornin' you've been huffin' and puffin' like the Big Bad Wolf over there. You look like you're about to explode, your face is so red!"

I felt self-conscious and a little bad for my apparent public brooding. But only for a minute. Because I felt justified. The way I saw it, Dr. Harrison's *good news* was what was wrong with the Christian faith. It was the reason why Clint was going the way he was going. It seemed so disconnected from life.

"Yeah, you know what Ains, I've got problems," I huffed as

we made our way over to the lunch line. "I've got a problem with the fact that we're supposed to go out and sell Jesus like he's some Kirby vacuum!"

"What do you mean by selling Jesus?"

"No. That's right. Selling *Heaven*."

I could tell by the look on her face that she wasn't tracking. Even more: she didn't seem at all bothered by the morning training, which made me skeptical to open up more.

"Forget about it, Ains," I demurred as we exited the line. "Just processing the morning. That's all."

We found a table in the corner. I desperately wanted to eat in silence, to recharge my introvert batteries and avoid any conversation about the shift in my spiritual life. My Energizer Bunny companion wouldn't let me.

"It seems like you're doin' a whole lot more than processin'," Ainsley said as she ate a forkful of salad. Then she added: "Are you going liberal on me, Pete?" with a smile and a wink.

Liberal?

My gut twisted at the drop of that word. I wanted to turtle inside myself at the accusation. Growing up, you never were caught committing two cardinal sins: backsliding or going liberal. The first would earn you a therapy session to break you of your sins. The second a prayer meeting to expunge you of your aberrant, heretical beliefs.

"Why? You have a thing for liberals, Ains?" I joked as I chomped on my turkey sandwich that tasted more like the cardboard packaging the deli meat came in.

"Funny," she retorted and returned to her salad, finally letting me sit in peace.

An hour later, we returned to our evangelism classroom for the next half of our training. Harrison had shed his sports jacket and tie before returning to his lecture of selling vacuum cleaner Jesus.

He began, "During the break I was pleased that a few of you were already thinking ahead with questions about the next topic in our training. How you engage and answer your prospect's questions."

There was that word again. *Prospect.* My gut turned over at the sound of the word.

This should be good...

"My answer," Harrison continued, "is that you don't. Don't even think about answering or engaging their questions."

I snapped my head up to attention and furrowed my brow, not sure I had heard him right.

Did you just say people's spiritual questions don't matter?!

I was surprised I didn't go and blurt out my question right then and there for all to hear.

"As much as you might want to stop the gospel presentation and answer your prospect's questions in that moment, don't. Don't let their questions distract you from your primary goal of getting the Christian message out there. I know it sounds counterintuitive, but I've seen time and time again how one question leads to an entire rabbit trail that derails the focus on the gospel presentation. My experience is that people's questions are usually just smokescreens, anyway. Walls designed to distract and detract from your God-ordained opportunity to communicate the Christian message."

Or maybe they are genuine emotional or intellectual barriers to that message!

I felt my nostrils flaring and my body becoming warm again as he continued speaking. I wanted to spit I was so irritated. Almost got up and walked out. And I should have. I really, really should have.

"Then what do you say when someone asks you a question?" someone asked from the back of the room.

Yes, what do you say, Mr. Silverhair? I crossed my arms and leaned back in my chair, waiting for his million-dollar insight.

"Here's what I say: 'Wow, that's a really good question. I see it's important that I answer it for you, and I promise I will. But why don't we put your question in abeyance for a little while and continue on. At the end, when I'm finished, if you ask me your question again I will be sure to answer it for you.'"

I found his response lame and offensive, but I saw others nodding along and taking notes. Including Ainsley.

Harrison went on: "What this does is two things. First, most people don't know what the word *abeyance* means. So they usually nod along and let me continue in confusion."

The room laughed in amusement at Mr. Silverhair's cleverness. I wanted to puke.

"The second thing it does is forces them to ask their questions again at the end. By the time we finish, they usually forget their question anyway, so there's no need to answer it. Win-win on both fronts."

This time Dr. Harrison chuckled at his own cleverness. I wanted to chuck my training manual at him because of his disrespect for people and their spiritual journeys. It's no wonder the world can't stand Christians, especially the silver-haired, coat-wearing, salespeople kind who trot out their nifty presentations—all the while treating people like objects to win for their spreadsheet, scalps to add to their belt.

"Now what's wrong?" Ainsley hissed in my ear in irritation.

I uncrossed my arms and sat up straight. "Nothing," I whispered back quickly.

I sat brooding the rest of the afternoon as Harrison walked the class through specific questions people often ask. Like how we can rely on a book written by dead guys so long ago; how we can be sure Jesus really rose from the dead; how we can say there is only one way to God. His answers betrayed his ignorance at why people asked such questions in the first place. Clearly this guy was culturally clueless.

After seven hours of lecture, the day was finally drawing to a close when Harrison announced the evening's festivities. "Folks, tonight we have a real treat. We are going out into the streets to put our *Everyday Evangelism* principles into practice."

As in street witnessing? Confronting people's spiritual destinies in Walmart parking lots and at bus stations?

Most of our fellow classmates reacted with a nervousness that slowly gave way to spiritual excitement. Even Ainsley seemed caught up in it all. I wanted to puke.

"You've got to be kidding me," I mumbled, shaking my head.

"Now, the main reason we're doing this," Harrison continued, "is to show you how to successfully execute your own on-the-job training back in your churches. Remember, the point of going out and witnessing isn't for the sake of prospects, but the trainees."

"Come again?" I heard myself blurt out. The room turned toward me. My face reddened.

Harrison looked momentarily thrown off. He searched the room for the voice behind the question before his penetrating eyes found me.

"Yes, young man," he said grinning. "OJT is more for the benefit of the person being trained than for the prospect to whom you are witnessing. It's all about equipping your people with the tools to evangelize than it is—"

"Actually, saving the heathen from going to hell. Got it, thanks." I was as surprised as anyone that I cut off our teacher— my boss. I glanced over at Ainsley who was staring wide-eyed, mouth agape. I knew I was rude. Disrespectful, really. But I couldn't take it any more.

"Just a joke, folks," I said smiling, trying to recover. A few chuckled nervously in the back.

Harrison didn't look amused, but he played along, quickly trying to return to the task at hand: preparing the group to sell Jesus to the Dallas masses.

"Of course, that's not how I would put it," the man said, "and every time we do go into the streets, several prospects become believers. It's really quite exciting! The numbers don't lie. One in three prospects will become Christians, just you see."

It's so simple, isn't it? Just a numbers game.

I didn't hear the rest of what Mr. Silverhair had to say, because I had quietly packed my bag and then walked out the back door.

That evening's little evangelism pow-wow would have one less member confronting poor, unsuspecting soccer moms and college students about their spiritual journeys.

Consequences be damned.

CHAPTER 8

"PETER DANIEL YOUNG! Where on earth are you going, leaving me like this?"

I turned back and saw Ainsley following me, her pace and face communicating clear annoyance. I turned to continue walking to our rental car to return to our hotel. I realized it was her ride as much as mine, so I stopped.

I turned toward her as she caught up to me. "You're not going to tell Roger, are you?"

"I don't even know what I'd tell him if I did! What is your deal, Pete? You've been acting like a nutso this whole day. I feel like there's something you're not telling me."

I sighed and leaned my head back, resting my hands behind my back.

I silently weighed whether I should let her in on everything I had been feeling, from the day's training venture and the last several months of ministry.

Silence grew as we stood in the middle of the megachurch parking garage.

"Are you game for going back to the hotel?" I finally said.

"Back to the hotel? But what about the on-the-job training?" Ainsley questioned.

"Screw OJT!"

I echoed more loudly than I intended. I glanced over Ainsley's shoulder and then around my own, hoping no one was around to hear.

"Truth be told, I really wasn't thrilled with the idea anyway," Ainsley admitted.

"Then let's jet." I hustled back to our rental still positioned between the Hummer and Cadillac. She reluctantly followed, and we both got inside.

"So, we're going to play hooky or something?"

Oh, Ainsley. Ever the rule-follower.

"Yes, like play hooky. I'm sure Dr. Silverhair won't miss me. And besides, I can't do it anymore, Ains."

"Anymore?"

I looked over at her as I pulled out of our parking spot, then said, "Let's wait until the hotel. Too much to talk about."

A dreaded local top 40s radio station serenaded us for the fifteen-minute drive to our hotel. It was dinner time, so we grabbed a table at the on-site steakhouse. Ainsley ordered a Diet Coke. I ordered a 20 oz. Deep Ellum IPA, a local favorite, apparently.

"So Peter, what's the deal?" she finally asked.

I looked down at the table as I picked at a fray in the corner of the tablecloth, plotting my course, wondering how much to share. Wondering whether I could trust my co-worker.

Ah, screw it.

"Last month, after one of our Monday morning meetings, Clint texted me in a panic to connect for coffee. So we got together at Saxbys and he basically laid it out that he's gone agnostic. Or at least has soured on Christianity."

Ainsley gasped. "No way! Why? What happened? Was it his mom's cancer?"

Our drinks arrived and we ordered: salmon for me, chicken for Ainsley. I took a large swig of my hoppy brew before continuing.

"It was a lot of things. But, yeah, I was shocked. Blown away, really. But here's the thing: he had all these questions that I had zero answers for. Zero, Ains!"

"Pete, you can't put this on you," she said, touching my hand resting on the table in reassurance.

I offered a weak smile. "Thanks. I don't blame myself necessarily. I guess I blame Christianity. I blame our *version* of the Christian faith."

This caused her to sit back. Her eyes narrowed slightly. Skepticism and concern crept across her face as she folded her arms.

"What do you mean by *that?*"

"What I mean is, why the heck are we offering people Heaven as a free gift, like some set of Cutco knives?"

"What's Cutco?"

"A high-end knife set I sold before—never mind, that's not the point. The point is we're so interested in saving people from Hell and getting them into Heaven that we don't even know what it is that people are looking for in the first place. And then the arrogance and audacity of selling people Jesus without engaging them in their deep questions about him and the Christian faith, not to mention treating them like they're training grounds for our army of Christian colonizers. I mean, what's up with *that?* Is *this* what Christianity is all about?"

The emotions from the past month came tumbling out of me, triggered by the day's teaching. If I left DC doubting the need to reimagine the Christian faith in light of our changing culture, those doubts were put to rest thanks to Mr. Silverhair and his out-of-tough, megachurch-inspired *Everyday Evangelism.*

Ainsley stared at me, blank-faced, as if nothing I was saying was registering.

"Does none of this register? Do you honestly think what our illustrious boss was describing would resonate with your gals in any way? Is Heaven, life after death in some land in outer space, really what they're looking for? I mean, is *that* the gospel, what the story of Jesus and message of Christianity is all about?"

These questions seemed to give Ainsley pause. She sat back and cocked her head to the side. I didn't get the answer I was expecting.

"So, what, you're no longer a believer or something?"

I closed my eyes and let slip a sigh, but quickly sat up straight. I said, "I'm finding I no longer believe in the Christian faith I've believed for two decades."

I was as surprised by my answer as Ainsley looked. I feared I'd said too much. I sat back, took a large swig of my IPA, then folded my arms and leaned forward against the table.

"Look, my issue isn't with believing. I do believe. Of course I do! It's just that I want to believe *otherly*. I want to believe other-than the versions of the Christian faith that have come before—the versions of the Christian faith Harrison represented in full today."

Before Ainsley could respond, our food arrived. We immediately set about our meals, giving the conversation room to breathe.

"I'm serious about what I asked before," I finally said after mowing through half of my salmon.

"About what?" Ainsley said mid-chew.

"Whether or not you're going to tell Roger about today. About this...conversation."

"I'm not even sure I'd know what to say. But no, I'm not."

"Good, because he wouldn't understand."

She set down her fork, swallowed, and wiped her mouth. "I'm not sure I understand."

"Look, it's not like I'm abandoning Christianity. I'm not abandoning ministry. I love my job, I love Jesus. I'm just struggling with what is important about the Christian faith, that's all"

"A crisis of faith," Ainsley said, defining what I had failed to define myself. Or perhaps failed to admit to myself.

"I guess that's what I'm saying. Yes, I guess I'm having a crisis of faith. But that doesn't mean I'm not a Christian," I quickly added, "or I'm going liberal."

She smiled. "That's good. The liberal part, I mean. Because you know what Roger would do."

"He'd throw my butt out on the street faster than you could say John the Baptist!"

We both laughed, deflating some of the tension.

"Crisis of faith is a good way of putting it," I said, "which scares me to death. At a number of levels."

"How so?"

"Well, I feel like I don't know what's up from down with what to believe, aside from core Christian beliefs. Like, did God use evolution to create? Is it even important *how* God created? What is the Bible and how should we think about the parts where it looks like God is behaving badly? What even is faith in the first place? Is it a prayer you say or things you do? What about people of other faiths? Are they doomed to Hell? And what even is Hell, anyway? Is it for real and forever?"

I shoved a forkful of salmon into my mouth, along with some couscous.

"Those are some super-deep questions, Pete. I'm not sure how I'd answer them myself."

"Now you understand what I'm saying. And then there's the whole ministry part of my crisis. How do I guide my students through their own questions if I can't even answer them for myself? I feel like a fraud, Ainsley." I tossed my fork on my plate and leaned back in my chair with a huff.

"Or maybe you're more authentic than you've ever been," she said, trying to reassure me.

Her response surprised me. She seemed to register that surprise.

"Think about it," she continued. "We're in these positions, placed on these pedestals by our students who think we know all the answers, that we're the experts on faith and spirituality. But maybe it's OK for us not to know all the answers. Maybe it's better for their own journey to know we struggle with the same questions they do. We're finding our way forward as much as they are. As much as Clint is."

I found comfort in what Ainsley was saying. A comfort that had been hard to come by since that fateful conversation in Saxbys several weeks ago.

"Do you struggle with these questions, Ains? Have you ever had a crisis of faith? How did you feel about today, with the way Harrison talked about the Christian message? With how he kept referring to our non-Christian friends as *prospects*?"

She set down her fork and knife and leaned back, crossing her arms. I could tell she was surprised by my direct questions. Was that because she couldn't identify with what I was going through? Or was it that she had been secretly struggling herself?

"I can't say that I've had a crisis, Pete. But the past few weeks some of my girls have been going through their own doubts, and some of their questions have caused me to step back myself."

"Really? Like how?"

"Well, one of my girls, Courtney, her brother was recently diagnosed with cancer."

"No..."

"Yeah. So that's caused her to question God's goodness, asking all of the 'if God is so good why is life so bad' kind of questions. Sure, I've got all the *right answers*," she said, making air quotes. "But they seem hollow. Courtney agrees."

I said, "Trying to explain the brokenness of creation by reciting all the right Bible verses and giving all the right theological answers isn't what Courtney needs."

"Exactly," Ainsley agreed. "Then another of my girls has been bothered by Hell, wondering what's going to happen to her Muslim boy interest if he doesn't become a Christian. Another freshman girl is questioning the Bible because of her science classes. I feel totally out of sorts lately, because the answers I've been trained to give just aren't working anymore."

"Then you understand what I've been going through the past several months! And why I'm so pissed that Roger wants to trot out Freddy Morris, thinking he's the answer to our students' paganism!"

Ainsley tried to suppress a giggle, but it slipped through her nose.

"Am I wrong?"

"No, I understand completely," she offered. "But what can we do? Tell Roger he doesn't know what he's talking about?"

"No. Tell him he doesn't know what the *heck* he's talking about."

She frowned playfully. "Pete...Don't be disrespectful."

I huffed, but nodded in agreement. "It's just so frustrating, because he doesn't know what it's like to actually do ministry in this world. He still thinks we're some sort of Christian nation that's backslidden. That people still respect Christianity and the Church at some level and that our students even know who Jesus is in the first place. They don't! We're postmodern and post-Christian, which means we need to do ministry differently, and we need better answers than the ones Dr. Silverhair has, when he's even in the mood to give them in the first place."

"What do you mean by *post*-Christian. And postmodern?"

I sat closer to the table, eager to share what Prosurgent Christianity had been teaching me.

"Yes, postmodern and post-Christian. This new group called Prosurgent has been helping me better understand this crazy new world we're living in as Christians."

"Prosurgent?" Ainsley asked, wrinkling her forehead in confusion.

"They're not important right now," I said waving her off. "Post-Christian means that people in the Western world have moved beyond Christianity as the only religious option. *Post* doesn't mean anti, but *beyond*. It's no longer a given that people go to church. It's no longer a given that people think the Christian way of living or thinking is the only way, or even the correct way. Does that make sense?"

"Sort of. I see that with my girls."

"Same here, with my guys. They don't hardly know anything about the Bible, the basic stories. They don't know anything about the basic beliefs of Christianity. Which isn't their fault. It's just reality. We're a post-Christian nation, and we're not ever going back to the way things were when Christianity dominated."

"So what of...postmodernism? Is that the word?"

"Yes, postmodernism or postmodernity. Roger would say it's another word for secularism and paganism," I said, rolling my eyes. "Postmodernism describes how people think about and view the world. Three guys represent this view. Derrida, Lyotard, and Foucault."

"Derrida, Lyotard, and Foucault?" Ainsley repeated. "They sound like dog breeds."

I smiled. "These guys represent how our college students view the world. Heck, they represent how *I* view the world!"

"*You're* postmodern?"

"Basically. Here's what I mean. So Jaques Derrida is big on the idea that we all bring something to the table when we interpret the world, including the Bible. As a white, American male from the Midwest, I read the Bible a certain way. As a white Southern Baptist belle from Louisiana, so do you."

"Gee, thanks," Ainsley said curtly.

"No, there's no judgment there! It's just the fact. So that impacts how we understand truth. It's like when there's a car accident and five people see it happen from five different angles. The same happens with truth."

"So all truth is relative now? We just make it up as we go?"

I stopped to consider this. "No, it's not that. It's just, that's how our college students *think* about it. And, let's face it, how many denominations are there in the world? In America alone? Hundreds, with lots of different ways of interpreting baptism and the Lord's Supper and how God created. Our students get this, so I think rather than hiding this fact I'm learning just to admit that multiple interpretations is part of being human. Even part of being a Christian. Doesn't mean there isn't one truth. But we're still finding out what that truth is."

Now I saw Ainsley stopping to consider this. She nodded, and said, "That makes sense. What about the other two. And just to warn you, my brain is beginning to hurt from this conversation!"

I laughed. "I understand. Mine is too. I'll move it along. So the other guy is Lyotard—"

"Like the little dresses ballerinas wear?" Ainsley interrupted.

"Cute. I like this guy because he's all about rejecting the big life-defining stories. Or at least rejecting how we prove them."

"You're losing me, Pete. Life-defining stories?"

"Yeah, like the Christian story. Or even the science and evolutionary stories. He's like, all your attempts to claim one universal truth are nonsense, because they're just one truth among many truths. One story among stories. And these stories are influenced by culture and powerful institutions. So when we say 'The Bible says…' or 'Christianity says…' our students are like, 'Whatever!' right?"

"I get that all the time now!" Ainsley exclaimed, getting more interested in the conversation.

"Well, that's because 'The Koran says…' and 'Buddhism says…' is just as legitimate a thing to say in the eyes of a postmodern person."

I saw recognition written on Ainsley's face. She seemed to be getting it.

"Doesn't mean we stop telling the Christian story," I added, "or believe those other stories are just as true. It just means how we prove our faith or use it to impact our students needs some tweaking."

"Makes sense. There was one more fella, right?"

"Foucault. And this guy will make even more sense. He's against institutions of power behind truth claims. He says what we say is normal and moral is really just a power play by institutions of power, rather than actually being moral or normal."

"Pete…"

"OK, I know. Your brain is fried. Take gay marriage."

"Whoa! Now we're going deep."

I laughed. "Stay with me. So Foucault would say the only reason same-sex relationships has been wrong for so long is because the powerful institution of the Church said it is. So, according to his logic, one powerful institution has been suppressing the rights of a less powerful group, gay people. He's like an archaeologist who digs beneath the surface to expose the power plays beneath what we call objective truth. He would say that truth really doesn't exist. It's all about power, nothing more. And postmodern people nowadays will fight against any powerful group that suppresses the rights of a minority group. It's not surprising that one of the top perceptions of Christianity is anti-gay."

"So let me see if I got this right," Ainsley said yawning. "Post-modernism says we all interpret truth according to our own perspective. That all truth stories are competing with other truth stories. And what we say is true and normal is really just about the most powerful winning out. Is that right?"

I sat and blinked in silence. "You pretty much boiled down my half-hour lecture in thirty seconds. Yes, that's it."

Ainsley smiled and leaned in. "So what do we do about it?"

"That's what I've been wrestling with the past month. And that's why I've been so irritated all day, because Dr. Silverhair doesn't get it. Neither does Roger. They don't realize we're like missionaries charting a new course for the Christian message in a foreign land and culture. Christians need to rethink how we interact with the world around us and how we answer people's questions. Frankly, we need to reimagine the Christian faith for a new day. A new postmodern, post-Christian day."

"Reimagine the Christian faith?"

By the sound of her voice I could tell Ainsley was skeptical. I'd had her up until that point, but I thought I just lost her.

"Yes, rethinking how we've been living as Christians and how we share the Christian message."

I hid my true interests and she seemed mollified by my answer.

"Maybe we need to create our own *Everyday Evangelism*, then," Ainsley suggested. "An alternative EE that will resonate with our students. After all, the reason Roger sent us here was to get trained to train our students, right?"

"Now we're getting somewhere! Yes, that's exactly what we need. Something that's not this cheap, greasy salesperson sort of way of sharing the story of God's rescue in Jesus."

"And in a way that actually answers people's questions," Ainsley added.

"Exactly!"

Our bill arrived. I paid for it with my ministry AmEx card.

"Whew," Ainsley sighed. "This has been the biggest mental workout I've had in a while, Pete."

"Thanks for listening and chatting, Ainsley. And thanks for not writing me off as a heretic or liberal or something worse!"

"Who says I haven't?" She grinned and winked, then said, "I'm not sure about this whole postmodernism thing, but I'm glad you're asking these questions. For my girls' sake as much as my own. Count me in. I'm with you in this."

I grinned back. "Thanks, Ainsley. You can't begin to understand how thankful I am to hear that. Especially since I'm not so sure our other ministry co-workers will be as thankful and supportive the further I go into this."

I signed the credit card receipt and we both headed to our separate rooms. As much of a pain as the day was, I was thankful for how it ended. Thankful I had a new ally in my journey toward reimagining.

However that journey turned out.

CHAPTER 9

I WOKE up with a throbbing headache and depressed. Not a good combination. I popped a few ibuprofens before showering, hoping the combination of steam and hot water would wash them both away before our flight back to DC.

As I got dressed, I couldn't shake my irritation with yesterday's teaching, and the fact Roger wanted us to not only use this method to reach people with Jesus' message of hope, but train our students to use it as well.

"Totally clueless," I said as I buttoned up my shirt.

So what should I do about it? What can I do about?

I considered Ainsley's idea about crafting an alternative to *Everyday Evangelism*. That I put pen to paper and whip up a proposal that will convince my ministry peers and bosses to reimagine how to share the Christian message in our world.

Yes, that's what we need. An alternative to EE!

I finished packing my clothes and stuffed my MacBook into my computer bag, along with my notebook and pens. Ainsley had already retrieved our rental car and was waiting for me when I arrived in the hotel lobby.

She honked and rolled down her window, and shouted, "We're gonna be late, get in!"

"Relax, we've got like an hour until we board."

As she drove, I considered what it might look like to do evangelism differently in our emerging postmodern, post-Christian world.

Emerging Evangelism. That's what I'll call it. Genius!

But closely trailing that thought was a searing fear.

What will my ministry think of me? What will they do to me? Write me off as a liberal heretic? Fire me as a liberal heretic?

Whatever. I needed to sketch this out for myself, not just for Campus Ministry.

We made it through security with a little more time to spare than when we flew to Dallas. I grabbed a coffee and muffin at a Starbucks while Ainsley dashed to our gate. I made it through just as they were closing it.

I settled into my seat and opened my laptop to write the evangelism method or program or whatever I was calling it that my students needed to lead them into following Jesus as King and Rescuer.

I started with how much of our culture neither understands nor accepts Christianity as being true, real, or valuable. What's more, not only has an entire generation been raised outside of church, it is being raised under the assumption that the Christian worldview is not all there is to life. Post-Christians have already encountered Christianity at some level and have their answer: *'Thanks, but no thanks!'*

I could feel heart thumping harder in my chest at the thrill of it all while I continued scratching out my thoughts for the foundation to a new way of sharing Jesus. After beginning with an analysis of culture, I turned to the difference between how we should share him based on what I had been reading from Prosurgent thinkers. The words were flowing easily as my excitement grew for the possibility of charting a new course for my ministry.

I sat back and smiled, satisfied at the work of art sitting on my screen. At least I thought it was pretty artistic. Didn't know if Roger would agree, but whatever. This was it. This was the beginning of how we needed to engage people with Jesus' message of hope.

Now the essence of that hope, the gospel. Or *God's Story of Rescue*, as I called it, something I picked up on from some of my Prosurgent readings. The language got at what the word *gospel* was in the first place: a story about the rescue from sin and death provided by Jesus' life, death, and resurrection. But it's a story that stretches well before Jesus and well after him as well.

I set my fingers on my keyboard and began to type:

This story begins at the beginning, with creation. The moment when God breathed all of this into existence—all of us into existence. And God's intent when he made us was for us to exist in an everlasting relationship with himself, defined by mutual love. We were made in his image as statues of the divine to channel and represent his rule on earth.

But then something happened: rebellion. Mama Eve and Papa Adam rebelled against God, plunging all of creation and all of us into chaos, sin, and death. Now things aren't the way they were ever supposed to be. And we aren't either. We do things God never intended when he created us, both to God and our neighbor. And we've been trying to find the fix ever since.

Thankfully, God didn't give up on us! From the very beginning God had a plan to rescue us from the fate of our rebellion and provide a way to be restored to him in relationship and be put back together again as whole people. That rescue began when God chose and called a person, Abraham, and then his descendants, Israel. God promised to be their God and they his people, but also bless the world through them. They failed miserably at their mission of acting as his agents of rescue, and eventually God took matters into his own hands by becoming one of us.

One day God became flesh and blood and moved into the neighborhood in the person of Jesus Christ. God the Father sent God the Son into the world to walk around in our human skin and experience everything that life has to offer. God understands our life of pain and suffering and struggle because he lived this life. While walking in our shoes, Jesus taught us what it means to live under God's reign and rule. He modeled for us how God intended us to live when he created us. Jesus gave us a taste of things to come by performing miracles that foreshadowed the day when this broken, busted world will finally be put back together again, when Jesus makes all things new. And he lived the life we could not live ourselves by living a life of obedience to his Father God, which was important for the climax of God's Story.

Because not only did God live the life we could not life, he died the death we should have died. Jesus Christ willingly crawled up on a Roman cross that served as an altar upon which the final sacrifice for the sins of the world was made. His body was beaten and broken apart, bearing upon itself the punishment for the sins of the world. His blood was shed, offering his life for ours. His very life dripped down the boards of execution that held his limp, lifeless body and puddled beneath it in a sticky mess.

But thankfully death didn't have the final word in Jesus' story. Now it doesn't have the final word in ours, either. Because on the third day Jesus defeated our last enemy by physically, bodily rising from the dead in full resurrection glory, paving the way for our own eventual resurrection. That first Easter morning launched a whole new revolution, as well as the final act in God's Story of Rescue: Re-creation.

The final movement in this four-act play began when Christ burst forth from the tomb to put this broken, busted world back together again, a life that continued in the most unlikeliest of ways: through his people, the Church. On the Day of Pentecost God unleashed his Spirit into the world upon his people to continue what Jesus Christ himself began. And that final act has been progressively unfolding ever since in both the miraculous and the mundane of life.

Eventually, God's Story will come to a close. Or, rather, the end will unfold into a new beginning. One day, Jesus will return to judge the world and bring Heaven to Earth, which is our ultimate hope. We do not hope for a future in outer space playing harps, dancing on clouds, and drinking really bad church coffee. No, our hope is in the resurrection from the dead, for life after death right here on Earth. Heaven really is a place on Earth! We were made for Earth, we are earthlings, and God's intent through his Son and Spirit is to re-create it to the way he originally intended it to be.

This Story is a hopeful story because it points to the hope of humanity in Jesus' life, death, and resurrection. Jesus is who people have been waiting for their whole lives, whether they know it or not. And we are called to bring and bear his Story of hope so that people trust him with their lives as King and Rescuer. That trust is the faith God has called us to invest in his Son. God invites us to trust his promise of rescue from sin and death in and through his Son, and to live a life of faithfulness in response to that commitment.

That's God's Story, and it's ours, too. Because Jesus wins, so can every person on the planet!

My fingers burned from nonstop typing as the magical, mysterious, revolutionary Story of God's rescue flowed out onto my MacBook.

This is exactly what Campus Ministry has been missing. This is what Dr. Harrison missed for ages: the unified, complete, holistic Story of what God has been doing in this world from the beginning of time.

I sat back in my seat and stared at my screen. I had a decision to make.

Submit or not submit?

Emailing my Word doc off to Roger would open up a box of questions and potential accusations that I wasn't sure I was ready to deal with. Ainsley's confusion and accusations were enough—and she was mild.

Why put myself through it? Why jeopardize my job, my career in ministry?

A smile crept across the corners of my mouth. For my answer was sitting in a coffee shop back home.

Those students, with all of their religious doubts and fears, their spiritual questions about faith and life and everything in between.

And Clint.

I opened my email program and wrote a note to Roger and Bernie. I thanked them for the training in Dallas and shared how

I had been thinking about the changes in our culture, believing we needed a different way to share what I called God's Story of Rescue. I said it wasn't meant as criticism against Dr. Harrison or their own ideas, but more a suggestion for how to best share Jesus' story with our students, and then train Christians to do the same.

I logged onto the plane's wireless connection. Then I sat back and re-read my email message. I hovered the cursor above the *Send* button, tingling with indecision.

Should I send it, or should I trash it?

I held my breath and clicked the button.

My stomach fluttered with a mixture of anxiety and anticipation and excitement. I took a deep breath, closed my eyes, and settled back into my seat for the remainder of the flight, praying to the good Lord above that it would be received well.

CHAPTER 10

IT HAD BEEN three days since I emailed off my proposal for the *Emerging Evangelism* alternative to *Everyday Evangelism*. And I still hadn't received a reply.

What does that mean? Should I start to panic? Should I start looking for another job?

Perhaps I'd opened their eyes to the realities of doing ministry among this emerging generation in a way that made sense to their culture. Perhaps Roger appreciated the method I'd laid out to not only share God's story of rescue with our students, but also train Christian ones to do the same. Perhaps he saw why *Everyday Evangelism* wasn't working anymore and wouldn't work in our ministry context among postmodern, post-Christian young adults.

Perhaps not.

As I walked through the front door of our ministry row house my heart began beating faster. Panic began settling deep in my belly.

Chill, Peter! Don't half-glass it.

When I reached the top of the stairs to go to my office, I saw

Roger meeting with Bernie and Peggy. He glanced my way through the closed glass door and returned back to his conversation with nary a smile. An unlikely response from Roger.

An ache began to needle the middle of my forehead as I sat down in my cubicle to check my email for the morning.

There was a message from Clint waiting for me. Before I opened it I noticed a message with two exclamation points indicating four-alarm urgency. The message was from Roger. Bernie and Peggy were carbon-copied. It read:

Hi Peter,

Thanks for your email and hard work considering how best to convert the students at Georgetown University. I've read through it, a few times, and want us to meet first thing in the morning. I've asked Bernie and Peggy to join us to discuss some things. Please see me when you arrive.

~Roger

I had no idea what I should think of the email. He wanted to discuss "some things"? How sufficiently vague. I hated vague emails.

I looked up over my computer monitor and back into Roger's office again. All I saw was Bernie and Peggy seated and staring forward, still in conversation with Roger. I read back over the email.

"Peter?"

I looked up. Tabitha was standing at the opening of my cubicle.

My eyes widened, feeling like I'd been summoned to the principal's office. "Good morning, Tabitha," I managed.

"Good morning. Roger was asking for you. You got a minute?"

I guess I wasn't too far off the mark. And this will take more than a minute.

"Sure thing. I'll be right there."

I grabbed my Nalgene bottle and filled it with water in the kitchenette before heading to Roger's office. Figured I should stay hydrated for the road ahead.

"Hey, Pete," Bernie said smiling with his thick Brooklyn accent as I entered.

"Hi, Peter," Peggy said more formally.

"Peter, thanks for joining us," Roger said with a weak smile. "Would you get the door?"

His tone was...different. Strained and betraying. Like he was trying to be nice, but hiding his true intentions.

I shut the door and sat in a chair between Bernie and Peggy. I could hear my heart in my head as I took a seat. I unscrewed the cap of my Nalgene, hands shaking slightly from adrenaline. I took a sip of water, then another as Roger began.

"Did you get my email?"

"Yes," I tried to say, my throat stumbling over itself. I cleared it. "Yes, yes I did. You said there were some things you wanted to talk about?"

"Yes, there are. First of all, thanks for writing your proposal, Peter. It's obvious a lot of time and thought went into it. It's also obvious you have a real heart for your students."

I continued listening as Roger laid down a ground of appreciation, greasing the skids for what was to come.

"But..."

Here it comes.

"I'm confused by some things in this paper. *We're* confused by some things," he added, nodding toward Bernie and Peggy.

He took out my paper. It was punctuated by underlines and

notations and circles and exclamation points. A red pen had sure had a delightful romp over nearly every one of my sentences.

I glanced from my paper to Bernie who was staring forward, still with a slight smile. Peggy was also staring forward, though more serious.

"OK," I managed. "What's the problem?"

"I have to say, Peter, part of my problem—" he stopped. "*Our* problem," he added, looking at Bernie and Peggy again to emphasize their united front, "is the tone of your proposal."

I took another drink of water. "Tone?"

"Yes, tone. There's a lot of pride here. A lot of arrogance."

Pride? Arrogance?

I didn't know how to respond. I felt my jaw drop and my eyes widen. I was paralyzed by his words because they felt like darts attacking my character more than addressing my ideas. I expected the latter; that I could handle. But questioning my character and motives?

"How is what I wrote prideful? And arrogant?"

"You have to understand that Dr. Harrison's evangelism method is a tried and true way of reaching the lost for Christ. Thousands of people have been saved through it—"

"During the stone age, maybe?" I mumbled.

I regretted my interruption and the words as soon as they left my mouth.

"See, that's what Roger is getting at," Bernie said, pivoting toward me with the gentleness of my grandfather.

I sighed. "Sorry. I didn't mean to sound so condescending and dismissive. What I meant to say was that his way of talking about Jesus and the Christian message might have worked back then, when Dr. Harrison wrote it and used it. I'm sure it did. And I'm sure it has led lots of people to Christ. All I'm suggesting is that it's time for new tools and new ways of doing things for a very different culture."

"You mean...postmodern and post-Christian tools?"

His question felt like a trap. As a former lawyer, Roger was good at laying them with carefully-crafted questions, intentionally or not.

"I mean tools for mission in a postmodern, post-Christian mission field."

"But that's just it. Why are you advocating that we use secular tools for spiritual work? Humanistic tools, even?"

"I'm not arguing anything remotely close to that!"

I knew I was becoming defensive. I felt like I was being attacked personally. I was also growing defensive because my co-workers clearly didn't get it.

"What I'm arguing is that our students are postmodern and post-Christian. They are beyond the modern, traditional way of viewing life and viewing truth. That's just a fact of reality. Same for being beyond the Christian story as the only one on the block to answer their spiritual questions, not to mention their life questions. All I'm saying is that we need to acknowledge this is the nature of our mission field, and then approach it in a way they need us to."

"I think I understand what you're saying," Bernie offered, ever my ally. "Like missionaries, using language and tools that meet the needs of that culture?"

"Exactly! Our students don't assume that Christianity is the starting place for truth. Heck, they don't even assume that *Heaven* is the starting place to satisfy their needs. The gift of some land in outer space after this life isn't what they're interested in."

Roger's face registered my little jab at Harrison's *Everyday Evangelism*. His eyes narrowed, then he smiled slightly before pressing in.

"So you're saying we need to shape the gospel to meet the

demands of this day and age? To make it more palatable to culture?"

"Not at all. I'd argue that's what Dr. Harrison did with EE."

Now I had everyone's attention.

"Listen," I continued, taking another drink of water and shifting in my chair. "When Dr. Harrison developed his own evangelism method, he did it to reach religious people who he assumed were interested in Heaven, and thought they had to earn it through good works. So he begins his version of the Christian message with Heaven being a gift that's not earned or deserved."

I stopped, weighing whether I should continue. I took another drink of my water as Roger, Bernie, and Peggy sat waiting for me to continue.

"But here's the thing. Not only is Heaven the last thing my students are interested in, I don't see how the gospel itself is interested in Heaven."

"Now what do you mean about that?" Bernie asked, his previously supportive tone dissipating. "You don't think God's good news is about Heaven? You're not saying there *isn't* a Heaven, are you?"

I shook my head. "No, I'm not saying I don't believe in Heaven. But where in Scripture does it say that Jesus died to pay for our sins and to purchase a place for us in Heaven, as *Everyday Evangelism* says? Where is it in the text?"

I was more forceful than I intended in my deconstruction of EE. But the question gave my bosses pause.

Roger leaned back in his desk chair and brought his hands together at his fingertips. "OK, Peter. Then what *is* the gospel all about, if it isn't about Heaven, as you say? If Jesus didn't die to pay for people's sins to provide the gift of Heaven, then what was the point?"

Again, it sounded like Roger was channeling his inner lawyer, laying a trap for me with his words.

I took a breath before channeling the Prosurgent writings I'd been reading.

"The resurrection from the dead," I said. "That was the hope of the ancient Church. Their hope was in *'the resurrection of the body and life everlasting,'* as the Apostles' Creed says. It wasn't in some world out there in outer space. It was *this* world. Heaven really is a place on Earth, thank you Belinda Carlisle!"

They didn't get my little joke giving a nod to the 1987 song by the lead singer of The Go-Go's.

"And I gotta ask," I continued, "What exactly are you accusing me of?"

Bernie turned toward me. "Now hold on, Pete, we're not accusing you of anything. We just have some questions about some of the things you wrote in your paper."

"Well, it sure feels a little like an inquisition. Like you're challenging whether or not I believe in the gospel. Whether or not I'm even a Christian."

"We're just trying to get clarity about what you believe *about* the gospel," Roger explained.

I was offended, though I tried to hide it. It was one thing to challenge and question my methods for sharing the gospel. It was another thing to challenge my belief in the Christian message.

"I believe what you believe. That all of us are sinners who have fallen short of the glory of God, and Christ died as a sacrifice for our sins, as Paul says. And that whoever believes in him will not perish but have everlasting life, as John says." I took a breath to calm myself. "What more do you want?"

The room grew silent.

"Nothing," Roger finally said, a smile lifting one corner of his mouth. "I'm just glad we could clear up some of the confusion."

Confusion? Accusation, more like it.

"Me, too. Glad I could clear up your...*confusion*, as you say." I sat matching Roger's smile, willing myself not to run out of the room and never return.

"Thanks again for your proposal, Peter. We'll talk it through and get back with you."

"Great. Thanks," I managed, standing up to leave.

Bernie stopped me. "Pete, can I have a word?"

CHAPTER 11

BERNIE LED the way to his office at the end of the hallway a few doors down, that wretched green wallpaper straight from the '90s and heavy, clingy potpourri choking my senses as I walked to what seemed like my second death. Dante insisted there were seven circles of hell. Surely I was teleporting from one to the next in this life.

I stepped out of Roger's office and into Bernie's, a small space painted blue and smelling of pipe tobacco. He swore to me that he never used at work, but I think he snuck a puff or two late at night after hours. Behind him, a Texas A & M diploma hung proudly in a crooked frame. Draped across one corner of it was a Medal of Honor he had received during his service in Vietnam.

Bernie plunked himself in his large leather swivel chair and scooted closer to his desk. "Have a seat, brother," he said, motioning toward a well-worn leather couch across from him. I flopped down and sighed heavily.

"So how ya doin'?"

I scrunched up my face in confusion. "How am I doing? Gee,

I was just basically accused of denying the gospel. So I'm doing just peachy."

"That's not what Roger was doing."

"Well, what then?"

"He was concerned about some of the things you were proposing, that's all. You have to remember, Roger is a big follower of Dr. Harrison. Went to his church and served on the leadership before coming to Campus Ministry."

I rolled my eyes, and mumbled, "If you ask me he's a lemming who's taking us all off a cliff!"

"Now, Pete. Behave."

"Seriously. I'm trying to do the right thing for our students by helping us reach them in a way that makes sense, using language that they understand—and I'm branded some sort of heretic! I feel so misunderstood."

I hunched over, propping my elbows on both knees and putting my head in both palms. I took a heavy breath, trying to control the emotions welling within me.

"Hey, I understand," Bernie said soothingly in his Brooklyn accent. "I know you were trying to do the right thing. I appreciate what you're doing, I really do. But, unfortunately, it's not going to happen. Not the way you want it to, anyway."

I looked up. "Just like that. Nothing?"

"Remember whose name is on the shingle out front. The Harrison Campus Ministry. He went to college here and he set up this shop. And Roger is a loyal soldier. So no, we're not going to use anything that's not Doc Harrison approved."

"Even if it's not best? Even if it's actually harmful to the spiritual journey of those students?"

Bernie fell silent, looking down at his desk.

"Here's what I'd encourage you to do, but you didn't hear this from me," he said chuckling. "Forget what you heard on your training and go do what you wrote about in this paper of yours. If this is where you sense the Holy Spirit leading you, then go and do."

I brightened, flashing a hopeful smile. "Really? I'd have your blessing?"

"Well, *secret* blessing." Bernie winked. "And it's not like you're teaching any of that commie-pinko liberalism crap."

Those words caught in my ear, but I let it go.

"Thanks, Bernie. I'm glad I can count on at least one person in my life as an ally."

He smiled as I got up to leave, then said, "One more thing before you go."

I sat back down, wondering what else there could be.

"I don't know how to say this, but I've noticed a...a change in you."

"A change?"

"Yeah, a change. Like you're wrestling with something deep that's got you on uneven feet. Is everything OK in your world? Is there anything you're struggling with that you'd like to share?"

I took a breath and considered whether or not I should share what I had been experiencing. Share Clint and Prosurgent and everything I'd been wrestling with the past month. I decided to go for it. If I was to venture down this road toward reimagining the Christian faith, I was going to need allies. And Bernie had been one of my strongest so far.

"Actually, I have been struggling the past month."

Bernie nodded and scrunched up his face with concern. "Do you want to tell me about it?"

"Remember Clint Winslow?"

"Clint. Yeah. Precocious guy, studying to be a biologist or something or other. Real involved in our ministry, if I remember."

"Right. Well, he's basically walked away from Christianity."

"No! Why? What happened?"

"It's like I shared in our meeting and what I wrote in my

paper. The answers that Christians are giving just don't connect to the questions people are asking—the questions *Clint* is asking. And, frankly, the ones I'm asking, too."

This last bit of revelation seemed to take Bernie aback.

"So you're questioning your own faith now?" he asked gently.

"Not questioning my faith as much as asking questions of my faith. If that makes sense."

"What kind of questions?"

"The ones Clint and my students and others are asking. Why could a good God allow so much pain and suffering? What happens to all those people in other countries who are never and will never be exposed to Jesus and the Christian faith? Are they going to fry? Forever?"

Bernie sat back and nodded in understanding as I continued.

"And the idea of making Jesus and his story about *Heaven* is just preposterous! Life after death is the least of my friends' concerns. Heck, it's the least of *my* concerns. How about life *before* death?"

"Well then, what is your concern? What you put in your paper?" Bernie asked, picking up my proposal.

"Maybe. But actually there's a whole group out there who are asking the same questions Clint is asking. The same questions I'm asking. They call themselves Prosurgent."

"Pro...Prosurgent?"

"Yes. Prosurgent Christianity."

"Never heard of 'em."

I sat up in my chair and grew animated as I described this new movement. "They're awesome! It's basically a group of pastors who've begun asking all sorts of questions about Christianity. They're trying to reimagine the Christian faith for our day, to help the Church rise forward. That's what the name Prosurgent means."

"Reimagine the Christian faith?" Bernie asked, skepticism lacing every word.

"Reimagine. I realize it might sound a little crazy."

"Sounds liberal," Bernie scoffed.

I rolled my eyes. "It's not liberal. And it's not conservative for that matter. You could say it's a third way, trying to help the Church move forward in our world."

"But is that what the Church needs? To move forward?"

I felt defensiveness begin creeping back up my spine. I knew Bernie was trying to be helpful. But I felt attacked all over again.

"These are good people who are just trying to find their way forward through the faith. And they're doing so through a little innovation in how they reach people with the way of Jesus."

Bernie smiled. "You know a wise man once told me—this was a few decades ago, when I was about your age—a wise man told me that innovation in the history of the Church has never turned out well. It's always led to heresy." He quickly added, "Not sayin' you're a heretic, Pete. Just sayin' that to warn you to be careful. You're too valuable to the Church to lose."

I smiled, wishing I had kept my mouth shut. "Thanks, I think...Don't worry about me. I'm not going liberal, not planning on joining the heretics' ranks. I'm just trying to find a way to best reach my guys, I guess. To meet them where they're at in their faith and offer some guidance."

"Give 'em Jesus and give 'em the Bible. Anything else is just commentary."

I chuckled. "Alright, chief. Will do."

"Now get out of there and get back to work."

GIVE 'EM JESUS and give 'em the Bible? I thought as I walked out of Bernie's office. So simplistic. *Unfortunately, it doesn't work that way anymore, Bernie.*

I returned to my desk, discouraged and unsure about how to be a minister in our world—how to be a *Christian* in our world. I settled into my chair and logged into my work computer to check my email before leaving again when I got a text. It was from Clint.

"*Can we meet?*" was all it read.

Now what? I was exhausted from the day and unable to think about engaging in another mind-draining conversation with Clint.

I shook my head and changed my mindset, thinking I was fortunate to be able to walk alongside him in his spiritual journey.

I went to write a response, but then remembered it was my guys lunch group meeting. Maybe Clint should come along. Could be good for him to engage his questions in that setting, as much as it would be for the other students.

I pecked off a text to invite him: "*Got your message, hope all is well. Sorry, but today's the guys group. The one I've invited you to a bazillion times? Just kidding! Feel free to come. We're meeting at Leo's. Noon. Look for you. If not I'll catch you another time.*"

I hit *Send*, then I leaned back in my chair and sighed. *What a morning...*

On my desk I noticed a copy of my *Emerging Evangelism* paper, the copy I printed for myself with my edits before I sent it off to Roger, Bernie, and Peggy. I snatched it, ripped it in half, and tossed it in the trash, anger rising at the response my ministry co-workers had to my genuine desire to find a way forward with mentoring my students and sharing God's story of rescue at Georgetown.

If anything, the morning conversation had strengthened my resolve to reimagine the Christian faith for our changed world. For Clint's and my students' faith. Like Bernie said, nobody had to know how I was sharing Jesus' story. Nobody had to know how

I was mentoring my students. I sure as heck wouldn't let Roger in on the secret. Even Ainsley, given her skepticism of Prosurgent.

Speaking of which, the next Prosurgent DC meeting must be coming up soon. I checked my calendar and scrolled to next week. Dang. It was the same day as the Freddy Morris event.

Maybe I'll call in sick...

A *bing* on my phone called for my attention. Clint had texted back: *"LOL that's right. Oops. Sounds good. See you soon. Got more ideas about Christianity. It's all good!"*

I was encouraged Clint sounded so upbeat. I wondered what had changed. I sent him a reply, telling him I looked forward to seeing him in a few hours. I also texted the other guys to remind them of our meeting and let them know we'd have a visitor.

As bad as the morning had been, I reminded myself that the text sitting in my phone was why I was doing what I was doing. Clint was why I was rethinking Christianity and rethinking how to communicate the Christian faith.

Both for his and my own spiritual sanity.

LEO'S WAS HUMMING with the usual lunchtime crowd when I arrived, the strong mixture of greasy pizza and burgers, Kung Pow Chicken and burritos provoking a greedy, ravenous response from my stomach. The on-campus cafeteria in O'Donovan Hall was also overcrowded as usual, so finding a table was proving difficult. I searched for an opening and spotted two of my students commandeering a round table in a far back corner.

"Hey, fellas," I said as I walked over, setting my bag down on one of the chairs.

"Hey yourself, chief," replied Logan Clarke, a sophomore quarterback on the varsity football team.

"What's up, Young?" Deon Johnson greeted me as he bit into his burger.

"Where's the rest of the gang?" I asked as I scanned the bustling space.

"They're around here somewhere," Deon said.

"Let me grab some food. By the way, we've got a visitor. You guys know Clint Winslow, don't you?"

"Is his roommate Hanish Sen?" Logan asked.

"Yeah, that's him. Make him feel welcomed if he gets here before I do. I'll be back."

I made my way through the lunch line, running into two of the other students, Thomás Cruz and Samuel Goldstein. They had finished getting their food, so they joined the two others waiting in the back.

As I watched them leave to go to our table, I was reminded how random our little small group was. There was Logan Clarke, a sophomore from Huntsville, Alabama, studying business administration on a football scholarship. Blonde and built like an NFL pro, at first glance you wouldn't think he was one of the more committed Christians in Campus Ministry. Yet he was, helping lead worship for the Sunday evening gathering and showing up to our events and studies without fail.

Then there was Deon Johnson, a junior African-American from Atlanta, Georgia. He had come to the group at the urging of his mother who was concerned he was "backsliding," as he put it when we first met. His parents had threatened to pull their financial support unless he got involved in the ministry. So he was more of a reluctant participant, though his interest in spiritual things had grown the past year of meeting.

Thomás Cruz, the son of a wealthy Mexican businessman was our group Catholic, which wasn't surprising since Georgetown University was the oldest Jesuit institution of higher learning in the United States. He came to one of our gatherings by mistake his freshman year, thinking it was a university-sanctioned Catholic service. He enjoyed the fellowship so much he stayed and then got connected to the small group. He was one of our more insightful members, giving a Catholic perspective to the rest of us Protestants.

And finally, Samuel Goldstein, a Jewish student from New York who came to recognize Jesus as the Messiah last year. This was no small feat, because he was also the son of a prominent

Rabbi to the large Jewish community in the city. He reminded me of when I rededicated myself to Christ five years ago my freshman year, bringing an eagerness for God and passion for the faith that tended to slip through the fingers over the years of Christian commitment.

It sure was an eclectic group of young men, but I loved it. I loved being able to come alongside them in their spiritual journeys, no matter where they were at.

As I paid for my meal, I saw Clint walk into the room. I called to him over the lunchtime din. He heard me and came over smiling.

"Hey, partner," I said. "How goes it?"

"Good, Pete!"

"You sure seem to be doing better than the last time I saw you."

"Yeah, I've been thinking through some things over the past few weeks about my faith and whatnot that I wanted to run past you. That's why I wanted to get together."

"Great, man. Go get some food, then we can chat."

When I finally reached our table, the guys were arguing over last night's Hoya football game, giving Logan an earful about how he fumbled the final play that lost the school the game.

"It wasn't my fault!" Logan insisted. "There was no good pass after our wide receiver went down. And besides, the sun was in my eyes."

The table erupted with boos.

"Oh, no you didn't!" bellowed Deon, tossing his leftover pizza crust at the quarterback.

"What's that for?" Logan protested, throwing it back at Deon.

He bit into the crust, and said, "For the whole sun-in-my-eyes excuse."

"It was!"

"I thought it was Dax's fault?" Samuel asked.

"It was the sun *and* Dax's fault," Logan said, grinning and setting off another round of boos.

I sat back and chomped on my salad, smiling as the table continued razzing Logan, who took it in stride. I finally jumped in to quell the rebellion.

"Alright, alright, alright. We now know Logan's a putz," I said, eliciting laughs from the rest of the guys. "But this time is Jesus time, so why don't we shift the convo."

"Yes, sir, pastor man," Deon said.

"By the way, this is my friend Clint. I think most of you know him."

"Hi," Clint said and waved. The guys offered their own greeting.

"So did you guys do your reading?" I asked, eyeing the table. "Last month when we met, we agreed to read through our book and talk about it, along with Mark 8."

"I got half-way through and stopped after he said the Bible was a product of man, not God," Thomás said. "The guy is off his rocker."

"Yeah, I finished," Logan said. "And yeah, I agree. He's off his rocker."

"Diddo on finishing," Deon said, "but I found his discussion of Christianity sort of interesting. Different perspective than what I had growing up, that's for sure."

"Does watching the movie count?" Samuel said.

"No way, dude," I said. "Epic fail."

"What book?" Clint whispered.

"*The Da Vinci Code* by Dan Brown."

"Hey, I picked that up a few months ago, too. Good read."

"Good read?" Logan turned to Clint. "In what way? The thing is heresy up and down!"

"By whose standards?" Clint retorted. "The Church's?"

"Who else's?"

"But how can the Church decide what's right or wrong when the Church invented it all to begin with?"

Warning lights began flashing in my head. Maybe bringing Clint to the table was a bad idea, given where he was at in his own spiritual quest.

The table grew silent. Logan and Thomás both looked shocked. Deon looked indifferent, yet I saw him nod his head slightly. Samuel sat as Samuel always sat: silent, head cocked to the right, and taking it all in with hand stroking his chin.

"Guys, let's take the convo back a few steps. Clint, thanks for sharing. I hoped the book would get a discussion going about Christianity, because the movie sure is."

"As well as it should," Clint interrupted.

"Now, what do you mean by that?" I asked, turning to engage him.

"I think we need a conversation about Christianity, about reimagining the Christian faith."

Reimagining the Christian faith? Interesting he was still echoing that language.

"How so? What do you mean by *reimagining the Christian faith?*"

"It's like we talked about last month. The way the Christian faith is answering the big questions nowadays just isn't working. The story the Church is telling about Jesus and his movement isn't working anymore either. Honestly, the story Dan Brown told is more compelling than the one the Church is telling!"

"What do you mean by *that?*" Logan sneered.

I could see his offense growing at Clint's words. I worried about what would happen at the table as the conversation progressed.

"It's like Brown said," Clint continued, "the whole Christian religion was created by men with political agendas. The Bible was put together by men who left out other books in order to push the man Jesus' divinity. And then the institution of the Catholic Church created all of these rituals and suppressed all of these people groups in order to gain and maintain power. Women, gay people, scientists, liberal Democrats in America."

This was a whole other level to Clint's turn I hadn't seen before. And I could hardly believe it. He used to be so committed to his faith, so passionate about the Church. What happened to make him shift so dramatically?

"I hear you with the Catholicism, my man," Thomás said. "It's why I walked away. Would have kept walking from Christianity had it not been for Pete here."

I smiled, feeling my cheeks flush from the sudden attention.

"What made you want to leave, Thomás?" I said, trying to shift the conversation away from Clint's little rant.

"I grew up going to Mass my whole life living in Mexico City. It was all ritual to me, nothing else. And the more I looked around me, the more I saw how anti-gay, judgmental, and hypocritical it all was."

Deon nodded, along with Clint. Logan shook his head and rolled his eyes. Samuel sat listening, hand propped under his chin.

I decided to move the discussion along, trying to bridge Brown and the Bible.

"Let me ask you all this. Actually, I want to let Jesus ask what he asked his disciples one day from our reading in Mark 8. Listen to verses 27-30."

I opened my Bible and began reading:

> *Jesus and his disciples went on to the villages*
> *around Caesarea Philippi. On the way he*
> *asked them, "Who do people say I am?"*
> *They replied, "Some say John the Baptist; others*

> *say Elijah; and still others, one of the*
> *prophets."*
> *"But what about you?" he asked. "Who do you say*
> *I am?"*
> *Peter answered, "You are the Messiah."*
> *Jesus warned them not to tell anyone about him.*

"So here's the question," I said, closing my Bible and setting it on the table. "Who do you say Jesus is?"

There was a long silence. The guys stared forward, considering the question.

"Gandhi on steroids?" Deon said, offering a laugh.

Thomás and Clint laughed too. Logan rolled his eyes. Samuel smiled slightly, but sat still and introspective, as always.

"What do you mean by that?" I asked. "Gandhi on steroids, as you put it?"

"I mean, the guy was this super loving, super nice guy who did all these great things for the people of his day. Like Gandhi, but souped-up!"

"So Jesus was a really, really souped-up nice guy. Anyone else?"

"God in the flesh," Logan answered. "The Lamb of God who came to take away the sins of the world, as the apostle John said."

"You mean the sins of the super-select few of the world," Clint interjected.

"No, I mean the sins of the world. As in *'For God so loved the world that he gave his one and only Son, that whoever believes in him shall not perish but have eternal life.'* Like John 3:16 says. The whole world."

"But that's not what all Christians believe," Clint retorted.

"What are you talking about?" Logan asked, throwing his hands up. "Of course Jesus died for the world."

"Not according to Calvinists! According to them, Jesus died

for a select few. The elect. And, of course, those Chosen Ones just so happen to be said Calvinists and their family members. Especially their kids. They even go so far as to limit who Jesus' blood covers to only the sins of the elect. Limited atonement, they call it. So, because my roommate, Hanish, was born in India and never had the chance to hear Jesus, then he's definitely not among the chosen. And Jesus didn't die for him."

"Not if you tell him about Jesus," Logan said proudly. "That's probably why God placed him in your life. To lead him to relationship with Jesus."

Clint narrowed his eyes and leaned forward. "But wouldn't it be better that I don't even tell him about Jesus? According to that logic, it's more cruel if I do tell him than if I don't. Because if I don't, he never really has a chance to reject Jesus, and then burn forever in Hell."

Clint was arguing circles around Logan, frustrating him and confusing the rest of the table.

"OK, let's set aside freshman Rhetoric 101 for just a minute," I interjected. "Let's get back to the question. Clint, how would you answer Jesus? Who do you say he is?"

For a moment I thought I saw his eyes moisten with emotion, as if he might break down right there at the table. It went away as he stared from me through the window to outside. He smiled and gave a short laugh before turning to me again.

"You know, a few months ago I would have spouted off what Logan just said. Jesus is God. Jesus is the Savior of the world. Jesus is the only way to the Father."

He grew still, then looked out the window again. He shook his head, and said, "Now, honestly, I don't know."

The guys grew silent. So did Clint.

"I don't understand anymore if God is so loving why there's only one way to him. I don't understand how a God like that can allow a whole worldful of people to just die and burn forever. I don't understand if God's so loving why his people are such jerks. I don't understand why science and faith can't coexist. I don't understand anything anymore! Thought I did. Was sure of it for so long. But now...I just don't know."

I was surprised by his honesty. I was also surprised that the smugness he displayed at the beginning of lunch had given way to a more gentle spirit. Perhaps it was a front to hide his doubts.

"Thanks for sharing, Clint. Thanks for being honest about your questions. About your doubts." I paused, wondering if I should play off of Clint's own self-disclosure about his doubts. I wondered what Roger would think. No, I knew what he would think. Which meant I should definitely ask the question.

"What about the rest of you? How about you, Thomás? Logan, Deon? And you Samuel? What doubts do you carry about the Christian faith? Even religion and spirituality in general?"

I could tell the question came totally out of left field. They definitely didn't seem to be expecting that. Probably didn't think they could share such things. Or even carry such things. But I could tell it stirred something up within them. Something they hadn't had the freedom to speak about before. Perhaps something that hadn't even surfaced fully.

What have I done?

I was surprised that Logan was the first to raise his hand. Literally.

"We're not in class, Clarke," Deon joked. "You don't need to raise your hand!"

Logan put it down. He frowned, and said, "Sometimes I wonder if the tomb is really empty. Like, did Jesus really walk out of that grave all zombielike and talk to the disciples and rise into the clouds. Did Jesus rise from the dead? I doubt that sometimes."

That threw me. Had no idea. If a guy like Logan could doubt

one of the central beliefs of the Christian faith, what about the others?

"I hear my brother Clarke," Deon said. "But I doubt something even more basic. Like, how can we believe the Bible in the first place? How can we trust some book written by dead white guys thousands of years ago?"

"It wasn't written by white guys, moron," Logan retorted. "They were Middle Eastern!"

"Whatever. I mean, it's a book. And then to find out from Dan Brown that there were other gospels that weren't included in the final product. What's up with that? And why do we follow only certain laws but not others? Like, we condemn gay people for getting it on in the privacy of their own homes, but then we don't condemn the guy up the road loading up on shell fish or the lady who's wearing clothes made of two fabrics."

"That's totally different!" Logan complained.

"Dude, I didn't interrupt you. So why you gotta interrupt me?"

"Because what you're saying is totally off-base."

"Fellas..." I interjected. "Logan, chill. Let Deon talk."

Logan frowned, crossed his arms, and sat back. "Sorry, Deon. I shouldn't have interrupted. Go ahead, I'll shut up."

Deon rolled his eyes. "Anyway, I just doubt the Bible, I guess."

"Thanks for sharing, Deon," I offered.

The two guys remaining looked at each other, as if waiting for the other to share first. Predictably, Samuel stayed silent.

Thomás said, "Alright, I guess I'll go. I doubt the Church, man."

"What do you mean by that? That you doubt the Church?"

"In Mexico the Catholic Church is the main gig, you know what I'm saying? But I just question why one institution should have so much power? Especially over people's fate, their salvation and their death. I've seen how they hold that power over people. I mean, you already know about the abuse that came from that power in the American Catholic Church. I saw it ten times as much in Mexico City. How can God use such a corrupt organization to do his bidding?"

Again, the guys nodded in agreement, understanding registering on their faces.

He continued, "And then I think about the natives who were there before the conquistadors brought Catholicism in the first place. See this skin?" Thomás held up his arm and pinched it. "This is Aztec skin, amigos. I may be the son of wealth, but I've got native blood in me. Which means I had ancestors die outside of Christ. What happened to them, you know? How is that just and loving?"

"I understand, Thomás," I said. "Thanks for sharing, as well."

I looked around the table. "Anybody else?" I asked smiling, nodding toward Samuel.

"Alright, I'll go," he said, "but I won't answer your question."

I smiled and furrowed my brow. "OK...Then what do you want to say?"

"It was interesting hearing your perspectives. I mean, thanks for sharing your doubts and all. But come on!"

The others shifted in their seats, looking offended at Samuel's comment. Even I was surprised that the normally polite and serene Sam appeared to be taking them to task.

"Of all of us, I submit that I have the most right to doubt Christianity. After all, I'm Jewish. So I memorized Torah from a young age. Genesis, Exodus, Leviticus, Numbers, Deuteronomy —memorized. Bet you all can't say you've had that kind of devotion to whatever faith you're now doubting. And then, I was circumcised on the eighth day, celebrated my bar mitzvah on my thirteenth birthday. My father is a prominent Rabbi, studying under Rabbi Yehuda Krinsky himself. So of all the people at this table to have reason to reject the Christian faith, it's me. Yet, after a decade of searching, I've come to realize that Jesus is who I've been searching for my whole life."

Samuel stopped. The table grew silent. Clint seemed especially interested in his response.

"But what about your own people, Sam?" he asked. "According to the Church they're screwed if they don't embrace Jesus as Messiah. You're fine with that?"

"My people aren't screwed, Clint, because the Holy Scriptures say Yeshua HaMashiach, Jesus Christ, came first for them and *then* for you Gentiles. The apostle Paul makes it clear that the good story of King Yeshua is a story that is God's power which brings salvation to everyone who trusts his promised gift of rescue and redemption—first to the Jews and *then* to non-Jews."

Clint huffed. "Fine, but if they don't believe then they're screwed!"

"Well, faith has always been central to Yahweh's covenant relationship with humanity, whether Jew or Gentile, stretching all the way back to Abraham. And my heart breaks for my people who have rejected Yeshua as the true Passover lamb that takes away the sins of the world." Samuel paused before continuing. "My heart breaks for my father and for my family. But that doesn't mean Yahweh isn't good. God's promised gift has been offered to all for the taking. And it's up to individuals to receive it, to take it. Now is the day of salvation, as the book of Hebrews says."

Clint continued pressing in, not willing to let Samuel's unwavering belief go unchecked. "But don't you find it a problem that the religion Christianity sets itself in competition with Judaism?"

"There is no competition, Clint. And it has nothing to do with religion. That whole idea is a modern construct, anyway. It has everything to do with the person of Christ, who is the climax of the Jewish story. He fulfills all of the longings of my people and all of the promises of Yahweh stretching back to the great exiles. So no, there is no problem because there is no competition."

Samuel parried Clint's rhetorical jabs well. I wouldn't have expected anything less from the philosophy major and captain of the Georgetown debate team.

He continued, "Look, it gets back to Peter's question. Or Jesus', really. He asks us, *'Who do you say I am?'* Either Yeshua is who he and the Church say he is, or he isn't. C.S. Lewis put it best: when it comes to Christ, you've got three options—he's a liar, a lunatic, or Lord."

That seemed to grab Clint's attention, because for the first time he was looking at Samuel while he went on to explain Lewis's argument.

"Yeshua said he and the Father were one, that if you saw him you saw the Father. He said that from the beginning he existed, just like the great I AM of Torah. He claimed to be the way, the only way to Yahweh. So take all of these statements and more and you've got to make a choice. Either Yeshua was right, or he was a liar."

"Or a lunatic, as you say," Clint interjected.

"Yes, or a lunatic. I mean the guy ran around claiming to be HaMashiach, the Messiah promised by Yahweh. He said crazy things like, *'unless you eat the flesh of the Son of Man and drink his blood, you have no life in you.'* He claimed that even though he was going to be crucified he'd rise from the dead. I mean, come on! Either Yeshua was right and deserves worship, or he deserves nothing more than a straight-jacket."

Now all of the guys were tuned into Samuel's impromptu sermon. Some of the surrounding tables were even giving us looks, either out of irritation or curiosity. Wasn't sure which.

"Now, I don't have it all figured out. I didn't grow up in the Church like all of you. But what I do know—no, what I've *experi-*

enced is that Yeshua really *is* Yahweh and HaMashiach. Jesus is Lord and the Messiah. He is the Father's promised gift to the world to rescue it and put it back together again. And I'm saddened you all seem to doubt that."

Samuel finished and leaned back. He took an apple from his tray and crunched into it, letting his words settle into his impromptu congregation.

I smiled slightly and looked at my watch. It was after 1:00 p.m., the longest one of our gatherings yet.

"Thanks for sharing some of your story, Sam. And, guys, thanks for this. Thanks for your openness and honesty. Thanks for listening to each other, even though it might have been hard at times. Know that you're not alone in your doubts. Know that Jesus can handle your doubts, that he invites you to explore those doubts. But also know that he is calling you out of doubt and into belief. But however long it takes you to get there, I totally believe he's with you every step of the way."

The guys nodded. I even noticed a small smile flash across Clint's face.

"But it's super late, and you've got class, so let's close by reciting the *Be Still*, shall we?"

We closed our eyes and I led them in what had become a way to center ourselves. They repeated the following words under their breath:

"Be still and know that I am God."

"Be still and know that I am."

"Be still and know."

"Be still."

I paused for several seconds to emphasize this last stanza.

"Be."

Be, the guys repeated as we closed what turned out to be our best small group time yet.

After they left for the rest of their day, I went back to the office, the past hour and a half replaying itself in my mind. As I reviewed the conversation and the questions, I was struck that no one said anything about Heaven, neither their need for it nor doubts about it. While some of the conversations came close to people's ultimate spiritual destiny, the questions weren't other-worldly but very *this*-world.

And that's what Dr. Silverhair and his lackey, what *Everyday Evangelism* and Campus Ministry didn't get.

But it was what Prosurgent got. It was why I was growing more attached to this group of kindred spirits and less interested in my own band of missionaries at Campus Ministry.

And why I was for sure skipping out on the Freddy Morris event next week and returning to Prosurgent DC.

CHAPTER 13

TODAY WAS the day we embarrassed ourselves to death.

As I wrestled with the morning traffic along Connecticut Avenue, frustration churned in my belly. I was stewing over a number of questions that I knew smacked of pride. But I couldn't help it.

Why don't they get it? Why can't they see they're doing more harm than good? Why won't they listen to me?

Something inside me wondered whether or not that was the true motivation for my irritation. Because they wouldn't listen to my ideas about reaching this emerging generation with Jesus' message of hope and rescue. Even after all the research I had been doing and books I had been reading about reimagining the Christian faith in light of our changing culture they still didn't want to hear it?

Burr, burr blasted a Mercedes behind me. I looked up and saw the light had turned green. A chorus of horns echoed behind as I jerked my hatchback forward. I looked in the rearview mirror and waved to the honker.

I continued along the major artery taking me to work and

continued mulling over my moment of honest self-reflection. Maybe it was true, that this emotion was somewhat an angsty, prideful reaction to feeling ignored and shrugged-off. Actually, the more I thought about it, the more I realized it was. I'd spent over a year with these guys, and Roger didn't think I knew what they needed?

It ain't Freddy Morris, that's for sure!

The street sign for Florida Avenue snapped me out of my angsty trance. I braked hard to make my right turn, getting another round of angry honks from Mr. Mercedes.

I waved again as I turned to make my way on Q Street and toward our ministry headquarters.

It had to be more than that, though. More than just pride and twentysomething angst. I jumped back to the conversation at Leo's. Here were five committed Christians—or at least committed to their spiritual journey, however that looked at the moment. And every one of them had deep questions about their faith. Even Logan, which was surprising. Especially with his questions about the resurrection. What was up with that?

I continued driving in silence, trying to make sense of this angst. Because it seemed deep-seated. Then I remembered.

Driving across Rock Creek Parkway I remembered as a child learning about the evils of evolution from my mother, Maggie, along with my brothers James and Johnny. Before middle school, Mom had homeschooled us three Young boys. Her science curriculum was from *Creation Studies Institute,* Morris's anti-evolution outfit.

We learned that scientists were hell-bent on destroying the fabric of our Christian nation by ramming through evolution into public science education. We learned that communistic countries, like the former U.S.S.R and Cuba, all had science curriculum based around evolution, which was designed to bleed God out of their society. We learned that everything from abortion and homosexuality to rap music and Disney could be traced back to evolution and a de-emphasizing of God in American culture.

As I continued driving on Q Street, barely squeaking through an orange light at 29th Street, I continued reminiscing about my childhood education and broader upbringing. Looking back, I really was thankful to the good Lord for how it rooted me in the fundamentals of the Christian faith, even though it was a thoroughly fundamentalist upbringing. But the more I thought about it, the more I traced my inability to answer Clint's questions and engage his doubts back to my childhood catechism—or lack thereof. Perhaps it was directly traceable to those lectures by Alfred Morris himself.

That was it. My antipathy, my apprehension, my defiance of Roger's Freddy-Morris bonanza.

"The guy ruined my faith!"

OK, not exactly. That wasn't fair. But it wasn't like he equipped me, either. And now I found the faith I had carefully constructed beginning to wobble as the scaffolding fell apart.

I took in a deep breath as I rolled past our ministry row house in search of a parking spot. My gut tightened as I parallel parked my hatchback a few houses down. I looked behind me as I negotiated the parking spot. That's when I noticed a tall, gangly man in a full-length wool coat and scarf get out of a taxi.

On instinct I jerked my brakes. It was him. Mr. Creation Studies Institute himself!

"Holy cow..." I said. Another car honked at me to finish parking.

I snapped back to attention and slid into my spot. I sat gripping the steering wheel, some new R&B song beginning to keep pace with my anxiety.

I slowly opened the door and carefully slid out of my car as Freddy ambled up the stairs. I saw him hesitate at the door. He turned around and looked in my direction. I crouched a bit at my corner bumper to avoid him seeing me. I knew I was being childish. I would see him in five minutes, anyway. Besides, what grown man crouched behind his rust bucket to avoid some Christian fundie superstar?

I saw him enter the building through my car windows as I continued crouching.

"Pete, whatcha doin'?"

I whirled around. It was Ainsley.

"Ains! What are you doing?" I huffed, then swallowed hard.

"What am *I* doing? What are *you* doing, all crouched and creepy down in front of your car, peering through your windows like that?"

She had a point. My heart was pounding. I tried to catch my breath and instinctively looked behind me, back toward our row house.

"Nothing. I was looking at something. *For* something," I tried to recover, fibbing in the process.

"In your car? With the doors closed?" She asked, eyebrow raised and arms crossed.

"No. On the ground. I thought I dropped something."

"You were there an awfully long—"

"What difference does it make?" I snapped. I huffed again and raked my hand through my hair. "Come on, it's butt cold out here. Let's get inside."

"Whatever," she said and brushed past me.

Here we go.

Ainsley left the door open for me as I trailed her inside our office. I heard loud laughter up the stairs. It was Roger.

Of course it is.

I closed the door and took off my gloves and scarf, taking as much time as I could to avoid what lay up ahead.

I heard a sharp Australian accent. My throat grew dry. My

heart galloped faster as I clomped upstairs loudly toward the bois-terous conversation. It sounded like Freddy himself was telling a story.

"Hey, Pete!" Roger bellowed. "Come meet our guest of honor, Dr. Morris."

Doctor? Yeah, right.

"G'day, mate," Freddy said, his hairy hand outstretched in a friendly greeting.

I hesitated slightly, but shook it with as much warmth as I could muster. "Hi, Dr. Morris. Great to have you with us today."

"Happy to be here, lad. It shall be quite a show, I reckon."

Yes, it shall be.

I dismissed myself to the kitchenette where I made a cup of peppermint tea before ambling to my desk. I set my tea down and flopped in my chair, trying to avoid Morris and the others.

I blew across the top of my mug to cool the minty brew. "How am I going to get out of this?" I mumbled.

"Get out of what?"

"Jeez!" I startled, twirling my chair around. "Ainsley. You've gotta stop doing that, sister."

"Sorry. I thought you heard me."

"No, I didn't!"

"OK. Chill, fella. Goodness, what's got you so uptight?"

I nodded toward the hallway.

Ainsley turned her head. "What? Dr. Morris?"

"Shh! Not so loud, Ains."

"Why, what's wrong with him?" she whispered.

"This whole thing tonight is bananas. If they think they're going to reach any one of our students with the gospel, they've got another thing coming."

"Oh, Pete. Are you still irritated about that?"

"Although, I suppose if God can reach Balaam through an ass, surely he can reach a Georgetown jock through—"

"Peter..."

"Alright, alright," I said as I turned around back to my desk. "Just don't expect me to show up with bells on as some opening act to Freddy boy."

Ainsley laughed. "Well, it's not just Dr. Morris, you know."

I swiveled back around. "What do you mean?"

"It's now a debate between Dr. Morris and some guy named Bryan...McLaughlin, I think."

I coughed on a sip of my tea, choking and searching for breath.

"Are you OK?" Ainsley asked.

I continued to cough, trying to bring relief to my burning lungs. I finally recovered and swiveled back to my coworker.

"Bryan McLaughlin, of Dogwood Bluff Community Church?" I asked.

"I think so. Sounds familiar. Why, you know him?"

"Sure do. He's one of those Prosurgent authors I told you about. Why didn't I know about this?"

"Well, you pretty much washed your hands of it two months ago when the original lecture idea was announced."

She was right. I felt a little foolish about my defiance and my bad attitude. But this had changed things. The evening might not turn out so bad after all.

"I guess you're right. But how did this happen?"

"It was Dr. Morris's idea, actually. He thought the lecture would be more productive if he went head-to-head with someone on the opposing side. To show the clear differences between orthodox teachings on creation and God and, well, unorthodox teachings."

I leaned back in my chair. "Interesting...What time is it again?"

"Starts at 7:00, but we need to be there at 6:00. Supposed to last an hour."

That would still give me time to get to the Prosurgent meeting at 9:00.

"Alright, see you then."

Maybe the evening wouldn't be so bad after all.

OUR MINISTRY OFFICES hummed with activity and antici-pation the rest of the day. Tabitha snagged me to help her stuff envelopes with information about Campus Ministry. Ainsley and Peggy were making hundreds of welcome bags for our student guests. Roger and Freddy were holed up in Roger's office preparing for the evening. Bernie was who knew where.

As the evening event drew closer, I waffled between sulking and celebrating—sulking because I thoroughly disagreed with this ministry approach; celebration because at least someone from my new-found tribe would represent a more sane Christianity to my students.

"Peter, dear, what's the matter," Tabitha questioned in her sweet Baltimore drawl.

I smirked as I stuffed an envelope. "What do you mean?"

"You're sulking."

"Sulking? I'm not sulking." I sealed the envelope and threw it on our pile.

"See, that right there. Tossing the envelope with info for our students."

"No, that's boredom," I mumbled.

"And that. You've been doing that the whole time, too. Come on Pete, spill it."

I rolled my eyes and took another envelope. I said, "It's just that I'm not all that keen on tonight."

"Mm-hmm. That part's obvious." She sealed her envelope and set it on her stack. "Why not?"

I looked over toward Roger's office, while stuffing the envelope in my hand.

"What, Dr. Morris is the problem?" she said.

I saw that Tabitha had followed my gaze. "Pretty much."

"Why? What's he done to you?"

"It's not about me, it's about my students. Well, one in particular."

A mixture of confusion and skepticism draped Tabitha's face. Her silence told me to offer more.

"It's just, the way he talks about creationism and Christianity—it's just so offensive, so off-putting to people like him."

"To people like him?" Tabitha asked.

I realized my slip. "Yeah. People like my friend, Clint."

"What's Dr. Morris got to do with Clint?"

"Everything!" I noticed my outburst caught Dr. Morris's attention across the way. He was looking straight at me. He smiled and nodded. I smiled back.

"He's basically left his faith behind because of people like the good Doc, people who make science and secular society out to be the enemy. People who make the gospel about the afterlife without any concern for this life. People—"

"Like Dr. Harrison and Dr. Morris and Roger?" Tabitha interrupted.

I was surprised by her insinuation, and it registered.

"Don't look so surprised, Peter. You've been storming around here the past few months pointing subtle, but noticeable fingers. I've seen it. I've heard it."

Heat crept up the back of my neck. I dropped my head in embarrassment. Had it been that obvious?

"And, yes, if you're wondering, it has been that obvious. Look, I get why you're frustrated, Peter. I look at our students at Georgetown and wonder what it's gonna take to reach them with the hope of Christ and his message of salvation and eternal life.

And then I look at some of the ways we're going about it and sometimes I shake my head and wonder."

"See, that's what I'm talking about!" I exclaimed again. This time Roger looked over.

"But what I don't do, Peter, is storm around like I'm God's holy prophet sent to set this ministry straight or Dr. Harrison straight! Or denigrate good and godly men who are just doing and saying what they feel called to. And for God's glory, I might add. Untold people have found a relationship with Jesus through their ministries. And I'd say that's something to respect, not wag a finger at."

Tabitha's words stung. But I had to admit it: she had a point. And my pride had blinded me to the ways God had used Harrison and EE in the past. Boy was I jerk.

I set another envelope down and sat back in my chair. Tabitha did the same.

"Look, dear. I didn't mean to hurt your feelings, but you need to realize how you're coming across. People have taken notice. People are concerned."

People have taken notice? They're *concerned?* Who people?

I hung my head, and said softly, "I had no idea...Gosh, I feel horrible. I mean, I know I've been critical lately, but I didn't know it was that bad. I guess I've just been frustrated with trying to figure out how to reach my guys, that's all."

"I think that's all our aim, Pete," she said as she stuffed another envelope, not looking at me.

I got up and gathered the envelopes piled next to my seat. "Well, I hope tonight is as impacting as we hope it will be. Truly, I do." I checked my watch and looked back at Tabitha. "I have to be somewhere in a half hour. Is it alright if I jet?"

It wasn't a lie exactly. I did need to be somewhere—anywhere but there!

"Sure thing, dear. And, hey, please don't take my comments

the wrong way. Only trying to help you see they might get you into trouble if you're not careful."

"For sure, Tabitha. And thanks. I'm glad to know how I'm coming across. Definitely need to watch my words a little more carefully. See you in a few hours."

I grabbed my bag, dashed out the door, and walked up O Street toward campus. I felt cold. Not only because it was end of November, but because of Tabitha's words.

I started shivering, a delayed physical reaction because of too much adrenaline in reaction to Tabitha's accusations. I pulled my hat tighter over my ears and bear-hugged myself, trying to rub some heat into my body and control the involuntary shakes.

I had no idea people were feeling this way about me. That they saw me as some sort of problem for challenging conventional Christian wisdom and trying to share the insights I'd been learning. Probably had been a bit of a jerk about it all. But still...

Whatever.

They didn't get it. They didn't get me. They didn't get my students. If they wanted to remain clueless about our shifting, changing culture—well, then so be it.

Again, whatever.

We'll see how tonight goes.

My guess was that it would show them a thing or two. Tonight would prove I was right.

CHAPTER 14

WHEN I ARRIVED at the Intercultural Center auditorium, I was surprised to find a healthy crowd already milling about inside. It looked like a third of the four hundred or so seats were already taken, way more interest than I thought there would be.

"Isn't this thrilling, Peter?" Roger said excitedly when I walked toward my ministry co-workers. "We're gonna pack this place out, I just know it!"

"Thrilling. For sure," I managed.

Tabitha walked over to me and smiled, handing me a pile of our lovely envelopes.

"Here, Pete. You're on greeter duty."

I took the pack and assumed my position at one of the entrances to the auditorium. I looked inside and saw Dr. Morris talking with some students near the front. I also saw someone else, an older man laughing with some other students. He had a small Buddha belly and a close-cropped beard that flowed up around his balding head.

Bryan McLaughlin! Has to be.

I peeked over at my team members, who were readying other

things for the evening. I figured I'd sneak down and say hello, just for a minute. I left the stack of our information envelopes at the entrance and strolled down to the front.

I was getting nervous as I approached him. But why should I? After all, it was my organization's event. It made perfect sense for me to introduce myself.

I caught him as he ended his conversation with the group of students.

"Hi, Mr. McLaughlin. Peter Young," I said, extending my hand. "I work for Campus Ministry."

"Great! Nice to meet you, Peter. But please, Bryan is fine. My father is Mr. McLaughlin."

I laughed. "Fair enough. So thrilled you're here this evening. Especially since I read a bit of your *A Reimagined Christian* book."

"Really? Thanks. That's wonderful."

"Yeah, it pretty much rocked my world! In fact, I got connected with the local Prosurgent chapter here in DC. And I've hung out with your associate, Darren Thomas, a few times."

"You better watch out for Darren. He'll turn you into a heretic, for sure!" We both laughed. "So tell me about your ministry. I must say, I was surprised by the invitation, considering my...opponent. Aren't you an extension of the Southern Baptists?"

You and me both, my friend.

"We are, actually. But we're not all Southern Baptisty. Well, some of us are. But not me," I quickly added. "I sort of was, but then I started shifting, and now I'm sort of reimagining the Christian faith. Along with you, I guess." I felt foolish stumbling over my tongue, a bit starstruck.

"And how's that going for you, Peter?" Bryan asked, furrowing his brow and crossing his arms with pastoral concern.

I looked toward the entrance and noticed Ainsley and

Tabitha had assumed my spot handing out flyers. Roger and Bernie were talking with a few students as they walked in.

"It's...been a challenge," I said, returning to Bryan.

He followed my gaze and smiled. "I bet. Venturing into new territory is a lonely endeavor, especially when there are those who'd like to hold on to the old homestead and refuse to venture out."

"Or want to deny there's even new territory to explore."

"Even more of a challenge."

I sighed, and said, "Well, nice to meet you Mr. Mc...I mean, Bryan. I should get back to my post. Good luck tonight!"

"Thanks. You, too. Hope to see you around. Perhaps at Dogwood Bluff sometime?"

"Maybe. I'll see about that."

When I reached the auditorium entrance, a large, growing crowd was echoing loudly in the ICC atrium and making their way through the auditorium doors.

"Sorry," I offered as I walked up to the entrance, taking the handouts from Tabitha. "Thought I should greet the other half down front. Man, what a crowd."

"It is indeed a crowd. You stay with Ainsley. I'll go over to the other doors with Peggy."

Had to give it to Roger, he sure had drawn a crowd. Lots of people seemingly representing the cross-section of the Georgetown University student body. Those who had come to many of our Christian events, and others who I guessed were interested in watching a Christian slug-fest over the super-controversial topic of Christianity and science.

Then I saw a few familiar faces bobbing through the crowd. Logan, Deon, and Samuel made their way over to us.

"Fellas! I wondered if you'd be here. Where's Thomás?" I said.

"Homework, I guess," answered Deon.

"Well his loss. He's gonna miss one heck of a party."

"Lots of people, that's for sure," said Samuel.

"Here's some of our info, in case you haven't read it the first twenty-three times I passed it out to you guys. You better go get some seats before the place fills up. And save me a seat, too, will you? I'll try and slip in once the event starts."

They filed in and found some seats on the aisle midway. I had mixed emotions seeing them. I was happy they were interested in spiritual things and took the time to check out the discussion. Yet I was concerned about how it would impact them.

I continued to greet more students, who were now coming in droves. I wondered if we would have enough seats now. I handed an envelope to a coed, and my stomach flipped. Clint was standing a few persons back. He waved and smiled. I did the same, but a part of me regretted seeing him, wondering if tonight would drive him that much further off the edge of his spiritual cliff.

Or maybe not. Knowing Bryan was here gave me hope. Perhaps he'd offer up a reimagined creationism for his reimagined Christianity.

"Hey, bro," I said, handing him one of our envelopes.

Clint and I clasped hands and embraced.

He said, "Thought I'd check out what fundie nonsense your organization is spewing this time around."

"Is that Clint Wilson?" an all too familiar voice bellowed from behind us.

"Hi, Mr. MacArthur," Clint said to Roger.

Roger walked up and slapped Clint on his back, trying to be fraternal. Clint jolted forward, and I caught him roll his eyes.

"We've missed seeing you at our events. But Peter, here, says he's keeping his eye on you and helping you work through some things." Roger laughed. I offered a strained smile.

Clint laughed nervously and looked at me. "Oh, he is."

"Good to hear. Well, you better get inside. The place is filling up quickly."

"Yes, sir."

Roger left us to accost some other students.

"Sorry about that," I mumbled. "The guys from the group study are down the center aisle about half-way. There still might be a seat for you. I'll try and join you all if I can."

"Sure thing."

The line began to thin as the seven o'clock hour approached. The place was packed. Several students were standing along the side wall and at the back. Some were even crouched in the aisle. Well over four-hundred people were packed into the auditorium to hear two versions of how Christians engage with science and the study of creation. I was eager to hear how both sides presented their arguments, especially Bryan's.

The lights dimmed and Roger took the stage, along with Freddy Morris and Bryan who shook hands and sat off to either side behind him.

Go get him, Bryan!

ROGER STEPPED up to the podium and adjusted the microphone. It responded with menacing protest, catching everyone's attention and quieting the room.

"Good evening, Georgetown University!" he said. "Welcome to what should be a rockin' good time as we explore two important, seemingly contradictory topics this evening. Christianity and science."

He stepped back and cleared his throat, then continued. "So one day a zoo-keeper was making his rounds when he noticed that one of his monkeys was reading two books, the Bible and Charles Darwin's *The Origin of Species*. He was astonished and asked the ape, 'Why are you reading both of those books?' The monkey looked up from his reading and said, 'Well, I just wanted to know if I was my brother's keeper or my keeper's brother.'"

Roger kept a straight face until he broke into a wide grin and started guffawing with rounds of belly laughter. A few students chuckled. Freddy Morris was similarly doubled-over in his chair with laughter.

Oh, Roger...

I shook my head and smacked my hand on my forehead, which made more noise than I intended. Tabitha looked over at me, looking annoyed.

I smiled and offered a short laugh. "Oh, Roger. Gotta love his jokes!"

"Anyway," Roger continued, "just a little faith-science humor to get things going tonight. Seriously, though, this is an important, serious discussion, because a lot is at stake when we talk about science and faith, *The Origins of Species* and the Bible."

Roger paused, taking a glass of water out from behind the lectern. He took a sip, then put the glass back and continued.

"Without further ado, I present to you our two distinguished guests, experts who will give us two competing perspectives on the interplay of faith and science in the Church.

"Our first lecturer comes to us all the way from Australia, at least that's where he was born. Since moving to America, he founded *Creation Studies Institute* and is the brain-child behind a new state-of-the-art Creation Museum. He is heard daily on his radio program and is a frequent guest on national TV talkshows. Dr. Morris has a bachelor's degree in applied science with an emphasis on environmental biology, as well as a diploma of education. After graduating from university, he began his initial career as a science teacher in the public schools in Australia.

"Our next guest is a local pastor who studied to be an astro-physicist before going into the ministry. Bryan McLaughlin is the pastor of Dogwood Bluff Community Church and has been writing on the nature of science and faith for quite some time. He is also the author of *A Reimagined Christian*, which seeks to reimagine what it means to be a Christian in our modern world.

"As you can see, this should be an excellent, lively discussion. But before we get to it, would you pray with me."

The room joined Roger in bowing for prayer, and I slipped down to an open aisle seat next to Clint, along with Logan, Deon, and Sam. There was a collective *Amen* when Roger finished.

"Our first presenter this evening is Dr. Alfred Morris. He will share an opening statement and then Bryan will, as well, followed by a casual back-and-forth discussion we hope will bring some clarity. Dr. Morris, will you please enlighten us."

"Yes, please," I mumbled to myself, folding my arms and settling into my chair as Freddy Morris walked to his podium on stage left, wearing a starch-white shirt, red bowtie, and tweed jacket.

"Thank you, Roger. And thank you all for the warm welcome at Georgetown University and for taking time to discuss such an important, vital issue for the health of the Church and the gospel of Christ—and on a Friday night no less!

"I realize that not all of you will agree with my point of view. Some of you are Christians who maybe are students in various science departments and have grown to believe Darwinian evolutionary explanations for the origin and progression of our universe."

I glanced at Clint, who nodded slightly. I wondered how he would take this discussion.

"Others of you aren't even Christians, but were dragged here by your friends or were curious to see what the bloke from Down Under was going to say or are sort of challenging me to prove my opponent wrong. Regardless, I know many in America find the Aussie accent to be charming, so I hope the bitter pill I offer slides down easily encapsulated in my pleasant dialect.

Even if you don't like what I say, I hope you enjoy me saying it anyway."

We laughed on cue, which gave Freddy a chance to take a sip of water.

"I want say from the beginning that many assume scientists and people who study or value science can't also believe in creationism. I think they're wrong. Genetics pioneer Crag Venter is a creationist. As is medical inventor Raymond Damadian. What I believe has happened is that science has been hijacked by secularists, who seek to indoctrinate the masses with the religion of naturalism."

"Here we go," I mumbled. Clint looked over at me and nodded.

"I believe there is a gross misrepresentation in our culture," Freddy continued. "I want you students to understand that the problem is this, I believe: we need to define terms correctly. We need to define creation, evolution in regard to origins, and we need to define science. In this opening statement, I want to concentrate on dealing with the word 'science.' I believe the word has been hijacked by secularists."

He cleared his throat and took another sip of water before launching into the heart of his monologue.

"What is science? The origin of the word comes from the classical Latin which means 'to know.' The dictionary will tell you that science is the state of knowing and knowledge. But there are different types of knowledge. This is where the confusion arises. There is experimental or observational science, as we call it, that uses the scientific method of observation, measurement, and experiment and testing. That's what produces our technology. Like computers, jet planes, and microwaves. Looking at DNA, antibiotics, and vaccines fits this category, too.

"You see, all scientists, whether evolutionists or creationists, actually have the same observational or experimental science.

And it doesn't matter whether you're an evolutionist or a creationist. You can be a great scientist regardless.

"I want you to also understand that what I call molecules-to-man evolutionary belief has nothing to do with observational science. Because when we're talking about origins, we're talking about the past. We weren't there, so we can't observe that. Whether the way all this developed was through molecules-to-man evolution or through the six-day creation account of the Bible in the book of Genesis. However, that is what's so fabulous about the biblical account. It tells us how all of this came into being, as well as who created it. None of it was random chance, but purposeful craftsmanship.

"When you are talking about the past, we like to call it origins-science or historical-science. I make no apologies about the fact that our origins, or historical science, is based on the Bible's account of origins. When you research science textbooks being used in public schools, by and large the origins or historical science is based on man's ideas about the past. Usually the ideas of Darwin. Public school textbooks seem to be using the same word 'science' for observational science and historical science. They arbitrarily define science as naturalism, and outlaw the supernatural. They offer evolutionary biology as fact. They are imposing the religion of naturalism and materialism on generations of students.

"I assert that the word 'science' has been hijacked by secularists in teaching evolution, to force the religion of naturalism on generations of kids. Secular evolutionists teach that all life developed by natural processes from some primeval form. That man is just an evolved animal. All this has great bearing on how we view life and death—even our own nature. Because we are not talking monkeys! We were created by God in his image and likeness. Unlike the evolutionary accounting of things, this history of our humanity gives us great dignity and worth. It also explains some other aspects of our story.

"It's hard for many of us to accept that when you die it's over. But you see, the Bible gives a totally different account of origins—who we are, where we came from, the meaning of life, and where all this is heading in the future. Romans 5:12 says that through one man sin entered the world, and death through sin. But John 3:16 says, *'For God so loved the world that he gave his only begotten Son, that whosoever believes in him should not perish, but have everlasting life.'*"

He paused to take a sip of water again, then said, "So, is creationism a viable model of origins in today's modern scientific era? The creation-evolution debate is really a conflict between two philosophical worldviews based on two different accounts of origins or historical science beliefs. I maintain that creationism is the only viable model of historical science, confirmed by observational science, in today's modern scientific era."

Freddy Morris stepped back from the podium, and we clapped. Some gave hoots of approval. No doubt Roger was among them.

Now it was Bryan's turn. I smiled in expectation at what he would say. I turned to Clint who had moved to the edge of his seat, apparently with as much expectation.

I hoped for his sake, as well as Logan's and Sam's and Deon's, that Bryan blew Freddy out of the water.

CHAPTER 15

BRYAN MCLAUGHLIN, who had traded the tweed blazer for a casual hunter-green sweater, stepped to his lectern and began. "Thank you, Dr. Morris, for your thoughtful opening statement. And thank you, Campus Ministry, for inviting me to give an alternative view of our origins and the interplay of faith and science. I have to say, I feel a little out of place, having left both my bowtie and Australian accent at home."

We laughed on cue. Bryan's jovial, mild-manner personality was disarming. A welcomed contrast to Morris's tone. He continued.

"In opening, I want to tell you a story. An ancient story that's been told for generations upon generations. One stretching all the way back through the early Church, past Jesus, past the prophets, past King David and even past King Saul before him. This story was shared by elders around campfires for nearly forty years stretching between two lands: Egypt and the Promised Land.

"Imagine that you are an Israelite who is lounging around somewhere in the Sinai wilderness after the exodus. It is dusk, and you are sitting around a campfire with the elders of one of the Tribes of Judah. As you are sitting there, a boy wanders over and tugs the robe tails of one of the elders. With the random curiosity that can only come from a child, the boy asks, 'Mister, where did all of this come from?'

"'What do you mean, young Jada?' the elder replies.

"'I mean, can you tell me how the birdies and bugs and my mommy and daddy came to be? How the world was made?'

"With the tenderness and care that can only come with age, the elder picks up the boy, plops him on his lap, and says, 'Ahh, Jada, that is a very good question. A very good question, indeed. Let me tell you...'

"'*Barashia barah Elohim...*'" Bryan quoted the first five words of Genesis in the original Hebrew.

"'*In the beginning God created...*'

"In the beginning God was Michelangelo in front of the unformed slab of marble before David emerged. He was Mozart before the keys of black and white on the verge of a magnificent never-before-heard-of concerto.

"Like Michelangelo and Mozart, God *created*. God breathed all of this into existence by his word. Out of the chaos and blankness of our unformed reality, God brought into existence all that we see and hear and taste and smell and touch. Out of nothing God created something. He created all of *this*.

"With a single word, an array of colors beamed across the blank canvas of nothingness and burst forth like a grand Fourth of July celebration. Out of the array of colors God separated the light from the dark, declaring what was light *day* and what was dark *night*. God looked upon this initial handwork, sat back and declared it *good*. That was Day One.

"Then, across the canvas of light and dark, the Creator spoke into existence a vault, a sort of roof that separated water above from water below—the sky. God rolled open the great big sky and called it the heavens. Day Two, complete and *good*.

"On Day Three, the Creator gathered together the waters beneath the heavens in order to form a space of dryness. He called the dryness land and the wetness he called seas. Then, at the Creator's word, came lush green grass, seed-producing plants of every kind, and magnificent trees. End of the Third Day, a *good* day.

"Light and dark, the heavens, sky and earth. These newly formed vessels now awaited their Creator to fill them with glorious objects and beings.

"Next, our Creator went back to the sky and filled it with lights of every kind and two great big lights—one to rule the night and one to rule the day, the sun and moon and stars. These great lights would help keep track of the seasons, days, and years. When he retired his brush for the day, God turned around and saw all that he had painted was beautiful and *good*.

"Now that things were just right, now that our Creator had crafted the perfect environment for living things, he beckoned forth creatures from every corner of the seas and heavens. From the seas bubbled up the most magnificent sea creatures imaginable. Out of the heavens flew birds of great variety and creativity.

"Then God blessed these creatures saying, 'Be fruitful and multiply and fill the water in the seas and let the fowl multiply in the earth.' That was Day Five, another *good* day.

"After God's great show of creativity in the sea and sky, the Creator turned his attention to the land itself. Onto the surface of Earth came animals of every kind. He made every kind of wild animal, crawly thing, and beast that you could dream of.

"An array of colors and sounds collided from all Earth's corners as sea creatures, heavenly fowl, and land animals all played their part in God's grand performance, all reflecting the majesty and glory and creativity of their Creator.

"At the end of his performance, God looked across the spectrum of all that he had created thus far and saw that it was all *good*.

"But then a hush fell across the entire expanse of creation. An anticipation began to well-up within the belly of the universe, for all was not yet created. Just when Creation thought all had been formed, our Creator dipped his hand into Earth.

"'What was he doing?' wondered Creation.

"Beady little eyes from every corner watched in eager expectation. Wings flapped as they hovered over Earth in wait. The wild beasts could hardly contain themselves and stomped in anticipation for the curiosity the Creator was causing.

"Then, at just the right moment, when everything thought they would burst with excitement, it happened: God's hand retreated from Earth to reveal a being not yet seen before, yet all too familiar.

"On the surface of Earth laid a being that God called *Human*. It was in an entirely unique category of its own, yet it mirrored the Creator that brought it into existence.

"Out of the dust of Earth, the Creator molded the Human out of the soil in his image and likeness. And then *bleeeew*. The Creator bent down and gave his very own breath to the Human in order to bring it to life. The Human became a living creature, whom God separated into Man and Woman.

"The climax of the story had finally been achieved! The crowning achievement of God's creative work had been accomplished in the creation of humanity.

"After this crowning achievement, God stepped back and looked at all he had accomplished and decided everything was just as he intended things to be. From light to the heavens and seas to Earth, from plants to fowl and sea creatures to wild beasts, and at last the image of God. Everything was *just right*. There was...*shalom*. Peace and wholeness.

"After the last work of art in his wonderful world had been crafted, God decided that all he had created was *very good*.

"The next day, the Seventh day, God was finished. God blessed the Day and hallowed it, because he created everything he intended to create. Then God rested. On that day, God set aside his brush and sculpting wheel after he crafted everything he intended to craft.

"The end."

Everyone had been on the edges of their seats in silence, hanging on his every word. At the end, the room spontaneously erupted in applause at Bryan's performance. The guys and I joined in as well. Bryan took the opportunity to take a sip of his water as the applause continued.

"What a beautiful story!" he said as the applause died down. "You see, this is how our elder Israelite and little boy Jada would have understood the opening chapters to the book of Genesis, as a story telling us *that* the world was created and *who* created it. Not—and this is important—not *how* the world was created, other than God being part of the process and guiding it along the way."

Here we go. The rebuttal.

"Because you'll notice that this narrative is carefully constructed around the seven-day week. And people who are brighter than I say that this narrative is clearly poetic in structure. You've got three vessels that are then filled with three separate items. The heavens, the sky and seas, and then land on one side."

Bryan stepped over to the right of his podium as he listed the three "vessels" as he put it, making a motion with his hands above his head, at the middle of this body, and then down by his waist to emphasize his points. He moved to the left when he continued.

"Then you've got the stars, moon, and sun; the birds and sea creatures; and then the land animals—all items in the universe which fill the vessels." Again moving his hands from top to bottom to show the connection with the "vessels."

I had never heard the creation narrative put this way before. Something about the way he taught it *clicked*. It made total sense!

"Understood in this way, as an ancient story and as a poem describing *that* the world was created and *who* was part of creating it, helps Genesis 1 make all the more sense. Because what the writer of this story in the ancient Near East was certainly *not* doing was giving us a scientific lesson on *how* the world was created."

I took note of the three words Bryan emphasized: *that, who, how*. Genesis 1 is saying *that* the world was created and *who* was part of creating it, not *how* it was created. This was different than what Freddy Morris said about Genesis.

Growing up under Morris's teachings through elementary, homeschool drilled into me that Genesis 1 was a play-by-play historical and scientific look at how the world was created. Which Morris had reiterated. Bryan's version was opening something else up within me: hope, that maybe science and faith weren't at opposite ends of the spectrum after all.

I prayed to God it was doing the same within Clint.

"I realize I am almost out of time for my opening remarks, but I want to get this in before we move on, because it's crucial. Crucial to the creation story, but also crucial to many of your stories. I know many of you are students of the sciences. You're physicists. You're chemists. You're biologists."

I caught Clint sit up straighter at the mention of his discipline.

"What's crucial to understand, and freeing really, is that when you realize Genesis 1 is a story, it's poetry, you realize science and faith are not at opposite ends of the spectrum. Instead, they're kissing cousins. Because the progression of the Genesis poem fits pretty well with the scientific account of how we moved from nothing to space and heavens and seas and land. From stars to sea creatures and birds to land animals, all before reaching the pinnacle of the evolutionary creative cycle: humanity itself. Rather than acting as a scientific play-by-play of *how* the world and all that's in it came to be, this deeply spiritual poem provides the narrative, Scriptural backdrop for the scientific explanation of the origin of species."

And with that, Bryan stepped back to take his seat as the rest of us clapped with approval. Far more approvingly compared with Freddy Morris, by the sounds of it.

Before Bryan sat, Morris walked over to his own podium. The pastor then seemed to remember he was supposed to do the same. So he went back to his podium.

Now the real action would start. Now the two would go head to head.

CHAPTER 16

FOR THE NEXT hour Bryan McLaughlin and Alfred Morris went back and forth, retreading the same ground and arguments from both sides of the aisle. Freddy Morris noted that his views as a creationist conformed with Darwin's views, noting cases of finches and dogs in which researchers saw a single origin for the animals. Then he insisted, "The word 'evolution' has been hijacked," where it's being used for both observable changes and unobservable changes. "The result," he said, "is that it indoctrinates students in evolutionary belief."

Bryan pushed back and insisted observable changes through science simply reflected unobservable reality, which the Genesis story pointed toward.

The evening seemed to be winding down. Until this happened:

"What's clear," Morris started, "is that the real agenda of the scientific establishment is to replace God with the idol of scientific certainty."

Bryan stepped back from his podium and put his hands on his hips. He looked at the floor for several seconds. I thought I could see him shaking his head slightly. He finally said, "Wow! I don't even know how to respond to that."

"It's true," Morris said matter-of-factly. "From the dawn of Darwin until now, the scientific community has been hell-bent on destroying belief in God itself. And what better way to do that than by dismantling the very foundation of that belief in creation? I've often used the illustration of a canon that's aimed directly at the foundation of a city—seeking to blow holes in the foundation. And that foundation is the reality of a Creator who fashioned the universe, particularly in six literal days."

"Fascinating, because I thought the foundation of biblical Christianity was the Way of Jesus," Bryan responded. "In fact doesn't Paul call Jesus a cornerstone, the *chief* cornerstone? I don't seem to recall him saying that Genesis or creation was our chief cornerstone."

I could see several students nodding with approval, including Clint.

Score another for Bryan. He was on fire!

"Yes, of course," Morris said nervously. "What I mean to say, is that Genesis 1 and 2 help form the foundation of the Christian faith. Creationism insists that there is a Creator who created the universe—a Creator we're responsible to, that we've sinned against, and that Christ came to save us. By undermining belief in a Creator, scientists are undermining the cross itself. And, frankly Bryan, this is my problem with people like you—Christian leaders are doing the very same thing that these scientists are doing! You are undermining the very essence of the Christian message by challenging six-literal-day creation that is clear biblical truth."

"Are you kidding me? He did not just say that..." I mumbled. Several others in the audience gasped and began chattering in confusion. I looked over at Clint. He was as wide-eyed as I was. "Give me a break," I said to Clint. He nodded.

Bryan seemed as taken aback. He smiled slightly and stepped back. He looked down and put his hands in his pockets. "Now what do you mean by that, Dr. Morris? That Christian leaders, like *me*, are undermining the cross and Christian message?"

"I'm sorry to be so forceful. I don't mean to be personal, but it's true. Here's the problem. The majority of Christians in churches probably aren't sure whether God really created everything in six literal days. Many believe it doesn't matter whether it took six days or six million years. However, it is vital to believe in six literal days for many reasons. Foremost is that allowing these days to be long periods of time undermines the inerrancy of Scripture, that the Bible is without error, calling into question the message of the cross itself. The whole message of the gospel falls apart if one allows millions of years for the creation of the world. You cannot be a Christian unless you believe in six-day creationism!"

Bryan smiled and stepped back slightly from the podium again, his hands cupped in front of him. This looked like a fight he wasn't interested in fighting.

Roger got up and took to the center podium again. He said, "Well, this has been a spirited debate, hasn't it? We've gone on now for just over an hour and a half, so why don't we wrap up with closing statements. Pastor McLaughlin, why don't you go first?"

Bryan stepped back up to his podium and gripped its sides, like a preacher ready to bring it. "You know, at the beginning I told you a story about creation, the Genesis story. The one that the people of God have told for ages to explain where all this came from. They told it in a way that made sense to their limited understanding of their world, but where God was at the center guiding it all.

"Well, there's another story. A story that impacted the earliest of Jesus followers. It was the Greek story, or more specifically Greek philosophy."

Now this is an interesting turn, I thought, shifting in my seat.

"Early on, the early Church had to make a decision about how to respond to Greek philosophy. In engaging with it, they tended to adopt a number of Greek terms, which impacted how they viewed God's story. Probably the biggest influence on the early Christians was the Greek categories of *natural* and *supernatural*—the belief there were two worlds: the ideal world, which was the real one, and the physical world, which was less so. For many Greeks, the ideal world was morally superior and the physical world was morally inferior—downright evil to some. So, there was this huge gulf between these two worlds—the higher one more real and more noble than the other, and the lesser one subject to chance and change and decay."

Bryan stopped gripping the podium. He chuckled. "I can see most of your eyes glazing over, which probably isn't only because of how late it is."

We chuckled along with him.

"Why am I telling this story? Because Dr. Morris would have you believe in this Greek story, the one which is filled with Greek idealism—a perfect, unchanging, complete, fully formed world manifest in six literal days. But that's not the universe God created. At least, as I read the story the ancient Jewish people told, especially in light of science. Both this ancient Jewish story and the science story give us one world, one universe. One with matter and life and God, not torn into two pieces like a loaf of bread—one that's real and one that's ideal. It's a beautiful, integrated, very good world, where what we call natural and supernatural are one and the same.

"This is a far different story than the Greek imposter story, isn't it? A far *better* story," Bryan said as he leaned into his mic. "It's an on-going, dynamic story—a coming-of-age story, really, that we are all part of. And God has been guiding it all along from that moment the *tohu wa-bohu*—the formless and empty universe, as the Hebrew says—burst forth those millions of years ago.

"Dr. Morris says that the very nature of salvation itself is at stake with how we talk about creation, and I agree. Because salvation isn't about restoring some sort of Greek ideal, but about moving the human story along another click through the person and Way of Jesus, who showed and taught us a better way to love and be human than the dysfunctional systems and stories of our world. He came not so much to restore as he did to reveal the next stage in our human development, which both the Jewish story and the science story attest to. Thank you."

"Wow," I whispered, joining the rest of the auditorium in clapping—no, in *cheering* for Bryan and his story.

"I agree!" Clint said, clapping and adding a few whistles to voice his approval.

As the clapping died down Freddy Morris moved to his own podium to share his closing statement.

"Pastor McLaughlin, that was some speech. Very compelling, very moving. But also very wrong."

I was thrown by how direct and argumentative he was, even for Freddy Morris. I also noticed how red his face was—how angry he seemed.

"This lecture was meant to showcase two Christian viewpoints, yet it's clear we are coming from such opposite and opposing sides that we can hardly be considered to be part of the same religious tribe!"

Clint turned to me, face etched with confusion and irritation. "Did he just claim Bryan wasn't a Christian?"

I matched his confusion and irritation. "Sounds that way."

"It's clear the major dividing line between us is the authority, authenticity, and inerrancy of Scripture itself—believing that it is the very Word of God, every word of it!" Morris pounded the podium four times to emphasis. *Every. Word. Of. It!* "Oh, he tells you this nice, fictionalized tale of Genesis, but that's exactly what it is. Fiction!

"To summarize, here are the things I've been saying throughout this debate. There is a book called the Bible. It's a very unique book, different than any other book out there, because it is God's book. In fact, I'd say no other religion has a book quite like this one, especially in the way it starts out by telling you that there is an infinite God. It talks about the origin of the universe, the origin of matter and the origin of light and darkness, and the origin of day and night and the origin of Earth. It tells about the origin of dry land and plants. The origin of the sun, moon, and stars. The origin of sea creatures and land creatures. Finally, it reveals the origin of men, the origin of women, the origin of marriage, the origin of different languages, the origin of clothing, the origin of nations. And yes, it also tells the origin of..."

Morris tried to pace away from the lectern, but the microphone wouldn't let him, which failed to pick up his...rant? Yes, rant. That's exactly what it seemed like.

He stepped back and grabbed the mic in hand, "It also tells the origin of sin and death, which are not merely Greek constructs but real things introduced into God's perfect, and yes, *ideal* world by rebellious humanity!

"That history also says that man is a sinner, and it says that man is separated from God, and it gives us a message that we call the gospel, which is a message of salvation, that God's Son stepped into history, died on the cross, and was raised from the dead and offers the free gift of salvation. The historical account of Genesis is true, and that's why the Christian message based on history is true—both the Genesis story and the Jesus story. If you search out the truth, if you really want God to show you what is real about his world about himself about ourselves and yourself, he will show you. He will reveal himself to you as you are searching out the silver and gold. Thank you."

He stepped back to his chair, and we gave him an appreciative applause, but less approvingly by the sound of it. I did hear a few shout "Amen" from the front right section, though. Roger, perhaps?

My boss made his way back to the stage and shook both Bryan's and Freddy's hands before turning to his microphone again to thank us for coming to the show and dismissed us.

And what a show it was.

CHAPTER 17

IT WAS JUST after nine o'clock. The guys stood to leave, but I managed to snag them all and set an impromptu small group meeting Monday morning for breakfast. There was no way I was going to let more than a few days go by without chatting with them about the evening.

As Logan, Deon, and Samuel left, Clint remained seated, staring at the stage as the echoing voices began to subside, the crowd thinning and retiring for the night after such a raucous evening. I sat down next to him.

"So?" I said grinning with raised brows, trying to get him to spill his thoughts.

"So what?"

I huffed and rolled my eyes. He smirked.

Clint said, "No, it was good. I mean, Morris's little speech was a rehashing of my childhood. Pretty predictable, so nothing new there."

"Yeah, me too."

"But, Bryan...He was different."

Clint stopped without continuing. He was staring off toward

the Prosurgent pastor who was mingling with some remaining students near the stage.

"Dude, you gotta give me more than that!" I said.

He smirked again. "I mean, it was interesting how he tried to hold onto both the Jewish story and the...science story, as he put it."

"Wasn't it?"

"I guess I've always seen the two in conflict, but he sees them, what, in tension?"

I nodded. "That's a good way of putting it. I guess I don't buy the whole evolutionary development thing quite like him—or you, I'd imagine. I mean, why would God need six billion years, let along six days, to create the world—"

"If there is a God who created it in the first place, you mean?" Clint interrupted.

"OK, if God created everything in the first place. I guess what it reminds me is that we need to do a better job of handling the Bible."

"What do you mean by that?"

I adjusted my posture, pivoting toward him in my seat. "It's like Bryan said. We all come to the text with these lenses—I guess in the past some sort of Greek lens. But what if we reimagine the Christian faith by peeling back the lenses, to get down to the essence of the faith. That seems to be what Bryan did with his introduction and the retelling of the Genesis story in a way it would have been told back in the day."

"You used that word again. I *so* dig it, dude!"

"What word?"

"The world *reimagine*. Reimagine the Christian faith."

I smiled. "Yeah, for a new day. Actually, Bryan is part of a group of people who are doing just that. They call themselves *Prosurgent*."

"Pro...what?"

"Prosurgent. It's a Latin mashup of *forward* and *rising*. Anyway, they're reimagining everything about Christianity. You caught some of that tonight. Bryan reimagining the creation story. And even a bit of what Jesus is all about."

"Cool..." Clint said trailing off, a smile of interest curling on one side of his mouth.

"It is. They actually have some groups around the country who meet together. There's one in DC. You should join me sometime. The guy who leads it, Darren Thomas, is a pretty cool cat. He's sort of restored my faith a bit."

"Restored *your* faith?" Clint turned toward me in his seat, crossing his lanky legs so he could face me. "What do you mean by *that*? I didn't know you were having some sort of crisis."

Yeah, he wasn't supposed to know that.

Just great...Now what?

My mind started trying to spool out an answer on the fly without giving too much away. Didn't know how much I should share, and how helpful it would be.

"I don't know if I'd call it a *crisis*, but I've definitely been... challenged recently about what I believe."

"I had no idea, bro! I thought we were pals. I mean, I shared my loss of faith with you..." He seemed offended and a little hurt by my not sharing with him.

"Sorry, man. I haven't really told anyone. And it's only been within the last month or so." This seemed to mollify him a bit. I chuckled, and said, "Actually, it started with you."

"With me?"

"Pretty much."

"Can't say I take pleasure in ruining your faith."

I smiled. "You didn't ruin my faith. You did challenge it, though, with your questions. Which got me asking questions myself. A whole bunch of them. And then we had this little evangelism training retreat last month. That's when I started asking a whole lot more of them."

"Like what?"

"For starters, what's the point of this whole Christian thing? Is it to avoid and escape Hell? Is it to escape to some land out there in outer space? And who is Jesus, anyway? Like, is he really God? And what was the point of him and his life? Just to die? If so, then isn't, like, most of the New Testament a waste? And what is the gospel, anyway, the Christian message? Some sales pitch we give people to convert them to join our organization called the Church? And what's the point of the Church, why do we exist?"

I realized I was verbal vomiting, not really filtering. I wasn't sure that was the best thing for a ministry leader to do. I looked over at Clint. Rather than appearing freaked out, he seemed intrigued. He was nodding and smiling slightly, seeming to appreciate my authenticity, like some deeper connection had been made by my sharing.

I continued, "Anyway, I guess what I'm saying is, I understand now what you're going through in some way. But, Clint, I'm also beginning to understand that there is a way to be Christian in our modern world. I don't think you need to toss out the faith. I think you just need to reimagine it by getting back to the core of what's important to the faith, its beliefs and practices." I turned toward Bryan who was still chatting with a few remaining students. "I think Pastor McLaughlin made that clear this evening."

Clint turned back toward the front, too. "Maybe you're right. I think after tonight I'd like to find out."

I was surprised. And excited! I tried to stifle a smile, but it slipped. "That's great. Thought tonight would have had the opposite effect. Frankly, I was scared stiff for you to come, thinking it would drive you further away from Christianity!"

"Well, what Bryan said was really enticing. And what you've

been saying, about reimagining the Christian faith and all is enticing, too. Maybe that's what I've been needing all along. Thanks, Pete."

We both stood to leave, two friends traveling through the *terra nova* of our faith, seeking to emerge into a reimagined Christian.

CHAPTER 18

WHAT A NIGHT, I thought as I punched snooze the next morning.

It was already 8:00 a.m., but I gave myself another eight minutes. I was normally an early riser, even on Saturday. But I figured I suffered and labored enough for the good Lord the previous night to give myself permission to sleep in.

I pulled the covers back over me and lay staring at the ceiling. I replayed the debate again, feeling vindicated by Bryan's performance and frustrated by Freddy Morris. Yet I was also encouraged with how Clint resonated with Bryan's reimagined version of the creation story.

Don't people like Morris realize what they are doing to people's faith? Can't they see?

The alarm sounded again. I turned it off and got out of bed to shower. As I let the hot water wash over me, my mind jumped to Bryan's book. I had been wanting to get back to his writings, but hadn't had the chance the past few weeks. Today seemed like as great a day as any.

After finishing, I threw on my jeans and a hoodie and headed back down to the Barnes & Noble perched on M Street in the heart of Georgetown. I got there just after the doors opened and headed straight upstairs to the Religion & Spirituality section, returning back to *A Reimagined Christian.*

Bryan had made something of a name for himself as an unknown evangelical pastor from the suburbs of Washington DC when he gave voice to what a new generation—and, frankly, an old one as well—had begun voicing. In light of the changes that had come to America's religious landscape over the past generation—through apathy with organized religion, the rise of the Nones (those who are now self-consciously religiously unaffiliated), and perceptions of the Church as judgmental, hypocritical bigots—many were clamoring for an alternative way of being Christian and believing in Christianity.

That's where Bryan came in.

He had become a sort of grandfather figure to the Prosurgent movement after *A Reimagined Christian* catalyzed a broader conversation about Christianity at the turn of the millennium. The tale he told of one fictional pastor journeying out of fundamentalism and into the lonely, uncharted territory Prosurgent Christians themselves were exploring gave a new generation the permission to question the faith that had been handed to them, while charting a new course forward into new Christian territory. He sought to better connect the Christian faith to the twenty-first-century world by reimagining and redefining what it meant to be a Christian in the first place.

After grabbing the book off the shelf and this time paying for it, I headed to Dean & Deluca for a replay of coffee and quiche. I settled into a table in the corner, my stomach growling in protest, perhaps only outmatched by my spiritual hunger for the three-course meal at the bottom of my Barnes & Noble bag.

I stuffed a fork-full of ham-and-brie quiche into my mouth, washing it down with a swig of coffee. I re-read some of what I had read a few weeks ago to refresh my memory of the story, smiling as resonance filled my soul.

It seemed silly to equate my real life with his fictional one, but Pastor Jack's ministry struggles were my own struggles—professional and personal. His questions were my questions. Like me, he struggled to connect the faith handed to him as a child with the faith he was trained to hand his people. He was my doppelgänger, a replica of myself who was asking the same questions, wrestling through the same ministry situations, searching for the same answers. And I was immediately drawn back into his story.

After reimmersing myself in the book, I blew through my coffee. I left it face down to keep my seat and went for a refill. As the server poured the fresh brew, I felt a sadness wash over me.

Who's my Neo?

Who was the one I could turn to with all of the questions and fears and doubts burning their way through my carefully constructed house of cards?

I retrieved my coffee and went back to my chair. What about Bernie? No way, too close to my ministry. Though I had a close bond with Clint, probably more so after the other night, I was his mentor—not the other way around. Then I considered Darren.

Lord, let it be Darren!

I thought about calling him, but returned back to my new friends waiting for me inside my book instead. Another half hour passed before something in the story jolted me. Jack received a visit from two people on his church's council. They came unannounced and as representatives of the full council in order to share with him some concerns they'd all had regarding a change in his preaching that seemed to reflect a change in his beliefs.

I was taken aback for Jack, as much as he was for himself. They trotted out some of the language he'd been using as proof to bolster their concerns: in one sermon he suggested the creation narrative wasn't about *how* God created, but *that* he was the one who brought creation into existence; he talked about how we needed to be careful of claiming our truth was the only version of truth, because we all bring things to the table when we study the Bible; he talked about how people needed to belong with us in community and become ready for Jesus long before they'll believe in him; he complained (rather loudly, according to one council member) about selling Jesus like a Kirby vacuum.

Knowing the backstory as the reader, I knew that Neo was the one who had helped him understand those things—and it seemed to be affecting his ministry. As I continued reading, sitting in Jack's britches on the couch in his living room listening to the laundry list from his elders, an uneasiness began to needle me. Because as I kept reading, I realized that I had voiced many of those same objections to my own ministry leaders.

As the story continued, the council members made it clear they were not accusing him of anything, just trying to "open up the dialogue" about where he was coming from. Jack took their attempt at reassuring him as their cue for him to explain himself. So he tried.

He shared that he had been "attacked by doubt" recently. He reassured them he was in no way compromising the Christian message or core teachings of the faith: "I still believe in the authority and sufficiency of Scripture. I still believe man is a sinner who needs a Savior. I still believe Jesus is the one who came to solve our problem by dying for our sins. I still believe in the necessity of new birth." Jack's explanations seemed to mollify them—for the moment.

But I wondered how much longer they would tolerate his shift. I wondered how much longer Jack would be able to hold back the rising tide squalling against the surge barrier of his faith before it burst through.

I wonder how much longer I'll be able to hold back the same rising tide, how much longer my own ministry will be able to tolerate my own shifts!

I continued reading, my heart thumping and chest rising in panic as I finished a few more chapters over the next hour, trying to keep the terror at bay. Because I realized that my story was Jack's story—and at some point I feared there was going to be a knock on my own front door with a council of people looking for answers.

I swallowed as I reached the end of the chapter. The final sentence was a summary of my own story as much as Jack's:

As the year winds to a close, I find myself wearing new clothes, a new identity: I am Ponce de Leon hacking my way through the Florida jungle in search of the Fountain of Youth. I am Christopher Columbus wrestling the unrelenting, unexplored seas to discover a new route to the Orient, only to discover the New World instead. I am Lewis and Clark journeying westward through the continental divide to explore and map a way across the Western half, only to discover the Pacific coast.

I set down the book and stared out at the Saturday morning shoppers strolling up and down M Street. I liked how he framed his journey, one mirroring the famous European explorers during the Age of Exploration. I felt the same way about my own journey. I continued reading:

Like them, I have felt this yearning desire to leave behind the familiar in search of the unknown, to chart a course through new territory—*terra nova*, as Neo says—in order to make a new life for myself. But, like them, both the journey and the destination are neither simple nor easy. There are naysayers, there are storms. You must leave behind the old in order to discover the new. Letting go and losing is the only way to get and gain.

As they say, "the Lord giveth *and* the Lord taketh away."

I read that line again, mumbling it to myself: *The Lord giveth and the Lord taketh away.*

"So true," I said, closing the book. I flipped it over and caressed the cover, wondering about my own journey and destination, a voyage out and away from the land of fundamentalism into the *terra nova* of...

What, Prosurgent Christianity?

I felt it was more than that. It was more about a reimagined Christian faith. How exactly that looked, I wasn't quite sure.

I wondered about my own naysayers, my own storms. The minor ones that had already passed; the mega ones cresting just over the distant horizon.

Am I ready?

I wasn't sure, but I sure as heck needed to be—for the same reason Pastor Jack needed to be. I could no longer stay where I had been, but I found it as difficult to go where I was heading. Yet I agreed: In order to discover, receive, gain the new thing that I sensed God was doing in my life—perhaps even the life of the Church itself—I had to push off the short of the familiar, the traditional, and rise forward into new, fresh spiritual territory in the near distance.

It was my destiny.

I sensed it. I knew it. I believed it.

CHAPTER 19

MY DRIVE to work was quicker than normal thanks to my later-than-normal start. Perhaps I should make sleeping in a habit.

After parking in the visitor parking lot at Georgetown University, I headed for Leo's. On my way, I felt my phone vibrating in my pocket. It was a number I didn't recognize, but with a Virginia area code. I answered it.

"Good morning, Pete."

It was Roger.

"Oh, hey, Roger. Good morning to you, too. What's up?"

"Well it's 8:30 and you're not in yet, so I wanted to make sure everything was alright."

That's odd.

"Umm, yeah. I'm heading over to Leo's to meet the guys for breakfast. They wanted to chat more about the wonderful event on Friday. I thought, what better way to extend the impact of Dr. Morris's message than with a follow-up small group meeting."

I embellished a little, pouring on the excitement to make Roger feel good and dissipate whatever concern he had for calling. "I should be in the office around 10:30 after I'm finished on campus."

"OK, great. That's just great, Peter."

Not exactly the reaction I had expected. Couldn't he be a bit more enthusiastic?

He continued, "When you do get in, could you stop by my office? At 10:30, right?"

My eyes widened slightly, my ticker skipped a beat. "Yeah... 10:30. Sure thing. No problem."

"Great. Thanks, Peter. See you soon."

I looked at my phone as the call ended, then shoved it back in my pocket. A gust of wind sent snow avalanching off some branches over the path leading to Leo's, covering my head and shoulders with the cold, wet white powder.

What does he want? I wondered as I brushed the snow off of me and out from under my collar.

I shivered, trying not to panic. But Roger's removed, guarded, business-like tone was so unlike him. I opened the door to Leo's and sighed, trying to set aside whatever was coming in order to be present for the fellas.

When I walked in, I could see our round table in the corner was already packed with the guys. Logan, Deon, Samuel, Clint— even Thomás had joined us. Looked like they were already eating and engaged in what looked like a lively discussion.

After grabbing my customary breakfast sandwich—ham, egg, and cheese—Greek yogurt, and large coffee, I joined the guys.

"...well that's because he's an ass!" I heard as I walked up.

"Thanks, Clint," I said, sitting down next to him. "I appreciate that. Glad to know how you *really* feel about me."

The guys laughed.

"Not you, dork," Clint retorted, slugging my shoulder.

"Ouch! Be gentle, man. I'm breakable."

"Whatever," he said, returning to his oatmeal.

"So who's the horse's rear end?"

"Morris!" Clint bellowed.

"I think kangaroo or koala bear is more appropriate than donkey, given he's from Down Under and all."

Clint rolled his eyes before shoving another spoonful of cooked oats in his mouth. As he munched, he said, "Seriously, you were there. I mean, he basically accused Bryan of not being a Christian—all because he didn't hold to *his* version of science and creation! It's guys like him that make me seriously regret not leaving Christianity sooner."

Wow. This was going to be a tougher conversation than I thought.

I said, "OK, let's back it up. Where's this coming from?"

"Logan—"

"I—" Logan said interrupting Clint.

"Go, go!" Clint said, his bedhead-hair bobbing as he huffed and waved Logan onward, returning to his oatmeal.

"As I was trying to say, I said Morris sounded reasonable—"

"Reasonable my ass!" There went that hair again.

"Clint, seriously, eat your oatmeal," I said. He huffed again and stuffed a large spoonful in his mouth. "That's better. Now keep that spoon in there for a while." I smiled and winked. He rolled his eyes again. "Go on."

Logan said, "I just thought he sounded reasonable, *as a Christian.* I mean, what did you expect the guy to say?"

"Well, it's not like Bryan ain't a Christian neither," Deon jumped in. "And he's actually a scientist!"

"No, he has an undergraduate degree in astrophysics. That doesn't make him a scientist. Morris is a scientist—"

"No. A science *teacher*, moron!" Clint said, interrupting again.

"Clint. Spoon?" I nodded toward his bowl, then ruffled up his hair, making it worse than his bed had already made it.

"Whatever," Logan said. "All I'm saying is, as a Christian it makes sense he'd believe that every word of Genesis is literally true. So why are you so surprised? I mean, that's what makes us... well, Christian! The Bible said it, I believe it, that settles it."

"Oh, come on!" the other guys said in unison.

"Why not? I mean, didn't God reveal himself to us? In a book called the Bible? So if the Bible says we were created in seven literal days—"

"Six," Clint interrupted.

"Huh?"

"The Bible says God created the universe in *six* days. He rested on the seventh."

Deon snickered. I tried not to, taking a bite of my sandwich.

Logan smirked. "Whatever. If the Bible says God created all of this in *six* days—six literal days, then why not believe it if that's what God said?"

"Just like the Bible says the world is flat?" Clint again retorted.

"What are you talking about?" Logan said in exasperation.

"Hello...Isaiah and Revelation both talk about the four corners of Earth! When the devil took Jesus up on the mountain top he showed him all the kingdoms of the world. How could you do that unless it was flat—or the authors *thought* it was?"

"What's your point?"

"My point, is that one day along came a scientist named Galileo who challenged the traditional teachings of the Church that the Earth wasn't flat but a sphere. And look where that got him—death by house arrest!"

"Actually," Samuel piped in, "Galileo was condemned a heretic for suggesting the Earth revolved around the Sun, not because the Earth was flat."

Logan smirked and crossed his arms in satisfaction. Clint rolled his eyes and pressed forward.

"Whatever. My point, is that here is this scientist, challenging the traditional teachings of the Church and what happens? He's shouted down, condemned, accused of attacking the cross for gosh sakes! Just like people like Bryan by people like Morris."

"It's not like Morris and others are burning people at the stake, Clint," Deon interjected. "Morris is entitled to his opinion as much as Bryan is."

"Of course he is. My only point, is that people like him attack people like Bryan in the same way the Church attacked Galileo and others after him. And history has proved over and over again that the powerful institution of the Church is usually on the wrong side of history when they try and suppress minority voices. Look how dead wrong they've been on slavery, women, and gay people."

"Oh, come on!" the table uniformly said again.

"Now Morris is a racist, misogynistic homophobe?" I asked Clint. "I don't think that's fair to equate this discussion on science and faith with social injustices like slavery. Besides, if you want to talk history, it's actually been Christians who have been at the forefront of liberation movements. In fact, the Church was the one who preserved knowledge and championed education in the first place during the so-called Dark Ages, allowing the Renaissance to happen and free inquiry to flourish."

"OK, maybe you're right—"

"But let's bring the conversation back around again to Friday night and science and faith," I interjected, "and Logan's point about the Bible. I mean, he makes a good point. If God did give us this book, a book God meant to reveal things about himself and us and our world, and it says God made the world in six days—made us, as well—what do you make of that?"

Logan seemed satisfied I had given him props for his point. I wasn't sure I believed what Logan was saying, but it was an important point for the discussion. The table went silent, reflecting on my question.

"Now, I wasn't there, mind you," said Thomás, "but to say that you must take every aspect of the Bible literally is a little silly. I mean, what about Jonah?"

"What about Jonah?" Logan asked.

"Well...So you believe a big fish literally ate some dude and burped him up out on land?"

"Yeah. I do! I mean, what did they teach you in that Catholic church of yours, anyway?"

"Logan...come on," I said trying to diffuse the situation. "Not necessary, man."

He went silent and looked down at the table. Then he said, "You're right, Thomás. I'm sorry."

Thomás shook his head. "No offense taken, amigo. But I do wonder what they taught you in that backwoods, fundie church of yours!" He smiled and winked. Logan smiled and nodded back.

"I think the point Thomás makes is a good one," I interjected. They all turned my way, perhaps not expecting me to side with someone challenging the literalness of the Bible after just giving props to Logan. I shifted in my seat, knowing I needed to tread lightly, while also trying to push them a little—perhaps toward the *terra nova* I had been exploring myself.

"I think back to what Bryan said, about knowing why something in the Bible was written. What did the author intend when he wrote it and what did the audience believe about it when they heard it. I think Bryan's case about Genesis 1 was pretty convincing—that it was this tribal story that was told from elders to their people around their campfires. They didn't mean it to be some literal, scientific explanation about how the sun came to be. How their livestock came to be. Even how *we* came to be. The point was to remind their people that God was part of creating all this—not the gods of Egypt or Assyria—but Yahweh. I think how exactly that happened is left up to science, which I think God gave us, by the way, to understand his world."

"Then where does it end?" Samuel questioned me.

Typically, he had remained perched in the corner, silent but for correcting Clint. He simply leaned back and listened, taking it all in and holding his chin with one of his hands, adjusting his glasses with his other every so often. Now he was coming out to play ball.

"What do you mean, Sam? What do you mean, 'Where does it end?'"

He leaned forward and put both elbows on the table, staring back at me with hands raised for a fight. "Jesus said, when you saw him, the Son, you saw the Father. He claimed to be God himself. Should we not take him at his *literal* word? Or what about the resurrection? Is it no longer a *literal* resurrection, but a metaphorical one?"

Sam's questions stopped me. I hadn't thought of it that way before. I definitely would have said there was a level of literalness to Scripture, like Jesus' divinity and his resurrection from the dead. So why not accept the creation story as literal, too?

"They're not the same thing, Sam," Clint argued back.

"Why not?"

"Because one is about science and the other is about faith."

"But wouldn't scientists deny the *literal* idea that God became human? Or the *literal* idea that a dead man came back to life again? I don't know of any scientist who denies that God created the universe, the creation account, who also accepts Jesus is God and Jesus is physically alive."

Clint opened his mouth to respond, but closed it again.

"Holy cow, is Clint speechless?" I exclaimed, high-fiving Sam. "Way to go, bro!"

The table cheered for Samuel. Clint slugged me in the shoulder again.

"You make a really good point, Sam." I continued. "Because if we say one part of Scripture isn't literal, what about the rest of the parts? I think this brings me to the last thing we should think about before we head off to our day—because I know you've probably got classes soon."

Logan and Deon checked their watches. I checked mine too, noting it had been over an hour—and then remembered my meeting with Roger right afterwards.

I looked up to bring our discussion to a close. "OK, so here are two Christians—definitely different kinds of Christians. I mean, here's a sort of conservative, traditional one. Then you've got this, I guess you could say liberal, progressive one. And here they are, arguing from the same Bible and coming to two different conclusions. What do you make of that?"

The guys grew silent again, considering my question. Minutes ticked by before someone spoke up. This time it was Deon.

"Maybe it means this whole Christian thing is way more complicated and complex than we give it credit."

"That's good," I said, encouraging him onward. "What do you mean by that?"

"It's like you said. Two guys committed to the same thing, but coming at it from two different viewpoints. Doesn't mean that one is wrong and one is right. Just different."

"I don't know about that, man," Logan said. "Either Morris is right or Bryan's right. They both can't be right."

"But why does it have to be an either-or scenario?" I hadn't meant to say that. I was thinking it, had been since Friday after reading through Bryan's book. Seeing Logan's confusion made me regret my slip.

"What do you mean, pastor man?" Deon asked.

"Yeah, what do you mean that it's not either-or?" Clint asked.

Logan didn't say anything, but I saw the same question written across his face.

I took a breath, and said, "I guess what I'm learning is that there's a tension, or maybe more a spectrum within the Christian faith between what's real and what isn't."

I could see I was not getting through, perhaps making things worse. An analogy popped into my head that seemed perfect.

"It's the difference between tents and tarps."

"Between tents and tarps, pastor man?" Deon asked.

"Yes. Tents and tarps. So get this, tarps are tied down with rope, while tents are supported by poles. Remove a supporting pole and the tent begins to droop. Remove lots of supporting poles and the thing collapses altogether. When it comes to the Christian faith, isn't there a tent under which Baptists and Presbyterians and Orthodox and Roman Catholics can unite? Can't we name the tent and describe the poles that support it?"

"I think I'm tracking..." Logan said.

"Let me take the analogy a bit further," I offered. "So what happens if you remove certain poles out from under the tent of Christianity? Take the pole of baptism. Some Christians baptize infants. While they say there isn't salvation in that act, they believe babies are sealed or covered in God's grace and preserved for the future."

"I was baptized as an infant," Thomás interjected.

"I sure wasn't," Clint responded.

I continued, "Then there are others who only baptize *believers* after a certain age. That was me, that was my church. I've even read about one denomination that recognizes both infant and adult baptism. Which I sort of like, because I would argue the pole of baptism isn't a major pole. Remove that one and the tent doesn't collapse."

I saw a bit more recognition on the guys' faces, encouraging me to press forward. "But I'd also say this isn't true for some other poles."

"Like what?" Deon asked.

"How about the deity of Jesus? What would happen to the tent of Christianity if that pole were removed? Or, as Sam said, the belief in a literal, bodily, witnessed resurrection? Take out the pole of Jesus' deity or the resurrection and we've got a major collapse on our hands!"

"I see," Deon said smiling. "So what about creation? Morris would say it's a major pole. Take it out and the whole Christian tent folds right in."

"He probably would say that." I hesitated before moving forward. "But I disagree a bit. I think Bryan is more on target than Morris, because he recognizes how the story functioned for the original audience. Does Christianity fall apart if God didn't create in six days—especially considering how the original listeners probably heard it and how little science they actually had in their day? I don't think so. I think we're at this point where we Christians need to perform a renovation of the tent to figure out what poles are really necessary. We need to be careful which poles we take away, for sure! But maybe the ones we thought were load-bearing columns are really just decorative studs."

Clint and Deon nodded along with me. I caught Sam nod as well. Logan just leaned back with arms folded, eyes squinted, as if he wasn't sure what to make of what I was saying.

"Sounds liberal to me, Pete," he finally said.

I smiled. "I understand that. It did to me, too, a few months ago when I started searching for answers to some of my own deep questions. But what some may say is *liberal* I have grown to think is *reasonable*. More reasonable than the way I used to think, at least."

I hated to end there, but it was now 9:56, and I knew the guys had to get off to classes.

"Sorry to end there. Hope I didn't cause more confusion. Let's pick this up again soon, alright?"

The guys all agreed and headed out for their day.

"Logan," I shouted as I caught up to him after he jetted. "Wait up."

He stopped just outside the cafeteria and turned around. "What's up, chief?"

"Just wanted to make sure you were good after our chat—to make sure *we* were good. You seemed a little turned off by some of what I said."

He didn't smile like I had hoped he would. We continued walking. He said, "I guess I was a little confused. Seemed like you were siding with Clint, who's, like, totally left the faith behind."

My stomach sank as we opened the door to step outside. "I'm not siding with Clint. I think he's asking some good questions. But don't worry, I'm not going all agnostic."

I offered a laugh. He stayed quiet.

"I didn't mean to confuse you, bro. Or frustrate you. You seemed a little angry with me, so I hope we're good." I slapped his back, hoping for something.

He lifted his head and smiled. "Of course we're good. Actually, I think the reason I was so angry with you, especially with Clint, is that the conversation just brought up all these emotions I thought I had dealt with."

We continued huffing across campus trying to make Logan's class, our breaths floating behind us in the frigid early-December air. I recognized a hint of the same confusion and frustration I had heard in Clint's voice—the same confusion and frustration I had myself. I treaded lightly, not wanting to crack what might be an icy-pond faith.

"I understand that, man. Been going through some of that myself. If you want to talk about it, I'm here for you. I'd be down with getting coffee or something sometime, just to listen if that's what you need."

We walked into the engineering buildings, relieved to find warmth again. Logan brushed snow out of his hair and turned to me. "Thanks, man. Let me think about it. I mean, I think I'm fine. I should be fine. It's nothing, really. Thanks, though."

I didn't press him, but only said, "No problem. And if you ever want to chat, let me know. You better get off to class. Looks like you're late as it is."

"Alright. Thanks, Pete. Appreciate you, bro."

I returned back out into the wintry DC wonderland, satisfied with the morning conversation, but now regretting what awaited me back at the ministry headquarters.

Whatever. I'm sure it's nothing.

CHAPTER 20

"'MORNIN' Tabitha."

"Good morning, Peter."

She didn't look at me when I walked past. Seemed to be avoiding eye-contact. And using my formal name was a bit unlike her. I tried to ignore the feeling that something was brewing, but couldn't.

I went to my desk to set down my bag, but stopped short. Something about the space felt...off. I noticed my computer was shut down, which I never did.

Did somebody go through my stuff? Surely not...

I set down my bag and took off my coat, then I headed to Roger's office. I knocked on Roger's door window. I could see Bernie was there. I didn't know he was joining us.

"Come in," I heard.

Roger was seated behind his large desk, Bernie was seated in one of the chairs in front of it. The other one was mine, which Roger motioned toward me to sit in.

"Hi, Bernie," I managed. "Didn't know you were joining us."

He smiled as I took my seat, but said nothing.

As I did, I looked at Roger's desk and noticed a single typed sheet on the ministry's letterhead. At the top was my name in full, Peter Daniel Young. At the bottom were what looked to be three signature slots, with two of them already signed.

I took my seat. My heart started galloping out of the room.

Am I being fired?

It had finally come to that. They were kicking me out of the ministry.

What, for asking questions? For giving alternative answers to their nice, pat traditional *ones?*

I tried to labor my breathing, I wiped my perspiring palms on my jeans. Either way, one thing I knew for sure: the meeting was going to suck.

"Let's get to it," Roger said flatly.

Roger rolled his big leather chair up to his desk, hovering over my execution orders. He picked it up, the air stinging with anticipation, then set it down again. He took in a deep breath and blew it out through his nose.

"Peter, this isn't easy. You know how much I love you—*we* love you," he said, motioning to Bernie, who nodded in agreement. "You have been a tremendous asset to the ministry. It's obvious the students at Georgetown have really taken to you—your guys' small group, especially. You've helped the kingdom advance in that dark place. But—"

Here it comes...

"Some things have to change."

Maybe they're not firing me after all...

I shifted in my seat and changed positions. "OK, what's up?"

"Over the past few months we've noticed a...shift in you. You've been defiant of ministry initiatives. You've been defensive. And doctrinally..." He trailed off, then huffed and threw up his hands. He said, "I just don't know what to make of you, Peter!"

His brow was furrowed now, with a frustrated, disappointed expression. I even caught a hint of fear.

"And I have to say, others have noticed your doctrinal shift, too. And have expressed concern."

And who would that be?

I jumped to my conversation with Tabitha a few days ago. I bet she said something—some*things* by the nature of our discussion. Or did Ainsley say something after our trip? Surely not. But maybe. It sure did explain why Roger was so up in arms. I probably sounded like a flaming liberal back in Dallas. I don't think Bernie would have said anything, especially considering he basically encouraged me to defy Roger's order to do ministry as I saw fit.

"Who?" I asked.

"That's not important," Roger replied curtly, waving my question away with his hand. "What *is* important is how you've been carrying yourself around here of late. What's going on, Pete?"

"I don't know how to answer that. I feel like I'm being punished for just sharing and being honest and asking questions. It's like there's an *our-way-or-the-highway* mentality, here."

I paused. Roger was leaning back in his big, leather swivel chair, his right hand stroking his shaved chin.

"Such as?" he asked, the lawyer beginning to emerge.

"I know you weren't all that supportive of my alternative evangelism plan. My guess is because it wasn't Dr. Harrison stamped and approved. And then there's my small group study. You weren't too keen on that book either."

"It sounds like you're still using it?"

"Yes, I was."

Roger sat up suddenly and scooted to his desk. "Even after I expressly forbid you to do so?"

"Sorry, I didn't realize you expressly forbid me from doing

so." I felt defensiveness creeping up my spine, and an urge to fight.

Stay calm, Petey. Stay calm.

"Yes, I strongly encouraged you to do a *Bible* study, not some *book* study." His emphasis on *Bible* and *book* betrayed Roger's normally calm demeanor. "And it's this defensiveness that's also causing problems. We're only trying to do what's best for our ministry and the expansion of God's kingdom. And yet, when we try to help correct you, the walls go up."

And you know better than me how to run my ministry...how?

"I'm sorry. I don't mean to be defensive," I said instead.

"Well, your defensiveness especially comes through with your changes in doctrine."

"What changes?" I shot back, knowing I just played into his defensive accusations.

"Like your beliefs about creation, for instance."

"Really? And how have I changed?" This question seemed to throw Roger. He stumbled for words.

"Well, you haven't exactly hidden the fact that you weren't happy we invited Alfred Morris to our lecture."

"But that was for entirely different reasons than doctrine."

"If you don't disagree with him doctrinally, then what was your problem?"

Roger leaned back in his chair, as if waiting for me to hang myself.

"Oh, I don't agree with him, for sure. I don't think the point of Genesis is to give us an account of the creation of the universe with scientific-textbook certainty. The point isn't *how* God created, but *that* he created. My problem was bringing someone to debate the issue of religion and science who has zero credibility among the people we're trying to reach, someone who actually dismisses and vilifies science. Believe me, it was far more about *mission* than about *doctrine.* At least you made up for it by inviting Bryan."

Roger leaned forward suddenly in his chair. "You were *happy* we brought in Bryan? You agreed with him?"

"Sure was, and sure do—" I stopped short, recognizing the trap I'd just stepped into in my frustration.

Roger simply nodded. "I see."

I looked at Bernie, who had his head down, hands in his lap. He seemed to have little interest in taking sides.

Thanks, Bernie.

Roger continued, "But the biggest concern has been your whole postmodernism kick and quest to...reimagine the Christian faith, is it?"

Reimagine the Christian faith. Definitely Ainsley. How disappointing.

I leaned back and crossed my arms. "What about it?"

Roger followed my lead, leaning back as well. "What does that even mean? Why do you think it's OK to reimagine Christianity? And who or what is this whole..." Roger paused to look at a legal pad on his desk "Prosurging people, anyway?"

"Prosurgent," I corrected.

"Fine, Prosurgent. We've seen you've visited their website quite a bit and been in communication with some of them."

What is this, the Gestapo? My mouth dropped slightly. I felt my face grow warm with irritation. *I must be in the seventh circle of hell.*

"You went through my stuff, my computer and email?"

"Peter, it's *our* stuff. And, yes, we did. As your employer, we were trying to see what's been going on with you."

I should have quit then and there. Should have got right up and walked out, never to return again.

But I didn't. Instead I dug in.

"Prosurgent is a group of post-evangelicals who are trying to reimagine the Christian faith in light of our post-Christian, post-modern culture—in a way *New Tribes Missions* would for an unreached tribal people group. They recognize that people in our day are just like them—they haven't been to church, they don't understand Christian lingo, they don't accept or recognize Christianity as the standard answer to their questions about faith and life. So, yes, we—" I caught myself. "*They* are trying to rethink what it means to be Christian. Because, let's face it: for so long we have been blinded by the fact our way of believing has been controlled by a worldview inconsistent with our world, and the Bible itself."

"Such as?"

"Well, such as the gospel."

I realized I was already taking on water, so why not let the ship sink to the bottom—Titanic style.

"The *gospel*?" Roger exclaimed, almost choking on his words.

"Yes. The gospel, the Christian message."

His brow furrowed and he tilted his head slightly. "What do you mean by that?"

"Not to disparage Dr. Harrison, and I certainly believe that God has used him and his ministry to reach people, but I was pretty offended at the main premise of *Everyday Evangelism*. The idea that the good news about Jesus is fundamentally about Heaven—some land out there in outer space. How is it good news that 'Jesus came to pay the price for our sins to purchase us a place in Heaven?' Doesn't his life, death, and resurrection matter for our lives *right now*? And where in the Bible does it say the gospel is about Heaven in the first place?"

I stopped, meaning the two questions to be legitimate ones for Roger to answer. Why should he have all the fun?

He seemed caught off guard, as if expecting my questions to be rhetorical ones. "Well, of course he matters *now*," he said, sitting up straighter. "But obviously our lives right now are just dress rehearsal for the next one. This world is not our home, we're just passing—"

"See I totally don't buy that," I interrupted, shaking my head. "And that's where I take issue with your gospel—" I stopped abruptly, knowing I was on the knife's edge of crossing the line. "I don't mean *your* gospel. I mean the kind I've been struggling with." I wasn't sure that recovery was any better.

I paused and gathered my thoughts. "All I mean to say is, I want a gospel that matters right here, right now." I leaned forward, pointing to the ground. "As much as it matters for down the road. And my students do, too, Roger. That's why I'm reimagining. For them, as much as for me."

"But the gospel is the gospel. Yesterday and tomorrow. It doesn't change. Just like God doesn't change. So, to hear you say you want to reimagine the gospel is concerning, brother." Roger said this last line softly, like a parent might to a wayward child.

He didn't answer my other question, about where the Bible defines the gospel as about Heaven, but I let it go. It was clear Roger didn't get it. He was blinded by his own lenses, which had skewed how he viewed the Christian faith. Just like Darren said the first time we met.

I sighed, mustering up the energy to try one last time to help him understand. "Look, if it makes you feel any better, I still believe the gospel is the power of God for salvation for everyone who believes, like Paul says. I still believe Christ died for our sins and physically rose from the dead that third day. I guess I'm just trying to figure out how best to communicate that to my students, that's all."

This seemed to mollify him. He smiled slightly and nodded.

"Well, that's part of the problem, too, Peter."

I squinted and tilted my head. "What is?"

"Sharing this with your students, these Prosurgent ideas. At minimum they're inconsistent with our ministry philosophy.

That, combined with these other issues here that need to be worked through, is enough to warrant an action plan."

Action plan?

Roger picked up what I thought was my death warrant from his desk and began reading:

"Peter Daniel Young. Be it known that Campus Ministry has witnessed you exhibiting several qualities recently that are contrary to the mission, values, and culture of this ministry, including:

"Defying ministry initiatives and ministry supervisor advice and direction, including the Executive Director; defensiveness when confronted and given direction; doctrinal shifts which appear to be liberal and go against the Ministry Statement of Faith.

"In light of these concerns, we are placing you on a ninety-day probation period where your attitude and beliefs will be monitored by both your immediate boss and the Executive Director. Over the next three months, we are requiring immediate and sustained improvement with consequences up to and including termination."

I was too numb from both shock and the beating I had just received to register any reaction. Probably a good thing, since defiance and defensiveness must change—immediately!

Roger said, "Now, if you understand and agree with this report, we need you to sign, here." Roger took a pen and placed an "X" on the unsigned line I spotted earlier, and then handed me the sheet of paper and the pen.

I looked it over, feeling so misunderstood, so rejected, so alone. And I was supposed to just sign away my rights for a job where I felt I no longer fit in? Did I really have any choice but to sign, even though it was total bull?

"Before you sign," Roger interjected, "I want you to know that these Prosurgent ideas have got to stop."

I set down the pen and stared at him, blank-faced.

"No more mention of them at meetings. I'd say no more investigation on your part, but obviously that's your call. Definitely no more use of them or mentioning of them with students in your ministry. Do you understand?"

Yes. I understand you're now my personal thought police, as well as the Gestapo.

I didn't respond. Instead, I bowed my head, signed the piece of paper, and handed it back to Roger.

He nodded. "Good, now here are two more: one for you and one for me. This other one is going in your file."

Great. I have a 'file.' I should feel honored, really. Like one of Hoover's commies.

I signed those two, kept one, and handed the other one back to Roger. I glanced at Bernie again. He was staring forward, hands still folded on his lap.

"Luckily, the semester ends soon for Christmas break, which we're including in the growth plan. So that'll shave off some time."

Lucky me.

"Is there anything else?" I said softly.

"No, that's all. Thanks for your candor, Peter. I really think this is going to be a good chapter for you. Thanks for being willing to listen to us and to change. We appreciate it."

Don't mention it, I thought, smiling and excusing myself.

CHAPTER 21

"HEY, PETE."

I was sitting in my cubicle, elbows propped on my desk holding my head up, breathing heavily. My pent-up adrenaline was giving way to a near panic attack. My hands started to tremble, the sensation working its way down into my gut. I felt like I was going to puke.

"Peter?"

I turned around and saw Ainsley standing behind me.

"My goodness, you're white as a sheet. Are you OK?"

I swiveled back around and put my head back in my hands. "Fine," I grunted.

"What happened?"

"Ainsley, I really don't want to talk about it!" I sighed and turned around again. "I'm sorry. I didn't mean to snap—I shouldn't have snapped. It's been a rough morning. I'll be fine. Thanks, though." I managed a smile and forced myself to stay facing her, confused why she ratted me out.

"Sorry, I'll let you be."

She turned to leave. I couldn't help myself before she left our office area.

"Why'd you say something to him," I said, loud enough for her to hear as she walked away.

She stopped and slowly turned around. "What? What are you talking about?"

"Roger. You told Roger about our conversation in Dallas, didn't you?" I faked a smile and took a breath, trying not to sound combative, merely inquisitive. I was on probation, after all.

Ainsley's eyes widened slightly before searching the ceiling and floor. "He asked me how the trip went, and I said it was great. Really informative. Told him I thought it'd be a great addition to my ministry work. I meant to leave it at that. But then he asked about you."

"Asked about me?"

"Yeah. Asked what happened that you left in the middle of Dr. Harrison's presentation. Apparently, the head honcho mentioned something to Roger."

I closed my eyes and smiled. "Right. Of course. Then what?"

"Then I said you had been acting a little strange. And then I told him about the conversation we had. I may have said it was a little...unsettling."

"Unsettling?"

"Yeah. I have to say I was a little surprised by some of the things you said."

"And you didn't think to talk to me about them?"

"Of course, I didn't," she huffed, "because you're not all that easy to talk to when you've got your mind set on something!"

I was doing it again. Defensiveness. There it was. I took a breath and smiled again, this time sincerely. "You're right. I'm sorry. For being defensive—in the past, right now. And I'm sorry I freaked you out in Dallas."

She stepped back toward me and folded her arms. Then she

continued quietly, "I didn't mean to rat you out. I just didn't know what to say when Roger cornered me like that." Then she whispered, "You know how he gets."

"Oh, I know."

"I didn't get you in trouble, did I?"

I paused to think. Then I said, "Nope. I got me in trouble."

She frowned. Behind her Bernie peeked into our office space. "Hi, Ainsley. Pete, can I see ya a second?"

"Sure thing."

Sorry Ainsley mouthed to me as I left. I patted her shoulder with understanding as I passed.

I followed Bernie into his office and closed the door behind me. I sank into his leather couch as he sat in a chair next to me. Bernie placed his thick hand on my shoulder.

"How ya doin' kiddo?" he asked me, his thick Brooklyn accent soft and fatherly.

"How do you think I'm doing," I mumbled back.

"Ass probably hurts real bad," he whispered, then giggled. He enjoyed throwing that word into a conversation every once in awhile. Straight-laced Christian as they came, which made it funny.

I furrowed my brow and smirked.

"Oh, come on. Cheer up! It'll be OK."

"OK? I just got my—yes, my *ass* handed to me in there!" I whispered back.

He nodded. "You'll get through it. Don'tcha worry."

"I don't know, Bernie. I feel like I should just quit now."

"Quit? You can't do that. Can't give Roger the satisfaction."

Roger had been something of a nemesis for Bernie, as the two had had their own share of disagreements the past few years. In fact, when Roger first started, apparently Bernie had a run-in with him that almost cost him his own job. Hadn't told me what, exactly, but from what tidbits I had picked up from him and others, it wasn't good.

I sighed. "If I stay it's not for Roger's sake, but my guys'."

"Yes, exactly! Do it for those students God has given to you. What will they do if you leave?"

"Or get fired?" I said, turning toward Bernie.

"It won't come to that. I'll make sure of it. All you've gotta do is lay low and just do your thing. Come in, preach the gospel, *yes sir* Roger, and you'll be fine. Believe me, I know."

"But how will I change. I mean, apparently I'm one big screw-up!"

"Don't say that. You're not one big screw-up. Yes, you've got some things to work through. Some character issues that even we've talked about over the last year."

"Defensiveness and defiance."

"Right 'o partner."

I shook my head and sighed again. "I understand. I saw myself doing it with Ainsley right before you walked in, actually. But how will I change? And immediately?" I felt my chest tightening, my throat closing in. The anxiety was returning again in force. Emotion started pushing its way out.

"That's what you've got me for!" He smiled his big, cheesy Bernie smile, which made me laugh. "Seriously, it'll be rough. Change always is. But you can do it. Well, actually you can't. But God can. Believe me, I know from personal experience. I mean, I was a lyin', two-faced, no good, rotten son of a gun. And Jesus changed my life. Think about Philippians 2. *'Therefore, my dear friends, as you have always obeyed—not only in my presence, but now much more in my absence—continue to work out your salvation with fear and trembling, for it is God who works in you to will and to act in order to fulfill his good purpose.'"*

I sat up for Bernie's impromptu sermon, letting Paul's words sink deep.

"It's a double-sided coin, our transformation is. We're told to work out our salvation—to do all we can to love God and love people, and with fear and trembling. But it doesn't end there. We're not alone! God is with us. He's working on us. Not only is he helping us to *want* to love him and others. He's helping us actually do it, to act on that desire. All so he can fulfill his good purpose—in us and through us and out into the world."

I sat up straighter, considering Bernie's encouraging words.

"Peter, God is with *you*. He's working on *you*. He will help you want to love him and others, and he will help you do it. Again, I know!" He sat back and stared off, as if considering whether to say more. "Over a year ago, close to when you started, Roger and I had it out. He had been appointed Executive Director six or eight months before and he'd come in here like he owned the joint. Made all these changes, told me how to run my ship. And I didn't like it. I mean, I *really* didn't like it. And then when you were applying for this job and I was in the process of hiring you, Roger tried to put the brakes on it."

I lifted my head and cocked it to the side, confused and disheartened. "Roger didn't want me? Tried to *prevent* you from hiring me?"

Bernie turned and looked at me. "Basically. Now, don't let that discourage you, Pete. He just thought you were too young and inexperienced, being only a year out of college and all. But I thought you were perfect. Took a likin' to ya. So I told Roger that...in not so many words." He stopped, looking off again. He chuckled. "Actually, I told him off. Called him up and gave him a piece of my Brooklyn mind. Chewed him a new one."

I laughed. "You did? What happened? I mean obviously you're still here."

"Yeah, I'm still here, but for the grace and mercy of God and Roger over there. The next day, he called me into his office for a conversation very similar to yours. Said I was way out of line, had been for months. Put me on probation, like you, and demanded that I, quote, *Make immediate and sustained improvements with consequences up to and including termination,* unquote."

"Sounds like a favorite line of his." I sneered.

"Tell me about it. But let me tell ya, Peter Daniel: it was the best thing that could have happened to me. I was a royal you-know-what. How I treated Roger was totally off-base. He should have kicked my fat heinie to the curb. But instead, he showed me grace—just like he's shown you grace."

I didn't want to admit it, but he was right. As much as I might not agree with Roger on most of what he accused me of, there was some truth to it. As witnessed with Ainsley.

I sighed and ran a hand through my hair. "Yeah, I guess you're right. He has shown me grace."

"You're darn tootin'. And it's times like these we can either retaliate and lash out or sulk away and moan and groan. Or, we can recognize it's a gift from God to change and shape us more into his Son, and ask him for the help with the process."

I smiled. "Thanks, Bernie. For your words, but also for being here for me. I don't know how I'm gonna change, with my defensiveness and defiance. That part I agree with, because I've definitely got some problems there. But about the other 'd' word, doctrine—I'm definitely not so sure about that one."

"What do you mean?"

I paused, considering my words. "When we chatted a month ago you gave me your secret blessing to sort of mentor my guys as I saw fit after Roger put the kibosh on my proposal."

Bernie laughed. "Shhh! But, yeah, understood."

"And then you said that you noticed some changes and I shared how I'd been wrestling with my faith and told you about that Prosurgent group?"

"Yeah."

"Well, I'm pretty much there with them. Like, I agree we

need to reimagine the Christian faith for our day—much like the Reformers did for theirs and then the early Church fathers did for theirs."

"What do you mean you're *there with them*?"

"I mean, I think they're right. Not that I'm throwing out sin or Jesus' deity and the resurrection or anything. But, well, take the debate we hosted. I'm with Bryan. We need to move the Christian faith forward if it has any chance of connecting with our world. I see it with my guys. And so, when Roger says I need to drop this talk about Prosurgent or stop ministering out of that... Not that I've even mentioned the group or anything to them. The point is—I can't do it. I *won't* do it. And this isn't me being defiant, or whatever. It's me caring about my students, my friends. Because ministering Roger's way will not work."

Bernie leaned back in his chair. He pursed his lips together and folded his arms. "Far be it from me to counteract Roger and his direct order. And I'm not telling you to defy him or anything..." He paused. "Pete, are you teachin' anything the Bible doesn't teach?"

I paused. "No way."

"Are you teachin' heresy?"

I smiled and furrowed my brow. "No. Not that I know of."

"Are you givin' 'em Jesus and the Bible?"

"Nope—I mean, yes. Of course I am."

"Then your issue's moot. Follow your ministry gut. And as far as I'm concerned, we never had this conversation." He looked down at a magazine on an end table, picked it up, and began reading, a wry grin sneaking across his mouth.

I picked up on the hint and quietly exited Bernie's office, not before saying a quick prayer of thanks for the ally I had in Bernie.

CHAPTER 22

I WAS DONE BEING WHACK-A-MOLE.

For the next few weeks, I worked hard to keep my head down and not tick anyone off. Which wasn't too difficult since it was fall exams time. Then I headed back to West Michigan for Christmas break, giving me a chance to recuperate from my beating and consider my life direction.

Yet I was far from thrilled with the idea of going home. Last my parents knew, I was nicely tucked away inside their bed of fundamentalism, towing the family line of faith I had walked since I was baptized at eight.

What will they think of Prosurgent and Bryan? What will they think of my reimagining the faith? What will they think of my new found faith?

The remains of what my guys termed "snowpocalypse" nearly grounded my flight Saturday afternoon a few days before Christmas. A Winter Storm Warning threatened to dump eight to ten inches from late afternoon to the next morning. Thankfully my fight was just inside this window, so we managed to make it out before the heavy snow started.

After sleeping through the bumpy direct flight back home, I was greeted by Mom, Dad, and brother Johnny.

"Petey!" My quarterback youngest brother said, nearly tackling me to the ground, looking all-American as ever with his blue eyes and blond hair.

"Dude, watch it! I'm not one of your varsity football pals. I'm fragile."

He laughed and slugged me in the arm.

"Hey, baby!" my mom, Maggie, said as she hugged me, a short, trim woman with curly hair and wearing her trademark floral dress.

"Good to see you, mom."

My dad, Danny, trailed Mom and Johnny, hands in his jean pockets and wearing a slight grin, gut extending beyond his belt.

"Dad," I said. We looked at each other, hesitating before awkwardly hugging.

"Son. Good to have you back home."

"Good to be back."

The drive home was a good one. The family caught me up on everything that had been happening the past few months. I didn't call home nearly enough, so the drive made for a good time of family bonding.

Johnny's senior year sounded like it was going well: he made captain of his varsity football team; he was also accepted to Grand Valley State University on a football scholarship, a local state school that had come into its own after languishing for decades; he dumped the girl he started dating during the summer. I didn't know he was dating anyone. Apparently, he was still a free agent.

Mom's job at the bank was uneventful, as usual, which suited her well. She started a ladies Bible study at Coopersville Baptist Church, though the ladies were far too inconsistent with attending for her liking. She also shared some news that was hard to hear: Dad would lose his job sooner than expected, though they weren't sure when. The local stamping plant for General Motors that Dad had worked since he was a teenager was shutting down in the next year. Dad didn't say much about it; Mom did all the talking.

Thirty minutes after leaving the airport and driving up I-96, the pungent aroma of rotting garbage punctured our car conversation. Even in the winter, the landfill that sat just south of Coopersville stood as a beacon announcing one's arrival to "Salad Bowl City," as I called it for the fields of celery and lettuce and sod that surrounded the town—though back in the day, it was a timber hub for the hungry furniture mills in Grand Rapids. A short ride west through Main Street and then north through town brought us to Cooper Manor, an out-of-place Victorian mansion that once belonged to the founder of Coopersville, Benjamin Cooper.

Here we are. Home.

A fantastical canopy of snow draped the boughs of the large sycamores that dotted our front yard. The fading winter sun had kicked on a series of Christmas lights adorning the roof, windows, and doors of the great house. I didn't know how he managed it, but every year since I was a kid Dad had risked life and limb to make sure Cooper Manor was a shinning example of Midwest homeownership. This year was no different. I could see my old bedroom on the second level, commanding one of the four large turrets that anchored each corner of the house.

Lord, let this be a drama-free trip, please!

The smell of freshly baked bread and beef stew quickly overwhelmed any anxiety rattling in my belly as we entered our home, replacing it with hunger pangs. I dropped my suitcase and walked over to the large pot, lid *rat-tat-tatting* from the steam.

Mmm, I let out as I lifted the Crock-Pot lid to have myself a look inside. "This looks awesome, Mom!"

"Thanks, Petey. Made it just for you. Your favorite."

"Thanks! Can't say I can remember the last time I had home-cooked food."

"What, you can't cook yet, big brother?" Johnny jabbed.

I ran into him with my shoulder as I left the kitchen. "Funny, baby brother." I walked into our darkened living room and started up the stairs, searching for signs of life. I found none.

I returned back to the kitchen. "Where's James? Thought he would have been at the airport. And it doesn't look like he's here. Is he working?"

Dad let out a short snort. Mom glanced his way. He said, "Work? Yeah, right." He walked over to the Crock-Pot to take a whiff himself.

"JT's gone," Johnny offered.

I whipped my head toward him with furrowed brow. "Gone? What do you mean, gone?"

"He left," Mom added softly, looking at the floor. "First of November."

I was shocked. I had no idea. "Why? Where is he?"

"You'd have to ask him yourself," Dad said between sips of stew.

"Danny, get your mitts out of Petey's stew!" Maggie chided.

This didn't make any sense. A year ago, my middle brother, James Thomas, had moved back home to sober up after a heroin scare left him nearly lifeless in a Grand Rapids ER room. Gave up dealing the drugs he was shooting in his arm with the help of a program my parents paid for out of pocket. Honestly, I was floored he agreed to it. Was even more surprised he had agreed to move back in with them to stay sober. But he did. He'd even gotten—and held—a steady job at a pizza joint. With ministry and life in DC, I'd lost touch with JT. And now he was missing?

"So, what, he's missing or something?"

"No, not missing," Mom said.

"He moved in with his girlfriend, apparently," Dad added, trying to steal a roll before being slapped away by Mom. "Ouch!"

I folded my arms and leaned against the counter. "We'll see him for Christmas though, right?"

"Who knows?" Dad said.

"No, we will," Mom said, nodding her head with conviction. "At least, I hope so..."

The room fell silent for a few beats before Johnny interrupted. "Can we eat? I'm starved."

"Spoken like a true teenager," I said.

"I'm not a teenager!" Johnny protested.

"Dude, you're eighteen."

"Yeah, but I'm an adult."

"You're a teenybopper."

"Boys!" Mom interrupted as Mom usually did. "Sit."

After having my fill of stew and rolls, I hit the sack early, settling into my childhood bed, the only thing left in my room from my previous life.

I lay on my back, staring at the shadow puppets left by the trees out front, made by the full moon reflecting off the snow. I thought about JT. He had called a few times during the summer, but I was too busy to answer. He never left a voicemail. I told myself I'd call him back, but never did. I mean, what would I say, anyway? We lived two totally different lives, had zero in common. If I was honest, I just didn't want to deal with JT's stuff.

Maybe I should track him down while I'm here. No, I'll see him at Christmas. That'll be good. Will give us some time to catch up without it being awkward.

"I hope he comes for Christmas," I said as I rolled over onto my stomach. "Either way, JT's problems are JT's problems."

Then a thought needled my mind.

Just like your problems are your problems, Pete?

That conviction hit hard. So hard that I turned back over.

I had Bernie and Darren, even my guys, to help shoulder my burden. But who did JT have?

I shook away the conviction and turned back on my belly. It was not that I didn't agree. It was that I didn't want to deal with it. I had a suitcase full of troubles of my own to lug around. How could I bear my brother's burdens? Was I my brother's keeper?

Sleep came quickly and I faded to black, resting up for what I expected would be a challenging time the next several days home for the holidays.

CHAPTER 23

WHEN I AWOKE the next morning, I was startled by my surroundings, forgetting where I was.

Parents' home. Christmas break.

It was Christmas Eve and I found myself surprisingly nostalgic as I wandered downstairs before the rest of the house stirred.

An eight-foot Douglas fir commanded one of two large picture windows in the living room facing the road out front, still filling the room with the dizzying scent of pine. White lights made the ornaments dance in the pre-dawn darkness, taking me back to several Christmases from childhoods past. Presents were stacked beneath and around the base. At the end of the room stood a massive stone fireplace. Lining the top was Mom's collection of nutcrackers. I remembered sometime during my early teen years she started collecting them; had to be nearly twenty by now.

I smiled at the quaint scene, looking forward to spending some quality time with my family.

I wandered into the quiet kitchen and started a pot of coffee.

My book bag was propped against one of the chairs in the breakfast nook overlooking our snow-covered backyard. I reached inside for Bryan's book, figuring I'd get in some early reading before my family awoke. Perhaps they'll catch me.

If I was honest with myself, I sort of wanted them to. I had kept this new change from them, not interested in the skepticism and stares, the pointed fingers and accusations. I'd had enough of that with work. Sure didn't need it from my family, too. Especially on Christmas break.

And yet, what better time to talk about rethinking Christianity than with your family during Jesus' birthday celebration?

I got a cup of coffee, doctoring it beyond what I normally did in order to tolerate the cardboard-tasting supermarket brew. I found some leftover coffeecake in the refrigerator, and then I settled into a chair at the breakfast nook table to continue Jack and Nelson's adventure through spiritual *terra nova*.

Ironically, the chapter I continued reading happened to fall during the Christmas season. Things had continued to heat up for Pastor Jack after that fateful meeting with the church leaders in his living room. Jack was on the brink of throwing in the towel —not only his ministry, but also his faith. He couldn't see a way forward with either.

In Pastor Jack's world he was preparing his Christmas Eve sermon. It was in the predawn hours on the Monday before he was to deliver his homily on the world's most monumental event, and he wondered what was left to say that hadn't already been said. I took a swig of coffee, then settled in with the chapter:

As I sipped my coffee, I tried to let the predawn air rekindle my sense of wonder at the birth of Jesus, at the God of the universe becoming one of us. The past several months had left my struggling, child-like faith, all crusted over with age and familiarity, beaten down and shut down with fundamentalist force.

Don't ask questions, they said. And definitely don't give alternative answers to the ones given by generations past.

Jesus is the same yesterday, today, and forever, they said, even though they hadn't a clue how we've stuffed him into our own personal, prejudiced molds over the years.

Parishioners say they want their pastor to stretch their beliefs. They say they want them to take them to new levels in their faith and walk with Jesus.

That's bull.

What they really want is a caretaker, not an interior designer. Maybe rearrange the furniture a bit in order to vacuum and dust. But don't you dare pick new paint colors or reupholster the couch. Maintain, maintain, maintain. And if you're lucky—if you maintain the premises well enough—you might even keep your job.

"Boy do I get that," I voiced. Not that I had any experience in a church, but the past few months at Campus Ministry was clear they wanted nothing more than caretakers.

I yawned and took another gulp of coffee. Grimacing, I set down the mug and continued reading:

But as I was thinking about the past year and prepared to challenge my people—oops, caretake my people!—I remembered a saying my ministry mentor from seminary used to say:

"When Jesus came, he blew everything to pieces,

and when I saw where the pieces landed, I knew I was free."

Ain't that the truth! From my faith to my ministry, even to my family—all of it had been affected by the fallout and shrapnel of what I firmly believed was Jesus not merely coming into my life and faith to caretake, but *overhaul*.

And there was an emerging freedom that had begun to come out from underneath the rubble of my heart and soul. I could almost taste it; not yet, but almost. Thanks to Nelson, yes, but also thanks to Jesus.

When I stopped to think about it, wasn't that the same truth of Jesus' own life? When that tiny baby fell out into the world, grew into a boy and then a young adult, and died his gruesome death at the hands of the most powerful empire of the day—isn't *that* what happened?

KABOOM!

The religiously "separated ones"—the religious caretakers of the day—went nutso when Jesus came. He came teaching and healing in a way that challenged their precious status quo. So much so that the people recognized him as a religious authority—which of course the existing authorities hadn't given their stamp of approval.

There were the countless people who were touched by this world-rocking Jesus in various ways and who were never the same afterwards: the woman hemorrhaging blood, who had found healing; the centurion's child, who was brought back to life; the leper, whose skin was restored; blind man Bartimaeus, who saw for the first time in his life; the Roman soldier at the cross, who realized he was standing beneath the butchered body of the Son of God; the legion of Roman soldiers, who got the surprise of their lives when Christ burst from the tomb in full resurrection glory that Easter morning.

Of course the disciples' lives were blown to pieces, too. Not only did they leave behind everything they had ever known—sometimes people (poor papa Zebedee!), sometimes professions—their whole religious identity was thrown into disarray. I thought about the apostle Peter trying to defend those preconceptions in the garden of Gethsemane that night Jesus was taken away by the authorities. Months before, he had expressed his outrage that Jesus said he would have to suffer and die a death reserved for Roman terrorists. He thought Jesus' talk was crazy talk, because as a good Jew he knew a dead Messiah was a failed Messiah. If Jesus really was that guy he and his people had been waiting for their whole lives, then shouldn't he have ridden in on a white horse to fight the final fight against Rome and drive their pagan oppressors from the land—all in order to reestablish temple worship and the nation of Israel? Except those old religious ideas were blown to pieces by Jesus, so Peter tried to defend them by the sword.

Jesus has been blowing lives to pieces left and right for eons; he was doing it again.

In my life, in my world.

And there are those who would want to resist that— who, like the apostle Peter, would want to take up the sword in order to defend what has been, and what is expected of Jesus. But we all know what Jesus said about that: "for all who draw the sword will die by the sword."

I was no longer willing to die in order to defend the same-old-same-old Christianity that has been.

"When Jesus came, he blew everything to pieces, and when I saw where the pieces landed, I knew I was free."

For the first time in a long time, I was finally OK with that.

Wherever the pieces might land.

A bedroom door creaked and closed shut up above. The hardwood stairs groaned in protest as someone made their way down below.

I sucked in a nervous breath, my heart beginning to gallop forward and stomach beginning to clench with the anticipated conversation.

Ready or not, here we go.

CHAPTER 24

"'MORNIN', Petey," Dad grunted in a scratchy, sleepy voice. He yawned as he lumbered over to the coffee maker.

"Mornin', pops. I made a pot an hour ago. Not sure how good it is anymore."

"That's OK. A little burnt coffee never hurt nobody."

I continued to stare at my book, pretending I was reading it, while watching Dad out of the corner of my eye as he doctored his coffee with way too much cream.

My heart picked up speed as I anticipated the questions. What would he think of my...shift? Would he support it? Would he understand it? Would he *permit* it?

Dad and I had, shall we say, a tumultuous relationship in the last few years. It all began in college when he thought I should have studied something more practical. Perhaps his apprehension over my decision to study government was born out of his own lack of vocational and financial stability, with the auto industry reeling over lay-offs from jobs going over seas and all. He thought I should have majored in business, even chemistry—something more stable and secure.

The next domino fell when I moved to DC without a job. Not only did he expect me to find something closer to home—how he thought a degree in government would find use in West Michigan, I still didn't understand. He was adamant against the kind of risk I had no problem taking. Perhaps it was a generational thing, but he couldn't grasp packing up and moving somewhere without a job and barely any savings. Maybe it was my naiveté and oppositionalism, but I didn't care—about either the risk or his opinion. In the end, he supported my decision, loading up the family minivan and renting a U-Haul trailer himself to move me out to DC a few years ago.

But then I went into ministry after working in one of the most powerful offices in the country. He couldn't understand—no, *refused* to understand how I could be more interested in chasing my dreams and my gut than chasing a paycheck and the prestige that came from the kind of job I had. When I landed the job in the Majority Leader's office in the House of Representatives, he was beyond ecstatic, even sent me a congratulatory gift. I still have the fountain pen he gave me in my day planner.

When I started expressing to him my frustrations with my office and experience on Capitol Hill, he told me to buck up and take it. Said that was life, that every job had its ups and downs. Said I had to put in the time like every working stiff. And besides, since I was working in a position of power, what wasn't to like about it?

Again, he couldn't understand why I would rather do work that was fulfilling and meaningful to me than simply work for money or power. For a time I was being fulfilled, my work was meaningful—a dream job, really. But after what I had experienced, seeing the seedy underbelly of the government—especially the seedy relationship between the Church and State—I was done. I wanted out—no, I *needed* out. Dad didn't get it, he refused to understand me.

When the ministry job came around I thought he'd be thrilled. I mean, I was basically bred to be a pastor through years of Bible quizzing, jail ministry, and preaching competitions as a teenager. So when Dad tried to fight my interest, and then my decision, to leave Capitol Hill for Campus Ministry, I was totally thrown. I expected him to be thrilled. Not only because I had found something I thought would fulfill me and bring me meaning in life. But because I was spreading the gospel for goodness sakes. Even then, he still wasn't happy.

Which brought me to this moment in the kitchen peeking out from behind my book at Dad standing in his flannel bathrobe, staring outside at the rising sun with coffee mug in hand.

What would he think now?

Whatever. Let him ask. I welcome the chance to share my quest to reimagine my faith. Bring it.

He turned around and spotted me reading. I was having second thoughts.

He strolled over with his *Worlds Best Dad* Christmas present I gave him when I was in the fourth grade. He asked, "Whatcha reading over there?"

"Just a book," I mumbled.

He huffed and rolled his eyes. "I see that." He grabbed the book out of my hand. I sat back and took a breath, girding for the fight to come.

He read the cover and squinted. Then he furrowed his brow and frowned. "*A Reimagined Christian?* What on earth does *that* mean?"

He glanced at me, then fanned the pages before tossing the book back on the table.

I picked it up. "Just something I've been reading for my ministry."

"But what is a *reimagined* Christian?"

Good question. How do I explain all that this means—all that it means to me?

I took a deep breath and jumped into the deep end, risking drowning-by-argument.

"It's someone who realizes that the way of being a Christian in the past isn't working anymore. It means finding a way forward to create a sustainable faith in our modern world."

He scoffed and sat down at the table across from me. "Sounds like a load of liberal bull if you ask me. Where'd you get this book of yours?"

I smirked, shaking my head. "Liberal? It's a perfectly reasonable way of thinking through what it means to be a Christian nowadays."

"Yeah, well, last I checked God is the same yesterday, today, and tomorrow. That's Scripture, the only thing you need to figure out what it means to be a Christian. The idea that he changes and that we should change is liberal nonsense, designed to tickle the ears of backsliding, wayward Christians. Pure and simple!" He took a swig of his coffee and set his mug down with an irritated thud.

"Are you calling me wayward on top of liberal?"

"Sounds that way, by the looks of this book!" His voice began to rise, the same voice I recognized from my childhood.

"How can you say that, you haven't even read the damn thing!"

"Watch your mouth in this house," he interrupted.

I stopped and looked down at the table. I took a deep breath before diving back in.

"Sorry. I don't want to cuss and I don't want to argue. All I mean to say is, don't judge what I'm reading by the cover or title."

Dad leaned back and folded his arms. "Fine. Then what does this book of yours say?"

I considered my words, wondering how much I should share?

Would he get it? Would he really understand? Did he even want to?

"It's a fiction book, but the author, Bryan McLaughlin, is using it to sort of teach some things about our life as a Christian in our modern world."

"Such as."

"Such as the idea that often the way we talk about faith doesn't at all connect to the questions people are asking. Like, when we talk about science we talk like it's the enemy and whatever the Bible says just trumps scientific discoveries. Like, when we talk about other religions and how Christianity is somehow better than them—"

"Why would something like this be good or useful?" Dad cut in again, his voice like two raised fists itching for a fight and face twisted with the same desire.

"To help people like me who are knee deep in a crisis of faith!"

It happened before I realized it. I didn't even think about the words; they just came out. I saw his eyes widen before narrowing. His brow furrowed and his mouth dropped slightly.

"Crisis of faith?"

My eyes fell to the table again, my face sank. "Yeah," I mumbled. "Crisis of faith."

"Why is your faith in *crisis*? What are you talking about?"

He didn't have the tone of someone who was actually concerned about me or my life. It was the tone of someone ready to point fingers and judge.

"What is all this racket down here?"

We both turned as Mom walked into the kitchen. She was tying her pink bathrobe, hair and face frazzled like she had been rudely awaken from a deep sleep.

"Here I'm trying to sleep in for once, and all I hear is you two yelling at each other. Now what's going on?"

"Petey's gone *liberal*, that's what's going on! A liberal *back-slider* from the sounds of it."

I jumped out of my seat, ready to unload. "Are you kidding me?"

"That's what it sounds like! What else am I supposed to think, what with this *crisis of faith* nonsense."

I threw my head back and folded my arms in a huff. "Unbelievable..."

"Crisis of faith?" Mom asked, turning to me, her face registering clear confusion. "Petey, what's your father talking about?"

I was done. I wanted to run away. Run back to the comfort of DC. I turned toward Mom. Her face was etched with concern and fear in pained lines.

"It's nothing, Mom," I said, trying to sooth whatever terror was being stoked by Dad's outburst and accusations. A faith-crisis in those parts was almost as bad as coming out of the closet—the same shame and stigma would haunt my parents if people ever found out.

"Sure didn't sound like nothin' a few minutes ago," Dad said, spitting the words out before taking a sip of coffee. "Maggie, he's basically walked away from everything from his childhood. Everything we taught him."

"It's not that I'm walking away. I'm...*progressing*."

"Progressing? Becoming *progressive*, more like it."

The conversation was going to be nothing more than *ad hominem* attacks—personal accusations of going liberal and becoming progressive and back sliding. What was the point?

"OK, fine. I *am* walking away. I'm walking away from the faith I've been given—from childhood through college and until now. And you want to know why?"

I let the question dangle in the face of smirking, red-faced Dad.

"Oh, you meant for me to answer that?" he said. "Alright, I'll play along. No, Petey, I don't know. Why?"

"*Because it doesn't work!*" I exploded. The gloves were coming off now. "It doesn't connect to the real lives of real people. It doesn't answer their burning questions about faith, life, and everything in between. It's a folk religion more than anything, built on pillars of sandy, surfacy, simplistic, *simpleton* answers. For once in my life, I'm owning my faith for myself. Owning my beliefs for myself without anyone else spoon-feeding me."

The anger of a thousand paper cuts from my ministry came barreling out—misdirected at Dad, but directed nonetheless.

"What on earth is *that* supposed to mean? We raised you on the truth, Petey, on *biblical* Christianity. There was nothing *simplistic* about it!"

"Oh, come on, Dad. 'The Bible said it, I believe it, that settles it' isn't simplistic?"

He leaned in over the table, pointing a finger at me. "It's *truth*."

I leaned back and shook my head. "Look, I'm not abandoning the Christian faith. I'm not abandoning the Bible. I'm just asking questions. I'm thinking through my faith. I'm not content to just believe what I was handed by...by my past anymore. Why is that a problem?"

"What, you think I don't think through my faith? You think I just accepted what my parents handed me?"

"No, I *know* you didn't just take what your parents handed to you—you handed it right back, remember? Mom," I said, turning to my mother who was leaning silently against the counter, "you told me that story yourself. How when you both started dating you went to some Christian rock concert and evangelistic crusade or something. When the preacher asked if you were certain you'd go to Heaven when you died, you didn't know for sure, did you Dad? And when the preacher asked what you'd say when you got there, if you said you were generally a good person and read the Bible and prayed and went to church or that you relied just on Jesus' death and resurrection, you weren't sure how you'd answer, did you Dad? Then you went forward to pray to receive Christ as your Savior. That was after growing up in your nice West Michigan church all your life, after going to Bible club every summer and then during school, going to church three times a week. And you left that church—your *parents'* church and your *parents'* faith, didn't you?"

"It's not like you're saying," Dad objected. "It's not like I went liberal, like I *progressed,* as you put it, beyond normal Christianity into—into something *else!*"

Normal Christianity. I let that comment go.

"But you did question the faith of your childhood. You rethought what it meant to be a Christian and you went into new territory in your faith. That's what you did and that's what I'm doing. So you've got no leg to stand on when it comes to judging me."

That silenced Dad. He slouched back in his chair hard, causing it to bang against the breakfast nook wall. He folded his arms again, then looked out of the window with clenched jaw.

"I think what your father is trying to say," Mom said gently, gliding to my side, "is that we just don't understand what's going on. And we're concerned, like any parent would be. You may have grown up and moved out of the house, but we're still your parents, Petey."

"No, you're not," I said shaking my head. "You're my mom and dad, but you don't get to stand over me as a parent. I'm not a child. That's not what we are anymore."

Mom sighed and backed off. "I understand. But I gotta say, this whole new direction, this whole conversation, makes me worried! It's like I don't even know you anymore."

"So, what, is this going to come between us? Can I no longer set foot in this house because I may disagree with how and what you believe?"

"Petey, stop it!" Maggie yelled. Her blood-shot eyes began to leak. "Of course this isn't going to come between us."

I should have been melting under the weight of Mom's emotions. But I didn't. Instead, I dug my heels in deeper.

"Good. Because this ain't going away. This journey I'm on and the things I'm starting to believe. I ain't stopping them for anyone. Especially my parents."

I said it with more bitterness than I intended. It was coming out of a place of hurt and misunderstanding. Hurt that the two people in the world who should have been standing beside me were against me. Sick of being misunderstood, my motives and desires and spiritual direction.

My outburst was the shot that ended the battle. A deafening silence settled over the kitchen. The only thing that interrupted it was the creek of the floor down the hallway. I looked over to see Johnny creeping into the kitchen.

"Sorry to interrupt," he said, "but when is breakfast? I'm starving."

CHAPTER 25

MARK MY WORDS, I will never go back to that place!

For the final week of my vacation after Christmas, I avoided talking about my spiritual journey and direction, especially about Prosurgent. Dad tried to bring it up a few times through under-handed, passive aggressive comments, but I deflected each time. Mom remained mum about the whole thing, though I sensed at several times she, too, wanted to return to our blow-up conversation, perhaps to make sure we were still good.

To avoid the conversations and avoid my parents, I spent most of my time in Grand Rapids, reacquainting myself with a city I never really paid much attention to. I spent most days parked in a corner table at a coffeeshop that reminded me of Saxbys, reading and surfing the blogs of leading Prosurgent thinkers. I even finished Bryan's book. Mom and Dad finally got the hint and laid off the twenty questions about my spiritual life, and soon I was boarding another plane bound for DC.

After deplaning from my evening flight and hustling to the luggage return waiting area, I checked my messages as I stood to retrieve my suitcase. I had two separate texts from Clint and

Logan asking to get together: Clint said he was eager to continue the conversation; Logan said he was growing more anxious and confused about his beliefs and needed to talk. I realized I totally forgot to email him after our chat on the way to class before my sit-down with Roger and Bernie.

It sounded like they were both back in town for J-term, and I wondered if it would make sense to connect with them together. Seemed like they were wrestling with the same demons and could use the mutual support. I pecked off two text messages asking if it would be OK to connect the next day for breakfast or lunch together. Within a few minutes I got replies from both eager for the three of us to meet. After another round of texts, we agreed on a late breakfast at Leo's.

I got home a little after eight and made it an early night. I crashed hard. The next morning, I woke to what looked like half a foot of snow. I groaned, but meeting with Clint and Logan fueled me to get out of bed. I showered, dressed, and then headed out to Georgetown University, praying along the slow drive through barely-plowed streets that the good Lord would give me some insight into each of their journeys, and perhaps channel some of what I had been learning from Prosurgent leaders to help give them a more solid footing on their own separate paths.

I was surprised by how busy Leo's was for early January. I searched for Clint, but bumped into Logan checking out instead.

"Brother, Logan," I said.

"Hey, Pete!"

We clasped hands and embraced. "How was your break?"

He sighed. "Brutal. Up at dawn every morning to help pops with milking the cattle."

"You milked cows all break?"

"I didn't milk them. Our milking pumps did most of the heavy lifting. But there's still a lot of prep work, so I didn't get much rest."

He sounded tired and looked burdened—like something more had been weighing him down than bone-weary fatigue.

"Why don't you go find a seat and I'll meet you in a minute. Did you find Clint? I didn't see him around."

"He texted and said he was running late. He may not make it. We'll see."

After paying for my coffee and oatmeal, I found Logan halfway through his breakfast at our regular table.

As we waited to see if Clint would show, we chatted some more about his time home. Father was worried they could loose the farm that had been in the family for three generations. Mother was having some tests done soon to check out a lump in one of her breasts. Fought most of the time with his younger teenage twin siblings. Looking forward to wrestling next semester, but not the classes.

"How about your spiritual life? How's that going? You praying and reading your Bible?"

Logan's fork slumped slightly. He looked down before shoving a forkful of eggs in his mouth. "Yeah, about that."

"Don't tell me you're leaving your faith, too?" I said with mock accusation.

"What? No, it's not that. I mean, my prayer and Bible study life comes and goes. But I had some good time with God, for sure."

"Good to hear. Then what's up? I remember you saying something before break about some emotions that came to the surface during our small group convo. Emotions you thought you dealt with or something?"

"Mornin' sunshines," Clint said, sitting down with bad bedhead, squinty eyes, and a bowl of Cocoa Puffs.

"Mornin' to you, too," I replied. "Did you oversleep? Is that why you're late?"

"Yeah, sorry," he said, voice thick with sleep. "We had one helluva party last night."

Clint looked like he got hammered, which wasn't like him. I considered saying something, but let it go.

Instead, I asked, "So how were your Christmases?"

"It was great being home," Logan started. "Got pounded with snow and worked a ton. But there's something about the Christmas season that just sets things right, you know? And this year I was snagged by Mom to play Joseph in our Christmas pageant back home."

"I didn't know you acted," I said.

"I'm not sure I'd call what I did acting. But, man, playing Jesus' dad gave me goosebumps."

"He's not his dad, moron," Clint said, his voice still thick with sleep and his mouth full of cereal. "God is. If you still believe that sort of thing."

Logan rolled his eyes. "Whatever. But just being there on stage and playing the part made the whole thing come alive to me in a way I hadn't experienced it before! It was rad."

"Nice, man," I said, "What about you, Clint?"

"It was fine," he mumbled.

"OMG that's sooo awesome!" I said, laying on the sarcasm. "Sounds like a super cool, AH-mazing trip!"

Clint socked me in the arm. "Cut it out. Not in the mood."

"I see that, bro. Come on, what's going on?"

"It just wasn't a good time home, OK."

Logan and I looked at each other. I wondered how much I should press.

"What happened?" I said, shoveling a spoonful of oatmeal into my mouth and waiting for him to answer.

"The whole Christmas thing is just so ridiculous for people our age!" Clint finally said, throwing his hands up dramatically in the air. "Forget Santa. How moronic is it that grown adults like my parents still believe that some mystical phantom god impregnated a teenager. I mean, other religious traditions have the same kind of myth. And then there are the pagan roots of Christmas, the whole December 25 and Winter Solstice thing."

He scowled and stuffed his mouth full of Cocoa Puffs again. As he munched, he continued sharing. "Then they believe this, like, superman, man-god baby, or whatever, grew up and played Houdini—turning water into wine, walking on water, healing peeps. And then died, but only for a super-select few, of course. And then he went all zombie. I feel like I'm trapped in some weird Groundhogs Day time-warp thingy with a bunch of ignorant, backwoods hillbillies!"

Clint leaned back and folded his arms and sighed.

Logan and I looked at each other again. Sounded like he had a similar go with his parents as I did with mine.

"No offense, by the way," he added. "I mean about the whole ignorant, backwoods hillbillies thing."

I smiled. "None taken. Sounds like you had a rough Christmas with your parents."

"You could say that," he mumbled, then returned to his cereal.

"Did you get into it with them about your doubts?"

"Yup."

"And they didn't understand, did they?"

"Nope."

"Wrote you off as some sort of pagan liberal backslider?"

Clint nodded, his face flat and pained and steely.

I smiled weakly, recalling my own Christmas break. "Sounds a little like my own holiday, actually."

"How so?" Clint said looking up.

"I had it out with my parents, too. About some of what I've shared, this sort of quest I'm on to rethink the Christian faith."

Clint scoffed. "Yeah, well, where you're rethinking it, I've *rejected* it!"

His word choice thudded heavily on the table.

"I'm serious," he said looking at me.

"Sounds like it."

"The virgin birth is ridiculous. Miracles don't happen. And the resurrection...don't even get me started!"

"Believe me, I hear you. I won't get you started!"

"Nothin' but a bunch of ignorant, backwoods—"

"Hillbillies, I know. The whole lot of us. Me and Logan and your parents."

The table grew quiet. Logan looked at me, then looked at Clint and then back at me again. I saw irritation on his face. I smirked and shrugged my shoulders. It was becoming clear to me that not only was Clint trying to re-hash a fight he had with his parents over Christmas break, he was also trying to pick one this morning. With me. But I didn't give in. I didn't get it, and maybe I'd try to figure out why he was coming out swinging both fists, but I wasn't going to fight back. I refused.

"I don't get you man," Clint finally said, breaking the icy chill that had settled over the table.

I chuckled and smiled. "OK."

"I mean, I tell you I've rejected your beliefs, I razz you for them. Basically say they're, like, a bunch of bull—and you just sit there. Calm, cool, and collected. You don't lash out. You don't respond. You don't tell me off, tell me I'm full of it. What gives?"

I found Clint's observations striking. I hadn't considered my response in the moment. Just seemed like the best thing to do. No use getting defensive and fighting with the guy. And besides: what would be the point in reacting with indignation, anyway? But I was sure glad I had acted the way he said I did. Perhaps it would give me an opening to share some truth.

I cleared my throat, and said, "Honestly, I have no idea. I

mean, I'm glad I reacted the way you say I have. Don't get me wrong, I still struggle with doubt, with believing. But I still have faith. And I guess I'm secure enough in what I still believe that it doesn't really matter what you think." I stopped and shook my head. "That sounded way more condescending than I intended!"

We laughed. Clint said, "Don't worry, no offense taken. But let's talk about that."

"Talk about what?"

"Being secure in what we believe. How can you be so sure? Especially after you voiced your own doubts before Christmas break?"

I looked over at Logan, who himself seemed to be waiting for how I would respond. I realized in the moment that what I said would be crucial for both of them, but in different ways. Logan wanted to know I still had faith; Clint wanted to know I still had doubts.

What should I say?

"You're right, I did voice some doubts. But don't mistake that for disbelief. It's not that I no longer believe in the Christian faith. It's just that I'm beginning to believe...differently."

"What do you mean by that?" Logan interrupted. "That you believe *differently?*"

I noticed he pounced on the word *differently*. I prayed for the right words as I tried to untangle the Gordian knot of my spiritual quest the past several months.

I shifted in my seat, then said, "By believing differently I mean different than the way I've believed in the past. And different than the way some versions of Christianity have believed in the past."

"For instance?" Clint asked.

"For instance, and I know I've said this before, but I keep coming back to it: how I believe about science and faith. I get it, I sound like a broken record at this point, but I think it's an important aspect of faith. And, Logan, you know how important of a belief it's been for our people."

Logan smiled knowingly at this, though I could see the skepticism in his eyes, too.

I continued, "The kind of science and understanding of creation the version of the Christian faith we grew up with was born in a certain time and place, back at the start of the twentieth century. Fundamentalists—and I don't say that to name-call, but that's what they considered themselves, right? Guardians of the fundamentals of the faith. Anyway, certain fundamentalists at the start of the twentieth century staked the survival of Christianity on the one issue of creation and science. It climaxed with the famous Scopes Trial—"

"Pete, way too early for a history lesson," Clint complained, stuffing his mouth with another spoonful of Cocoa Puffs.

I held up my hand. "Hold on. Bear with me here, because it's important to what I'm trying to say. So, there was this substitute high school teacher, John Scopes, who was accused of violating some Tennessee law that made it a crime to teach evolution. The guy was found guilty and fined $100. The real show, though, was how the trial publicized the fundamentalist–modernist controversy. Which set modernists, who said evolution was not inconsistent with religion, against fundamentalists, who said the Word of God as revealed in the Bible took priority over all human knowledge."

I paused to take a bite of my oatmeal and collect my thoughts. After swallowing and taking a swig of coffee, I continued.

"So you had these two famous dudes, William Jennings Bryan prosecuting the teacher, and Clarence Darrow defending the guy. It wasn't just about whether evolution should be taught in schools. It was more than that. The whole thing was a theological contest pitting science against faith. Shoot, even Adam and Eve were on trial! While Jennings won, in reality the Church lost because of how it clung to old ways of viewing and reading the Bible."

"You mean *outdated* ways, right?" Logan said, a slight edge to his voice.

I considered this. "I guess. But think about what Bryan said in the debate with Morris, how Pastor McLaughlin put the whole creation story in context of the era it was written in. It wasn't that he was denying that God created. He was trying to show how the creation narrative isn't doing what many fundamentalists think it's doing."

"And what's that?" Clint said, edging closer to the table.

"Teaching us science. It's not a scientific account in the same way the Bible isn't a scientific textbook or encyclopedia. The Bible is God's Story to us about himself and us. What I'm learning is to treat it that way."

Logan folded his arms and leaned back in his chair, seeming to consider my words. Same for Clint.

"And so, to answer your question, Clint," I continued, "I still believe the Bible is God's Word. I still believe God created every-thing. I just believe *differently*. I'm sort of reimagining what the Christian faith is really about. Because I'm still hopeful that it connects to our modern world."

Logan sat forward loudly, suddenly, and huffed. "Dude, you sound like my old youth group leader!"

I was taken by surprise. I didn't know how to respond. First Clint, now Logan?

"Your youth group leader? I don't understand," I said.

"It's what I wanted to talk about before. My senior year we got this new youth leader from the West Coast. California, I think. About your age. Came in real sly-like by doing all this cool stuff. Went to all the school sporting events. Hung out at school. Organized a ton of fun activities. He was real popular. Really built up the youth group. But then he started teaching all this stuff that went against our church. Saying it was OK for women to preach. That God was active in other religions. That evolution was one of the ways God used to create the universe."

Great, now another fight on my hands...

Logan seemed as ready for a fight as Clint was at the beginning. I resolved not to fight him as much as I refused to fight Clint.

"Interesting," I simply said. "So what are you getting at?"

"What I'm getting at is, you're that guy!"

"Hey, man," Clint interjected. "Seriously? You're gonna come at Pete like that?"

I raised my hand. "It's alright. But, bro, I still don't know what you mean. You think I'm trying to sway you guys, or something? Like your youth pastor?"

"It just seems like all of a sudden you're quick to abandon our faith, man."

"Look, Logan, I'm not abandoning anything!" I felt the back of my neck grow warmer. I tried to simmer down, but I was hurt by the accusation—from one of my guys no less. "I still believe Jesus is the Savior of the world. I still believe he died to pay for our sins. Shoot, I still believe we're sinners in need of saving. And I still believe in the resurrection."

"But you don't believe in Heaven anymore, and now you believe in evolution."

"Not true, man. Not true. I already said I don't see why God had to take six billion years to create. But I also don't see why he needed six days, either."

"Because that's what the Bible says!"

Clint sighed. "Oh, here we go with that bull—"

"Clint..." I interrupted before he could derail the conversation.

He looked at me and sighed again, folding his arms and nodding for me to continue.

"Logan, I respect your view of Scripture. I do. In fact, I respect Scripture too! So much so that I'm asking questions about how we handle it and read it. Asking questions of the *traditional* ways we've handled it and read it—and then *communicated* it. Like the story of Jesus. You said I don't believe in Heaven anymore. Not true. What I don't believe in is how people have sold Heaven like a vacuum cleaner. Or, rather, sold Jesus on the hope of Heaven."

This seemed to give Logan pause. "What do you mean by that?"

"I didn't share much with you guys, but back before school started Ainsley and I went on an evangelism training trip to the church founded by the head of our organization in Dallas. *Everyday Evangelism*, it's called. The whole thing was built on the idea that Heaven is a free gift that's not earned or deserved."

"But, isn't it?" Logan asked.

"No!" I said, shaking my head. "Well, OK, God's eternal life is a free gift that's not earned or deserved. But Heaven isn't the point, Jesus is. And the *rescue* and *re-creation* he offers is his point. Rescue from sin and death, and the gift of re-creation at the resurrection from the dead when Jesus returns—not some mystical land in outer space. Rescue from shame and guilt in *this* life, and the freedom to live a brand-spanking new one *right now*, just like God intended when he created us. I don't know about you, but I'm not interested in life after death as much as I am in life *before* life after death. I mean, what does Jesus mean for my life right now?"

I saw Clint nod slightly out of the corner of my eye, which infused me with courage. I also saw some sort of knowing look in Logan's eyes. They squinted and the side of his mouth curled up slightly, like maybe I made some sort of connection.

"So, you see, I'm not abandoning the Christian faith. I'm trying to reimagine it outside the box we've put Christianity in over the years. No, I'm interested in absolutely *dismantling* the box we've put the faith in. For the sake of Christ and his Story."

I paused before continuing. "Actually, it's more than that. Because while these past few months of reimagining have definitely been about me and my own faith—trying to find a faith that's more sustainable in our modern world—it's been more than that. Because I want to dismantle the box for the sake of *you* guys and *your* stories."

Their eyes were fixed on me now. I found myself getting choked up as I continued.

"Like yours, Clint. Back when the school year started—that conversation messed me up, man."

Clint raised both eyebrows and chuckled. "Sorry, bro! Didn't mean to mess with you."

"It's fine. But, man, those questions...And I just didn't have answers for them, you know? Really, the faith I was given as a child and in college—even my ministry—they couldn't offer you answers. Which got me asking the same questions. So, thanks for that!"

He chuckled again. "No problem."

"But it wasn't just you. The other guys in the group had the same questions about faith and life and everything in between. Even you, Logan, voiced doubt. Wasn't it about the resurrection?"

"I wasn't doubting the resurrection," Logan corrected. "I just said, sometimes I wonder if the tomb is really empty." He quickly added: "But I still believe it!"

"OK, sorry. But still, there's that one percent of questioning—which I think is fine! And all these questions led me down the rabbit hole into this whole other world of people asking the same questions, this group called Prosurgent. Which gave me comfort. Because it made me realize that it's OK to ask them. There's nothing to fear with asking questions. It also made me realize there's so much about the Christian faith that has been filtered through our own prejudices and perspectives. And I think it's time to rethink what it is that makes up the essence of Christianity—what is central, what's always been central to the Christian faith.

"Which is what, exactly?" Clint probed.

I answered, "The rebellion of humanity. The rescue provided through Jesus' life, death, and resurrection. The necessity of new birth through faith in him—his death on the cross and resurrection from the dead. And re-creation, the beauty of a life put back together again, both in this life and the next. That's what's important. Not whether the world was created in six days!"

Clint leaned back and folded his arms. I could see his mind racing as he considered this.

"And all of this, this questioning and reimagining the essence of Christianity has not just been for me. It's been for you and your friends and that world out there." I pointed outside the windows overlooking the campus.

Logan leaned back as well. "I hear what you're saying. I guess I had always been afraid of questioning my faith."

I was surprised by Logan's admission. He was one to project confidence, never one to let his guard down. I was pleased.

"Why is that?" I asked.

He went silent for a few beats before continuing. "Maybe because of how my youth pastor was treated, especially by my parents."

My eyes widened slightly by the admission. I hoped he didn't notice. "Tell me about that."

He went silent again, as if searching for a way to explore the memory. Then he said, "Back when everything went down with Pastor Mike, there was this adult-only meeting with him in the sanctuary. No kids allowed sort of thing. Our house was up the road, so I biked there and snuck into a stairwell near the sanctuary. And the things they accused him of...The things my parents accused him of. '*You're a sorry excuse for a pastor,*' Dad said, '*You're a sorry excuse for a Christian if you think questioning the Lord and his Good Book will get you anywhere in life but a ticket straight to hell!*'"

He stopped and shook his head. "I'd never been one to doubt or question my faith. And after hearing that, there was no way in hell I'd go down that road."

I could see Clint look at me, but I kept focusing on Logan and his memory. I glanced at my watch. It was almost time to go, they had classes in fifteen minutes.

"I'm sorry to hear about that, bro," I offered. "I don't mean any disrespect to your dad when I say this, but I think he was dead wrong. Not only with the way he treated Pastor Mike, but especially with what he said about doubting and questions."

The resurrection story at the end of Matthew grabbed for my attention in the moment. So I pulled out my Bible and flipped to Matthew 28:16–20, finding what was tucked away in my Scripture memory.

"I know we need to go in a few minutes, but listen to this:

> *Then the eleven disciples went to Galilee, to the mountain where Jesus had told them to go. When they saw him, they worshiped him; but some doubted. Then Jesus came to them and said, "All authority in heaven and on earth has been given to me. Therefore go and make disciples of all nations, baptizing them in the name of the Father and of the Son and of the Holy Spirit, and teaching them to obey everything I have commanded you. And surely I am with you always, to the very end of the age.*

I set my Bible on the table, and said, "So, Jesus has just been raised from the dead and his friends meet him at this spot on a mountain in Galilee. They worshipped him there, but some also doubted. I mean, hello! The guy you've spent three years of your life learning from and serving with, the guy you've seen heal people and walk on water—that guy is now standing in front of you. And you doubt? And in the middle of worshipping? Yet what does Jesus do?"

I let the question settle in the middle of the table. I could see the two of them considering it before I answered.

"Does he condemn them for doubting? Ridicule them? Does he even address it? Sort of. To both the solid believers and the wavering believers he gives what's been called the Great Commission. He sends them on mission to continue his mission of rescue and re-creation. Amazingly, their weakness of faith didn't disqualify them! He took these doubting worshipers and continued to work with them on the path of their spiritual journey.

"And you know what?" I paused a beat before answering. "He still takes doubting worshippers like us doubting worshippers and works with us and our own journey. In Jesus, there's still hope for people who struggle to believe, because he is with us. Jesus says, '*I am with you always...*' not only to complete his mission, but to complete our spiritual journey! Paul speaks of not having already grasped the end goal of his own Christian life—fully knowing and understanding Christ and being like him. But one thing he did, he said in Philippians chapter 3: '*Forgetting what is behind and straining toward what is ahead, I press on toward the goal to win the prize for which God has called me heavenward in Christ Jesus.*'"

I closed my Bible and took a breath. I continued, "So here's what I'd challenge you both with: Don't give up! No matter where you're at in your spiritual walk, don't stop and lay down.

Don't head back to where you've been. Even if the only way you can move forward is on all fours crawling like a *dog!*"

The guys laughed.

"Do what Paul did: press on toward the goal of winning the prize. You know what that prize is? These words at the resurrection: *'Well done my good and faithful servant!'* And you know what else? Jesus is with you every step of the way."

I glanced at my watch again. Five minutes left. I said a short prayer, praying for both Logan and Clint. They thanked me for meeting with them and for the encouragement before heading off to class.

Lord, this is what I've been made for!

CHAPTER 26

I WAS RIDING high from the conversation. There really was such a thing as a ministry high, the feeling that came from coming alongside someone in their spiritual journey and nudging them along that well-worn path that much closer in their relationship with Jesus. And for once, I had felt—I mean, I really felt—it was Christ himself speaking and working through me. Which only heightened the euphoria!

Before going to the office, I stopped into Saxbys for a hot peppermint tea and took it to the seating area in the bay window where all of this began. Figured Roger wouldn't mind if I was a little later than I had originally said.

I stared out the window and sipped my tea, watching people pass outside and grinning again at all that had gone down—from that first conversation with Clint in those chairs several months ago to that table in Leo's with all of its conversations over the school year.

I took another sip, savoring its minty goodness and thinking about what God had called me to in my mentoring role. Over break, I had read the passage from John 15 about Christ as the true vine, and how we're branches of that vine. He urged his followers to remain in him if they were to produce fruit.

Today, I was in the vine! And I can't wait to see the kind of fruit that's gonna come from all of those conversations—especially in Clint's life.

I spent another twenty minutes just sitting and reveling in the morning—thanking the good Lord above for my work, for my vocation. Then I drained my tea and left for whatever was waiting for me back at the farm.

My breath billowed behind me as I huffed back to the office thanks to a recently settled polar vortex. Yet nothing could dampen or cool the fire growing in my belly for the kind of ministry I sensed Christ himself directing me into.

When I arrived at the Campus Ministry office, I took the steps up the stairs by twos, feeling like I should whistle or something to fully express my delight. I headed to my desk, passing Tabitha on the way.

"Hi, Tabitha!"

"Hey, Peter."

She looked sullen, like her cat had died. I stopped and turned back around. "Everything alright? You look like something died!"

She looked at the floor and sighed. She looked back up with a painted smile. "No, I'm fine. Tired is all."

"That's good. Not about being tired. I mean, I'm glad that it's not anything more serious."

"Yeah..."

"Hope you can put your feet up on your desk and take it easy today. Maybe even take a cat nap when Roger isn't looking." I winked and threw her a smile.

"I thought I heard you out here."

I startled and turned around. "Hey, Roger."

"Hi, Tabitha," he said flatly. "Peter, can I see you a second in my office?"

The look in his eyes and the same painted smile Tabitha had worn broke the floorboards keeping my stomach in place. My face went with it, sinking at the request.

"Sure," I offered. "Just give me a minute to put my bag at my desk."

Roger hesitated, like he wanted to protest. He relented. "OK, go and do that, and then just come on in when you're finished."

Not again, I sighed inside as I got to my cubicle. *Don't panic. Maybe they're letting you off the hook from your probation.*

My steps tried to keep pace with my heart as I shuffled to Roger's office. When I stepped in, Bernie was waiting along with Roger. They were sitting in their seats of choice.

"Close the door, Peter," Roger said.

I closed the door and caught Tabitha walking out of her office holding a box. I turned back around before I could see where she was heading. Instinct told me my office.

Not good...

I sat next to Bernie in the seat I had come to know and love the past few months. With how many times I sat in it, they should have replaced it with one of those actor chairs complete with my name.

Roger hesitated to speak, looking down at his desk and then up at Bernie before settling on me with a blank face.

He sighed before stepping up to the plate to deliver whatever it was he was trying to avoid. "Peter, we have received a series of...disturbing emails, from one of your guys over the past few weeks."

Disturbing emails?

I sat statue-still. I stared past Roger in disbelief, then shifted in my chair.

"OK..." was all I could manage.

"This student wrote to us concerned about some of the things that you have been teaching—suggesting they were liberal teachings."

I felt like a linebacker had just lunged into my chest, throwing me to the ground and landing on top of me. I could barely breathe. Who on earth would write such a thing? Surely not Clint. Or Deon. Maybe Thomás. Logan? Sam? My mind was intoxicated with confusion. I tried to make sense of what was happening. But sense was hard to come by.

"What's disturbing about this one particular email, Peter, is that it's dated just this morning, referencing a conversation that happened just today."

Logan. No way that was Clint.

My mind swam with a myriad of why questions. Maybe Logan just wasn't ready to deal with the idea of reimagining his faith, or ready to listen to someone he respected talk so openly about questioning. Regardless, I didn't fault him for that, or begrudge him for writing Roger.

But, man...

I sat up straighter, at the edge of my chair, trying not to let my face betray my betrayal.

"You know that in December we had a talk in this very room about several character problems. Defiance and defensiveness. We also talked about some of the doctrinal concerns we've had, and I explicitly told you to stop it with this Prosurgent nonsense —both involving yourself with this group and especially teaching it to your students. And yet..." He held up the printed email without saying a word.

I glanced at Bernie. In perfect Bernie form, he didn't make eye contact. Simply stared forward, hands folded on his lap.

Could really use your help right about now, friend. Especially after you told me to follow my ministry gut.

I stared at Roger waiting for him to continue. I saw his face begin to flush. Were his eyes moistening?

"It's for this reason," he began softly, "as well as the many other documented problems, that we've decided that you're no longer a fit here."

I sank into my chair.

It was happening. Really happening this time.

"You're dismissed from ministry."

I felt air hiss out my nose, like a tire surprised by a nail. I shouldn't have been surprised by the announcement. It was the way it was announced; it wasn't *that* I was let go, but how it was said.

It wasn't that I was *fired.* I was *dismissed from ministry,* like some false teacher strung up by his neck and left to swing for the ravens.

No one was talking. Roger was staring at me, eyes wet with emotion. Bernie was finally facing me, his face sullen and regretful.

Seminary.

The word came out of nowhere, stabbing the silence with a calling or a wish—I wasn't sure.

I clung to it, nonetheless, as the job that was far more than a job to me slipped from my fingers into the netherworld. It was my life. I had the privilege of stewarding the spiritual lives of college students during one the most pivotal times in their lives. You don't strap that role on like a line worker at an assembly plant or some dime-a-dozen marketing executive with a Fifth Avenue firm.

I was a campus pastor to a congregation of post-Christian twentysomethings trying my best to help them. And that role, that *identity,* was just ripped away from me.

And probably by my own doing.

"Peter?" I heard.

I lifted my head, not realizing I had let it drop in the haze of my execution. "Yes—" I cleared my throat. "Yes, I understand."

"We're going to need your keys. And here is your final paycheck."

Final paycheck?

So they had been planning this for at least two weeks. I smirked as I unwound the front door key to our building off from my key ring. I tossed it on Roger's desk. Roger watched it skip across it before handing me my check.

"Thanks," I said, snatching it and getting up to leave. It was the only thing I could think of doing at that point.

Roger stood too, extending his hand. I took it.

"We wish you all the best, Peter. We all believe God has great plans for you, that he wants to use you mightily for his kingdom."

Just not here, right?

He continued, "We just feel like you're not a fit here anymore."

"I understand," I said softly. "Well, thanks for the opportunity, anyway. Bernie..."

I seemed to jostle Bernie from a trance. He stood. We embraced.

"You're a good troop, Pete," he whispered in my ear. "A good troop."

My throat began to constrict in on itself. I wiped a tear that had slipped by my efforts to hold back the impending tide of emotions. Not yet. That would come later.

Both Bernie and Roger weren't as steely. Their eyes were beginning to overflow. I refused to stand there while they got to be emotional for ruining my life.

Without saying goodbye, I went to open the door to walk out, but I was stopped short by a box sitting outside the closed glass door. Tabitha's box. Inside I saw some items from my desk and the bag I had dropped off before meeting Roger.

"We'll mail you anything else Tabitha couldn't fit in that

box," Roger said behind his desk, as if understanding why I was still standing at the door. "Blessings on your life, Peter."

My eyes narrowed. A smile curled upwards. I grabbed the handle and yanked the door open.

The first thing I noticed as I picked up my box was how quiet Campus Ministry was. Eerily so. Like the Rapture had just happened, taking the world up to Heaven while I was left behind holding the box of my disintegrated ministry.

The next thing I noticed was Ainsley pulling herself back out of visibility's range in our office area.

Bye to you, too, Ains.

Peggy and Tabitha were nowhere to be found, either, though I suspected they were hiding with Ainsley. Was probably for the best.

The last thing I noticed, still standing in Roger's doorway, was a sense of relief. Relief from the watchful, wondering eyes of people who didn't get it. Relief from feeling like I had to hide my doubts and questions and fears about my faith.

And freedom...

Someone cleared their throat behind me. I realized I was still holding my box standing in front of Roger's office. I turned my head halfway toward the noise and took off, walking down the stairs and then out the front door—leaving behind my ministry and shedding my identity as a minster once and for all.

I walked down O Street back to my car with purpose, carrying the box of trinkets that had come to define my life, its weight seeming to grow with each step. To add insult to injury, the universe decided to give me a parking ticket along with giving me unemployment.

"Beautiful." I yanked the ticket out from underneath my windshield wiper, balled it up, and threw it in my box. I stuffed it behind my seat, brought my car to life, and started driving. No direction, no agenda. I was in a jobless, pink-slip trance, the world passing me by as I hovered through the streets, numb to the reality of what had just happened.

I just lost my job. I just lost my ministry. How am I going to get another job? How am I going to pay rent? How am I going to eat?

The questions kept rolling, waves cresting and crashing against me as I left Campus Ministry in my wake. It was only after I passed 37th Street that I realized my mistake: O Street dead-ends into Georgetown University. I passed through the university entrance as I had done hundreds of times for nearly two years. I circled around the statue of John Carroll, founder of the university. The names of my students flashed through my mind in rapid succession: Logan, Samuel, Thomás, Deon...Clint.

What would they think? What would they do without me?

Not that I was a special spiritual superstar, or anything, but they had come to depend on me like congregants depended on their pastor or priest. What would happen to their spiritual journeys now that I wasn't part of it?

A car behind me started riding my bumper as I slowly made my way around the entrance loop, breathing in my ministry stomping grounds one last time.

After I rounded the circle, I hit the accelerator to punch it back home. I passed my office again—my *former* office. My gut twisted with a mixture of anger and fear, reality finally settling in:

I had just lost my job. I had just lost my ministry. I was now unemployed.

Lord, what am I going to do?

CHAPTER 27

AFTER ARRIVING HOME, I shed my clothes and put on my sweats, then crawled into bed. I couldn't think of anything better to do during the mid-day than sleep it away. Initially, sleep was hard to come by. Then it was restless. I woke just after 6:00 p.m. I should have been hungry. I wasn't. My stomach was tied up in unemployment knots, growing tighter as I thought about the future. With all of its pesky demands for housing and sustenance and whatnot.

I got out of bed and took a shower, hoping somehow I would evaporate out of existence along with the steam. I just stood there and let the water run over me, my mind spinning out of control.

It's so unfair!

I willed the steaming water to wash away the anguish. It didn't work.

Here I was trying to do the right thing by my guys, trying to help them move forward in their relationship with Christ in their world—and I'm canned for it?

My anger continued to mount, rising in concert with the steam, fueled by my hurt at being so misunderstood—so *judged*.

Seminary.

There was that word again, like some telepathic smoke signal coming down from above.

"What does that mean? Why grad school for ministers? Is that what's next, Lord?"

Then seemingly almost out of the same netherworld, another word popped into my mind: *Labyrinth.*

"Yes," I whispered, "that'd be perfect!"

I checked the clock above my toilet. 6:23. I would make it just in time for the Washington National Cathedral's labyrinth contemplative service.

The labyrinth was an ancient spiritual practice going back through to the early Church. The earliest known labyrinth was found in a church in Algeria around AD 350. Many cathedrals in Europe during the Middle Ages constructed large labyrinths as a way to provide a stand-in spiritual pilgrimage for Christians unable to make the trip to Jerusalem, symbolizing the journey to the Holy Land. The most well-known of these was in the floor of the nave at Chartres Cathedral in France.

At first glance, the path of a labyrinth looked like a maze. However, there were no dead ends, it only looked that way. While it had multiple twists and turns, the path took the walker into its center, an area for resting, prayer, and meditation. The path was meant as a metaphor for the path of our lives. Along the way, the walker was meant to pause to pray, asking God for direction and insight into their life-path—whether aspects of it they had already traversed, or for what lay in the future. Just as the path of the labyrinth has several twists and turns, which creates a confusing, uncertain experience, yet always ends in a clear destination—the same was true for life.

I could think of no better way to contemplate the next leg of my own journey than with this spiritual practice.

I put on my jeans, then I threw on a charcoal grey hoodie and orange down vest. I slipped on a wool hat and gloves, deciding to jog the mile and a half to the cathedral. Even though the temperature was hovering just above freezing, I figured the exercise would do me good, preparing my body for the full-on spiritual experience.

Twenty minutes later, I arrived at America's church: Cathedral Church of St. Peter and St. Paul, as it was known. Its neo-Gothic, imposing body beckoned me to come and drink of its spiritual well to experience the goodness of God. I entered through a back door beneath the High Altar that I had accidentally discovered the last time I was there. The heavy walnut wood creaked as I swung it open. I labored my breathing and shed my vest as I walked through the low corridor of Indiana limestone in the belly of the cathedral, passing what looked like offices for the various clergy which served this active congregation.

After taking a few wrong turns, I found the stairwell I was looking for, which brought me up to an entrance off the nave near the War Memorial Chapel. Two massive canvas maps patterned after the floor of the nave at Chartres Cathedral had replaced the chairs which normally filled both annexes on Sunday morning. In the center, the faint sound of a harp ascended heavenward as an aural offering before the throne of God. It was a siren call of the labyrinth service inviting me to taste and see that the Lord was good—despite my circumstances.

A few people had already begun their contemplative journey, but most were still in the wooden chairs of the Great Hall, either kneeling or sitting in quiet reflection and prayer. I joined them, sliding my vest around the back of my seat. A Bible and *Book of Common Prayer* sat nestled in the chair back in front of me. I took the prayer book and traced the thin gold cross set in its jet-black cover with my finger as a way to ground my evening. I flipped the book open to the table of contents, searching for the Compline Office of the final evening prayers. It sent me to page 127.

I released the red-velvet padded kneeling bench from the chair in front of me and assumed a position of supplication. I began by whispering the opening line of the Order for Compline: *The Lord Almighty grant us a peaceful night and a perfect end. Amen.*

Amen.

Since I didn't have a guide for the prayers, I acted as both officiant and respondent. I continued: *Our help is in the Name of the Lord; The maker of heaven and earth.*

I prayed the prayer of confession, pausing afterwards to reflect and confess specific sins. Roger's continued accusations of defensiveness and defiance came to mind. Something broke in me as I considered them. He was right. I had been those things— and so much more.

Lord, I've been a royal prick the past few months, I prayed silently. *Can I say prick in the National Cathedral? Whatever. I have been. I'd been a jerk to my coworkers as I set out on this new path. Perhaps I deserved being fired today. I probably did. Please forgive me of the ways I didn't love my Campus Ministry neighbors.*

I crossed myself with the sign of the cross, and whispered, "Amen."

Then I continued from the prayer book: *May the Almighty God grant us forgiveness of all our sins, and the grace and comfort of the Holy Spirit. Amen.*

I chose Psalm 31 among the available psalters for my evening reading. I read the verses it listed, one through five:

> In you, Lord, I have taken refuge;
>> let me never be put to shame;
>> deliver me in your righteousness.
>> Turn your ear to me,

come quickly to my rescue;
be my rock of refuge,
a strong fortress to save me.
Since you are my rock and my fortress,
for the sake of your name lead and guide me.
Keep me free from the trap that is set for me,
for you are my refuge.
Into your hands I commit my spirit;
deliver me, Lord, my faithful God.

Glory to the Father, and to the Son, and to the Holy Spirit, I prayed, *as it was in the beginning, is now, and will be forever. Amen.*

Next, there was a passage from the Gospel of Matthew, the words of Jesus in 11:28-30:

"Come to me, all you who are weary and burdened, and I will give you rest. Take my yoke upon you and learn from me, for I am gentle and humble in heart, and you will find rest for your souls. For my yoke is easy and my burden is light."

Then I prayed the Lord's prayer:

Our Father, who art in heaven,
hallowed be thy Name,
thy kingdom come, thy will be done,
on earth as it is in heaven.
Give us this day our daily bread.
And forgive us our trespasses,

as we forgive those who trespass against us.
And lead us not into temptation, but deliver us
*   from evil.*
For thine is the kingdom, and the power, and the
*   glory,*
for ever and ever. Amen.

I concluded my mini-compline service with one of the Collects. The first one offered a simple, yet powerful prayer. It read:

Be our light in the darkness, O Lord, and in your great mercy defend us from all perils and darkness of this night; for the love of your only Son, our Savior Jesus Christ. Amen.

"Amen," I whispered.

I rose from the bench, sitting as I put it back into place. I looked up to see the labyrinth mats filling up as more people sought the solace and direction of the spiritual practice.

I sighed and stood to join them, excited, expectant, and nervous for what I would find inside.

CHAPTER 28

THE ELDERLY LADY playing the harp at the front of the nave smiled at me as I came forward. I removed my shoes and stepped up to the "entrance" of the mat. I hesitated, feeling a little silly.

I placed both feet on the mat and waited. Hoping, wishing, divining some sort of word from the Lord.

Nothing.

I walked farther inside before hitting my first bend. I stopped and waited again. I stared at the ground.

Again, nothing.

Frustration began to bubble up within me as I looked around at my fellow contemplators, all of whom looked as though they were making a connection with the Divine. I felt like I was doing it wrong.

But then I remembered the first time I came to the service. I had the same feeling of inadequacy and failure. And what I did then is what I did in that moment. I closed my eyes. I breathed in deeply then eased my breath out, clearing my mind of distraction and my heart of burdens. I prayed a short prayer from Psalm 119:

Lord, your word is a lamp for my feet, a light on my path.

Please help me understand that path, both past and present; reveal a way forward. Amen.

I took another breath before taking a step forward. When I did, my mind immediately jumped to the bend I had just passed and then to a moment during my childhood.

It was junior high. And I was in the middle of a long, awkward phase of growth when my body decided to fritz out on me—and my "friends" decided to make me and my awkward, plumped-out teenage body the butt of their jokes. For two years, I wasn't Peter Daniel Young, but rather Barney, the oversized purple dinosaur. It didn't help that Mom had the brilliant idea of dressing me in lots of purple that year.

Those were long, fallow, wintery years of pain and loneliness. Nowadays, they call that sort of thing bullying. I didn't understand it as such back then. I just knew I wanted out, even contemplated taking one with the handgun stowed away in Dad's dresser drawer.

But then college happened. God brought me to the exact place I needed: Freedom University. He provided a solid group of friends; helped me excel in my studies; created a unique friendship and mentorship between me and the college president; and even helped me become president of my class all four years, which was one of the best things to happen to me. Those were long, full, summer years of blessing and bounty.

As I continued shuffling forward I realized how God had brought me through that bend and stretch of pain and misery, how he had guided me by the hand into a land overflowing with milk and honey. I said a prayer of thanks to my Rock and my Redeemer for that period of my life, how he had brought me through it and set my feet upon a sure and steady plateau above my enemies. I continued walking, reliving the pain of those years of mockery and misery, and then contemplating the elevation and provision, the kind I needed when I started over again as a college freshman. I smiled with the bittersweet memory. Because as much as I valued those years, I couldn't go back to Freedom.

I looped around to the far side of the labyrinth only to encounter yet another twist in my path, rounding it into another stretch. My mind jumped to yet another moment in my story, a pattern I sensed was going to dominate the evening.

This bend came when I moved to Washington, DC. During my senior year at Freedom, I spent my spring break visiting the city to get the lay of the land and network with well-positioned alumni throughout the government. It was during that trip I resolved to move here and make my own Jesus-shaped mark on our nation's capital.

So with a thousand bucks to my name and a suit jacket full of prayers, I packed up every one of my earthly belongings and moved. I had found a five-month sublease in an apartment in Alexandria through our career services office that I figured would let me plant me feet. Had no idea how closely I would scrape the edge of that lease before finding a full-time job.

Those first few months were rough. I spent that hot, sticky DC August pounding the pavement in my shiny new, ill-fitting suit. I had to have handed out nearly a hundred resumes and applied for half as many open internships and entry-level jobs through the congressional job bank that month. And yet, no one bit at my fresh-faced bait.

Near the end of the month, I started to panic. I learned real quick that a thousand dollars in DC wouldn't take me nearly as far as it did at my alma mater or back home. So I took drastic measures to pay rent and eat—I became a sales associate at the local Christian bookstore.

Looking back, that was a bend in its own right, and an ironic bend at that, considering where I was now. It was also God making my path straight by providing what I needed at just the right time to carry me forward financially—and providentially.

Because one day, a congressional staffer stopped in to buy a new Bible for his son's birthday. We got to chatting and somehow or other we got on the subject of my background at Freedom University, my subsequent move to Alexandria, and my job hunt. Turned out, he was the Chief of Staff for the House Majority Leader, who happened to have an opening in their legislative shop—not just in their district office, but in the *Leader's* office. He offered me the job on the spot. I can't explain why, other than God's movement in my life to move me through that bend in the road and beyond it.

I smiled and shook my head again in disbelief as I continued looping around through another twist, thanking Jehovah-jireh, the Lord who provides, for all he had done for me. What an amazing year that was, helping the Majority Leader craft economic and social policy for America.

But as I came to yet another bend in the labyrinth mat, I remembered how unbearable it was toward the end, too. Within a few months, I had risen to the ranks of senior legislative aide at a mere twenty-three years old. And that put me in the enviable position of meeting with the high-rolling Christian activists from both sides of the aisle and both ends of the theological spectrum.

Toward the end of that leg in my journey, I remembered a poll shortly after the mid-term election by the *National Journal*. It asked Members of Congress, "If you could ignore one special interest group without having to worry about the political repercussions, whom would you ignore." For Democrats it was the environmentalists, unionists, and abortionists—in that order. For Republicans it was the National Rifle Association, National Right to Life, and Religious Right—in that order.

After I read that poll and experienced too many closed-door, off-the-record meetings, I'd had it. I was through trying to peck my way through the wall separating Church and State—in fact, I was ready to reinforce it at all cost.

Before I realized it, I had arrived at the center of the mat where a few others had arrived before me seeking solace and comfort for their own journeys. Embedded in the center were eight sort of cubbies for eight people to sit in quiet contemplation and prayer. I took a seat next to a well-appointed middle-aged man in a gray suit who was seated shoe-less and legs crossed with palms turned upward.

I matched his pose and took a deep breath, trying to drain my mind of distractions and use the time for prayer. I tried to focus, but the events of the day pressed in against me.

They did it. They really fired me.

I shook my head to extinguish the memory while keeping my eyes closed.

As I continued to sit, fear began seeping into every pore of my mind, filling it with every concern and possible scenario: eviction, starvation, car problems, life-time unemployment, homelessness—moving back home!

I pressed my hands against my temples, trying to stop the cascading emotions from overwhelming me. I couldn't stop them.

Lord, comfort me. Stop the doubt, quiet the fear. Help me to trust you.

Almost immediately, I was given a word—a verse, actually, from Psalm 34: *"Taste and see that the Lord is good; blessed is the one who takes refuge in him."*

I dropped my hands to my legs and opened my eyes, considering the words again. I repeated the phrase.

Taste and see that the Lord is good. Taste and see that the Lord is good. Taste and see that the Lord is good.

I stopped and closed my eyes again.

How is this good? How is this for my good?

I let my words dangle, hoping for an answer. I found none.

And yet...

I wondered if maybe that was the point. Maybe it would be

some time until I tasted and saw, some time until I realized how good this experience—all of these experiences, from my distant past to immediate present, really were good for me.

I smiled and nodded and stood. I took a deep breath and looked around the Great Hall. I got what I had needed. Time to return to the land of the living. I resumed the metaphor of my journey in order to return to my real one. When I did, I returned to the place in my story where I had left off, this feeling that I had come to the end of my Capitol Hill road. I could still remember the moment vividly.

It was springtime, and the cherry blossoms had just fully peaked. The Capitol grounds were blooming with soft pink flowers and the air was tinged with the sweet scent by which they get their name. I remembered walking out of the building one evening to a set of benches lining one of the walkways toward Constitution Avenue. I had just come out of a weekly meeting with a number of representatives from the Religious Right, and this time they were clamoring for my boss to do something about foreign abortion funding. It wasn't like I didn't agree, but it was the way they went about it that was exhausting and infuriating. So I took a stroll, and had what I can only describe as an apocalyptic vision. Right there on a bench outside the Capitol building.

Given the nation's high-alert status with terrorism, I probably shouldn't be admitting it. I remembered taking off my jacket, loosening my tie, and stretching my legs out on the stone path, and I was staring at the Capitol building when it hit me: *Peter, one day this is all going to burn.* I had this apocalyptic image of the thing crumbling to the ground and flames shooting from the rotunda high into the sky. I realized that all the glitz and glamour, the prestige and posturing didn't match up to a hill of beans. None of it mattered. It was all worthless.

That evening, on my way home, I met Bernie randomly on the Metro subway platform at Metro Center. I was switching trains during rush hour, and he was standing next to me. He noticed I was reading Dietrich Bonhoeffer's book *The Cost of Discipleship*, and he struck up a conversation.

As I continued walking the labyrinth, I found it odd that I obliged, given my introversion and shyness around strangers. But I did, which led to a conversation about my role with the Majority Leader and my disillusionment. For some reason, I mentioned I was fixing to get out and into a new line of work, maybe ministry. He mentioned he worked for Campus Ministry at Georgetown University. He shared about their vision and mission of reaching college students. I was intrigued, so he offered to show me the office one day and share more. When I showed up a week later, he gave me the nickel tour, then mentioned they were hiring for a campus liaison, preferably a younger guy who could lead Bible studies with the college guys. He asked if I would consider the position. I thought the idea was nutso. What did I know about spiritual mentoring, especially to college students? But when I left, I just knew it was the next step. The next day, I accepted the job and gave my two weeks notice to my office.

I finished tracing this moment in my story and noticed I was nearing the end of the labyrinth. I continued walking toward it, politely passing a young coed standing in contemplative prayer. I came to another bend and my mind jumped to my conversation with Clint at Saxbys. I continued walking and another series of events from the past few months fired in rapid succession: the *Everyday Evangelism* training in Dallas, and my near flip-out moment and then conversation with Ainsley; the presentation and rejection of an alternative evangelism training program; the Freddy Morris and Bryan McLaughlin debate; the sit-down with Roger and Bernie leaving me naked, exposed.

Before I knew it, I was one bend and four paces shy of the end. I took a breath and turned into it, knowing what it represented: my firing. As silly and melodramatic as it sounded, I felt unable to move forward, as if the metaphorical bend in my path was channeling all of the fear and insecurity of my literal one.

But then the second part of the verse I had meditated upon earlier in the labyrinth's center came rushing to my mind: *"Blessed is the one who takes refuge in him."*

The one who will experience God's joyous mercies and is divinely enriched, he is the one who turns to hide himself in the Lord.

I felt a new confidence rise up within me, a sense of anticipation for the good things and blessings of God I would experience despite the fear and doubt and pain. I stepped forward a few steps before reaching the end.

I looked down at my feet.

On one side, the one I was standing on, was the warm, soft, cream-colored canvas mat. The other side was the cold, hard, charcoal-colored stone tiles of the cathedral. Beyond my feet was gray, foggy blankness. It was't that it was dark; it was not yet formed. There were no more lines to guide me.

I looked up and turned around, looking at all that I had just traversed, all of the twists and turns, the bends and breaks in my path that had brought me to that point, that moment in time. Not merely in the labyrinth, but my path, my journey, my story on the hunk of rock spinning around our yellow dwarf star, lapping it every 365 days.

The wispy, shaky confidence that began to bubble had now solidified into a constant stream within. Because in looking back at all I had just travelled—in walking through the travelogue of my story, which I believed God had graciously allowed me to traverse in a loving act of remembrance—I could see how God was in it all.

And that gave me great confidence. No, wait, something even better:

Hope!

Knowing—*experiencing*—all of what God had already brought me through gave me strength for that day and a bright hope for that next step off the known path into the blankness of *tomorrow.*

So I took it.

I stepped out into my future, knowing that God really could be trusted with whatever came my way.

In my life. In my faith.

CHAPTER 29

WHAT DO normal people do who get fired?

I had no idea. Had never been fired before. I was lost, drifting through life like a phantom, untethered to anything of substance or significance and unsure of how to live my life.

A few days after my labyrinth experience, I sent a carefully crafted email to my guys letting them know I was no longer employed with Campus Ministry. I received emails from several students who were more acquaintances thanking me for my ministry and wondering what was next. I kept my answers vague, telling them I was thankful for the experience but felt it was time to move on.

The emails I got from Logan, Deon, Thomás, Samuel, and Clint were more heated. They were confused, they wondered why I had left, and they wanted answers. I felt I owed them the truth, so I told them. Their responses were more comforting than I expected. All expressed outrage at the injustice, threatening to boycott Campus Ministry activities and spread the news of my firing. I was touched, but I encouraged them to stay connected with the organization and promised to stay connected with them through text and email.

I had come full-circle: I had no job and had four months left on my lease. So I did what I did when I arrived in DC a few years ago: I got a temp job, this time working for a fortune 500 company as an administrative fill-in for a woman on pregnancy leave. The assignment would carry me through the next few months as I tried to figure out what was next.

Over the next several weeks I traded emails and texts with my former crew to stay in touch, but the connection began to fray as their semester demands took over and my new life prevented me from connecting with them over meals like I had before. It wasn't long until loneliness overtook me. I tried to connect with the guys after work during the evening, but homework, extracurricular actives, and college life stood in the way. Clint vowed to hang out with me soon, and we made plans at different times, but things always seemed to come up.

One day, it all caught up with me. The feelings of utter relational abandonment were especially acute. I sat eating alone at my temp office, and I vowed to break the chain of loneliness. It was the end of April, which meant it was the monthly gathering of fellow reimaginers. It had been a while, but I needed the spiritual oasis I knew as Prosurgent DC.

After work, I took the bus out of Tysons Corner in Northern Virginia where I was working to the Falls Church subway station and up to Dupont Circle Metro stop to The Front Page for the gathering. I made my way to the back room where we met, and I saw a familiar face.

"Brother Darren," I said as I walked up to the bar.

Darren turned his head and smiled. "Peter Daniel Young!" he said with a laugh. "Aren't you a sight for sore eyes, mate. I thought you'd died and gone to Heaven! Or Hell, depending on whether you've been excommunicated yet by the powers that be. Take a seat ol' chap, and grab this guy a Doghead IPA."

I took a seat next to him, and the bartender poured me a glass of water.

"You look more dressed up than the last time I saw you. What's with the tie? New ministry uniform?"

I looked down at the grey noose hanging from my neck. "Oh, that. I guess I never told you, did I."

"Told me what?"

"I had a bit of a career change."

"What? Why, how?"

My IPA arrived. I took a sip before answering.

"I was fired. Excommunicated, really. Like you said."

"No way, brotha," Darren said in his quiet Australian accent.

"Yup."

"What reasons did they give?"

"What reasons *did* they give? Let's see. They said I was prideful. That I was arrogant. That I was divisive. Oh, and that I was a heretic." I took another long swig of my beer.

"They said all those things? Really? Called you a heretic and all?"

"In a manner of speaking. Before Christmas, they sat me down and had a little pow-wow about my attitude, particularly my defensiveness and divisiveness about some of my new beliefs and things I was proposing. Said I had to drop my Prosurgent beliefs, stop attending Prosurgent meetings. Especially stop using and spreading said Prosurgent dogma in my ministry."

Darren laughed. "Who said this? Your boss? The bozo you told me about before?"

I smiled at the word *bozo*. "Yeah, Roger."

"Man, I didn't know the Gestapo was alive and well in this country! Banning you from thinking differently? And attending a

Christian meeting? What's next, they're going to start banning and burning our books? Burning our *leaders*?"

I smiled and took another swig. "Tell me about it."

"Speaking of which," Darren said, setting his drink down and rising from his stool. He walked forward to someone over my shoulder.

I turned my head toward Darren. My eyes widened. It was Bryan McLaughlin.

"Peter, have you met Bryan before?"

I stood, feeling my face flush with nervous excitement. "Yes. Hey, Bryan, my ministry hosted that debate with you and Freddy...err, Alfred Morris."

"That's right," Bryan said, smiling widely and taking my hand with vigor. "Peter, right?"

I smiled and nodded.

He said, "Great to see you again. How have you been?"

Darren said, "Do you smell the scent of burnt flesh and singed clothes on him?"

Bryan gave him a confused look.

"I was let go a few months ago," I offered.

"Burnt at the stake, more like it! Run out with pitchforks and torches, he was. And for, get this, attending our little Prosurgent DC! For gathering with us and, might I add, reading your book. So it's all your fault, Bryan. All your fault!"

I laughed as I sat back down, embarrassed to be the center of attention.

"Wow, sounds painful," Bryan said, taking a seat on the other side of me. "But what's that Aussie knucklehead talking about over there?"

"Well, the powers that be at Campus Ministry didn't take a liking to my spiritual direction and my quest to reimagine the Christian faith. And, yeah, reading your book didn't help matters. No offense!"

Bryan held up a hand. "None taken. Unfortunately, that reaction is a bit too common."

"It is?"

"Tell him about the time you came to speak at my old church back in Australia."

Bryan chuckled and settled back into his bar stool, "Ahh, yes. So Darren, here, has the bright idea to bring me back home to meet the family. It's this century-old Anglican Church of Australia outside of Sydney. We've got clergy and lay people there, a collection of them from different denominations. Anglican priests, Baptist pastors, charismatic network leaders— even some Roman Catholics. I'm there to talk about some of the ideas in my book, about what it might look like to live out this identity as a reimagined Christian and a reimagined Christianity in our post-Christian, postmodern world."

"Tell 'em about the fundie picketers!" Darren interrupted, snickering. "And, bartender, get this guy a Smithwicks."

"I'm getting there, I'm getting there. So, before the morning began, I was chatting with one of the organizers, and he warns me about some possible...guests. Apparently, some concerned churchgoers wrote some letters to the local paper threatening to picket the event. Even protested the church throughout the week before for, in their words, 'inviting a known heretic' to speak in their town."

Darren snickered again before returning to his beer. I couldn't believe I was sharing a pint with Bryan McLaughlin!

Bryan's drink arrived. He took a long swig and hummed with pleasure. "Love the Smithwicks. So, we begin, and the morning fairs pretty well. As far as I know, no picketers have shown up. But then, two hours later, at the mid-morning coffee break, I look outside and notice a handful of people running around the parking lot sticking these bright orange slips of paper under windshield wipers. I'm like, what on earth? So I go out and snatch one of them up. All the while the four or five people are still running around, totally oblivious to who I am! Anyway, the paper warns the people inside about this 'controversial religious teacher' who's this 'dangerous heretic' spouting 'unbiblical views.'"

I furrowed my brow and scoffed. "That's crazy."

"You're telling me. I'm like, 'Here I am, this mild-manner guy—'"

"Mild-manner guy?" Darren mocked. "Bloody hell you are!"

Bryan took another swig, then said, "Seriously, Darren, I never set out to create controversy. I'm not some well-known pastor of a megachurch with this multi-book platform built by the Christian Industrial Complex. I'm a simple pastor of a country church who started asking questions about what it means to be a Christian in our day and age. I didn't do it for the money. I didn't do it for the fame. I definitely didn't do it for the attention—who needs that kind of thing when you've got people running around parking lots pasting orange slips of paper to car windows!"

"Then why'd you do it?" I asked.

Bryan grew quiet, almost reflective, as if chasing a memory of intention.

"I'll tell you why. I do it for the twentysomething guy manning the video equipment at the conference that day, who came up to me to tell me that for the longest time he refused to associate himself with the word 'Christian,' because of all the baggage that word came with. I do it for the Catholic lady who said I was giving voice—and permission—to the questions she'd been asking for years, yet was too afraid to ask because she felt so alone in them. I do it for the seventy year old lady who came up at the end who's scared for the faith of her grandchildren and encouraged me to keep at it, because somehow what I say seems to connect with young people."

He paused, took a swig of beer, then he said, "Frankly, I've done it for people like you, Peter." He poked his finger at my shoulder as he took another swig.

I smiled and cocked my head. "What do you mean?"

"I mean, for people like you in ministry, who are faced with the kinds of questions fundamentalists just don't get—because they don't know anybody who's asking them! So they're not getting them, and they wouldn't get them in the first place." Bryan took another swig of beer. "They think people are asking about how to get to Heaven, whether the Bible is inerrant, whether Jesus' atonement is substitutionary or a recapitulation or moral or an example or a ransom, or any of the other insider baseball questions Christians think the rest of the world is asking."

I nodded knowingly, scooting closer to him on my stool. I resonated with what he was saying, because of how closely his reasons had connected to my own.

"I certainly didn't do it for the controversy." He paused, then added, "But I guess I've also done it for myself—even for my family, for those closest to me. I may be over fifty, but that doesn't mean I've stopped growing as a person, especially as a spiritual person, as a Christian. I'm on a quest for an honest, authentic, sustainable faith as much as the rest of those people—for a faith that makes more sense to me and others. There was a point in my ministry, a few years ago, that that journey was starting to fray my faith, like a ball of yarn that had almost run out of string on its way down a hillside. *Something isn't working in the way we're being Christians and doing the Christian faith anymore!* I remember thinking.

"For a few years, I took long walks alone, just praying and thinking and wondering what would happen to me and my faith if better answers never came. And here's the thing: I didn't have anyone to share this with! So, I created two characters to share my journey. You know them as Pastor Jack and Nelson Edward."

"Whoa," I said quietly. "I had no idea about this part of your story."

"Well, it is. I created the people I wished I had to help me work through my spiritual stuff. And, along the way, I vowed never to let anyone else who was experiencing what I experienced not have people to walk with as they worked through their own spiritual stuff. I guess, I hope that what I've learned—what my characters have learned—will provide some sort of spiritual companionship for the path they are walking on."

I smiled. "I'll tell you, Bryan, they have. *You* have," I corrected myself. "More than you could ever know. So thanks."

Bryan smiled back. "Thanks for saying that. Keep at it, brother. It'll be alright. I have a strong sense that God isn't through with you and your ministry yet. Think of this as just one bend in your path with Christ. One day, you'll discover what it means to be a reimagined Christian and follow a reimagined Christian faith as much as I have. And then you'll be able to be for others who are asking the same questions what Pastor Jack and Nelson Edward were for you."

I liked that idea. Not only of getting to a place of understanding and living what it means to be a reimagined Christian. But especially being the kind of person Bryan had been for me, even through his characters.

We finished our beers as a crowd began to trickle in toward the backroom.

"We should probably take our little meeting of heretics to the back room, wouldn't you say?" Darren suggested.

"Onward ho, to reimagining the Christian faith," Bryan said, standing up.

Yes. Onward.

CHAPTER 30

A MIXTURE of slushy snow and rain from a winter that was hanging on for dear life was pelting my car as I parallel parked it into a spot on O Street. After managing to squeeze it in between an oversized Cadillac SUV and BMW sedan, I turned off my car and sat still, staring at the Cadillac's bumper.

Clint had texted days ago begging me to meet. So we set a time to rendezvous at our old stomping ground at Saxbys. I was sad it took so long to connect, but thankful and excited, nonetheless.

I felt my chest tighten as I sat, my breath fogging the windshield as I stared out through drapes of clumpy, wet snow. I thought I could handle seeing my ministry building across the way. I was wrong.

I closed my eyes and breathed in deeply in order to stuff the anger and rising resentment back inside.

"Whatever," I mumbled as I swung open my car door, resolving not to let it get in the way of my time with Clint—one of my last times, probably.

I hustled across the brick sidewalk and went to open the door to Saxbys, when a tall man with head down opened it from the inside.

We locked eyes. It was Roger.

He startled back slightly and blinked rapidly, as if he couldn't believe what he was seeing. I couldn't either.

"P-Peter," he stammered. "Why, hello! I, uhh, didn't expect to see you. Here, especially. Why *are* you here?"

He spit out the question with an air of accusation as much as bewilderment, like I had no right being this close to my former place of employment—and Georgetown University for that matter.

"Just meeting one of my guys," I said with pleasure. "Clint, actually."

"Really..." he said as he turned around. "I thought I saw him here."

I didn't say anything. I simply continued standing in the descending slush.

He stared at me in silence, tipping his head back. "Do you really think that's appropriate, Peter?"

"Appropriate?" I asked, confused.

"Yes. With you being...well, dismissed and all?"

I couldn't believe the gall. And I couldn't help myself. "Roger, chill."

I stood my ground, staring at the man as he retreated, then frowned slightly.

"I should run," Roger said as he held the door for me. "You know how it is, lots of the Lord's work to do!" He smiled and headed out the door. "Have a blessed day."

I watched him shuffle across the street through the door window. "Have a blessed day, yourself," I mumbled. I turned around looking for Clint. I found him in our usual spot, already nursing a cup of coffee.

He looked up, smiled, and came over.

"Dude, was that Roger?"

We bear hugged. "The one and only."

"What a windbag. The biggest a—"

"Clint."

Chided, he stopped and looked down.

"Whatever, right?" I said. "I'm not gonna let that dampen our pow-wow."

"Thanks for meeting."

"Wouldn't have missed it. Let me get something to drink."

After getting my own cup of coffee and a scone, I sat across from the guy who was largely responsible for setting the events in motion that led to the current juncture in my journey in the first place.

"Gotta tell you, Pete," Clint said, "when I got your email that they canned you I flipped. I mean, I almost got the guys together to march down to your office with pitchforks and torches to burn the place down!"

I smiled and chuckled, touched by his passionate protest of my being let go. "Thanks, I appreciate it. I think?"

"I mean, how could they do that? How could they fire the guy who was single-handedly responsible for bringing me back to my faith?"

I looked up, startled and confused by his admission. *Did he say I brought him back to the faith?*

Clint continued, "I mean, did you kill somebody or something? Did you embezzle money from the place or get a girl pregnant?"

I laughed. "No, it was nothing like that."

"Then what was it?"

I took a breath and looked outside, choosing my words carefully. Everything inside me wanted to let loose against Campus Ministry, Roger in particular. But I didn't want to sour him against one of the only lifelines he had left to the Christian faith.

I settled on: "It's...complicated."

He continued pressing. "Come on, man. I'm not a little kid. I'm your bro! Spill it."

"As far as I can tell they disagreed with my...ministry and spiritual direction."

Clint furrowed his brow and slumped back in his chair. "Your ministry and spiritual direction? What the hell does that mean?"

"I know that's vague and doesn't make sense. They just disagreed with how I went about doing ministry and some of where I was going in my own faith."

"Like actually engaging and entertaining our questions? Like challenging us to own our faith for ourselves? Like questioning the faith yourself rather than rely on pat answers?"

I took a sip of my coffee. "It wasn't only their fault. It was partly mine, too. I was pretty arrogant the past several months with it all. But, yeah, something like that."

Clint shook his head, and said, "That just pisses me off! Good riddance, Campus Ministry."

Again, I was touched and couldn't argue with him. But I changed the subject, bringing the conversation around to why we were meeting.

"Let's take the convo back a step. You said that I brought you back to the faith. What did you mean by that?"

Clint's face brightened and he shifted to the edge of his seat, coffee sloshing over the side of his mug in response to his excitement.

"That's what I wanted to talk with you about. So I've been doing some thinking—"

"You, thinking? No!"

Clint laughed. "I know, right? I've been doing a lot of thinking the past few months since we last chatted. And some *observing*, really. I've been watching you, Pete."

I sputtered on my coffee, burning my chin as some of it spilled over the side.

"Ouch!"

"Dude, you alright?" Clint said.

I wiped my chin with my shirtsleeve. "I'm fine. What do you mean by that? You've been watching me?"

"Not like a creepy stalker bromance. I mean, I've been taking note of how you've been wrestling with your own faith the past few months. Seeing how you've handled my doubt."

I cocked my head slightly. "OK...What do you mean?"

"I mean, you're not afraid to ask questions. I've never known a pastor like that before. But then you're also not just tossing away the faith, you know?" He took a sip of coffee and sat back. "Unlike me, who let everything go when the questions started coming and answers were hard to come by."

"It's not like I've been a good Christian boy myself holding on to what I've always believed," I said. "It's tough to keep on believing in the face of doubt."

"I know, but you held on! And then, even when you started shifting in your beliefs, you didn't just flip sides. You went to the middle."

"What do you mean by that?"

"Like with creation and evolution. You clearly were no Morris fan."

We both laughed. I said, "Understatement of the year."

"But then you also were a little skeptical of Bryan, even though it seems you're more where he's at than the creationist guy. You said it yourself, you don't understand why it had to take six billion years, let along six days, to create the world. You're like the master of the Golden Mean, as they say."

"The Golden Mean?"

Clint's face fell and he cocked his head to the side. "Oh, come on. You've never heard of the GM?"

I laughed. "The GM? Uhh, no."

"It's Aristotle, man! You disappoint." He shook his head. "Anyway, the Golden Mean is the spot in the middle between two extremes." He spread his hands apart to illustrate. "It's the sweet spot right there, in the middle. Like believing God created, like the Bible says, but also being willing to listen to what science has to say about the world."

I nodded. "That sounds about right. But I'm not sure I've mastered any sweet spot. Definitely still knee-deep in figuring things out."

"But that's the thing, you're figuring it out—right here..." Clint brought his hands to the center and cupped them. "That's where you're at."

He paused, then put has hands on his lap and looked down. He said, "That's where I want to be as well. Which is why I've been praying and reading the Bible again. But just the story of Jesus in the Gospels. Not ready for anything else yet."

A few beats skipped by before it dawned on me: *Does this mean he's coming back around?*

I tried not to get hopeful, but I pressed in for more, trying to draw more out.

I said, "Dude, that sounds like some sort of conversion to me."

Clint laughed. "I don't know if I'd call it a *conversion* so much as a realization. And maybe...maybe a sort of rededication."

Surprise turned to giddiness. Somehow I had a hand in God's work to bring Clint back around in his faith.

"That's quite the change, bro. From fundie to atheist and then back again?"

"I wouldn't say I was an atheist. And *definitely* not a fundie!"

"I'm kidding. Sort of. Seriously, though, this is epic!" I shifted in my chair and took a sip of coffee. "Tell me more about this. I'm curious about what it is you've realized. And what's this rededication about?"

"You're the one who helped me realize it, actually. That the Christian faith is still relevant to our world. That I don't have to pitch my childhood faith in the trash to still believe in Jesus and follow him. There's a way about the Christian faith that's still sustainable. And all it takes is a little reimagination to figure out how to still be a Christian. Doesn't mean you throw out what's basic to the faith. Like Jesus, for one, as well as sin and salvation. It just means believing in him and following him might look different in our day than it has in the past. And that's OK, because every generation rediscovers what it means to believe in him, to follow him anew. Shoot, Jesus himself talked about new wineskins replacing old ones, didn't he?"

I smiled and nodded. "Spoken like a true pastor."

Clint smirked. "I don't know about that."

"Seriously! You've got a way about you—a way with the Bible and the faith that the world needs."

He smiled and shook his head, and took a sip of coffee. "Well, I owe it all to you."

"Come on..."

"No, really! You saved my faith, Peter. It's because of the time you spent listening to me and drinking coffee with me. It's because of your *patience* with me that I'm at this point of rededication."

I felt my face flush. I took a sip of coffee, then said, "Thanks brother. It's been a pleasure. And so thrilling to see you shift and change, to grow and move forward in your walk with Jesus. It's been an honor. Truly, it has."

"Well, I need help with one more thing."

"Anything. What is it?"

"Will you pray with me?"

I raised my eyebrows, not expecting that.

"Pray for you? Sure. What for?"

"Not pray *for* me. Pray *with* me. I feel like I need to, like, recommit myself to Jesus and his Way."

"Like, pray the Sinner's Prayer?" I asked dumbfounded, and looked around. "Right here in Saxbys?"

"Not the Sinner's Prayer, exactly. I'm not coming to faith the first time. I did that when I was six. But, yeah, something like it. Do you think I can do that? Do you think he'll take me back?"

There was an eagerness and earnestness in his voice. An urgency to his question.

A smile curled at one end of my mouth. Clint's desire to publicly proclaim his new faith direction with me was humbling. Convicting, even.

"I absolutely *know* that he will! I mean, think about the apostle Peter and how he totally denied Jesus before he went to the cross. The guy basically rejected him in that denial. And what did Jesus do when he comes back to life? He went and sought Peter out, who was doing the very same thing he was doing when Jesus called him in the first place. Fishing!"

A hopeful smile stretched across Clint's face.

I continued, "It was as if Peter put a big exclamation point on his abandonment by going back to his former life before he met Jesus. It's like he thought it was over, that his relationship with Christ was dead and gone—literally, because he was crucified. Peter didn't remember what Jesus said, about him rising back from the grave. Or he didn't believe it. Either way, there Peter is in the boat. And what does Jesus do? He reveals himself to Peter and Thomas and Nathaniel on the shore while they're fishing. And when they realize who it is, they eat with him, and then Jesus confronts Peter.

"Remember that question Jesus asked the apostle Peter? That painful question? '*Simon son of John, do you love me more than these here fish?*' Of course I love you, Peter says! Jesus asks him two more times, '*Simon, do you love me?*' As you can imagine,

Peter's hurt that Jesus would ask this. He says *'you know I love you!'* And all three times Peter says this, Jesus responds by saying *'Then feed my lambs.'* Stand up, Peter, and go out and join me on mission again! Follow me and my way, a way that's going to lead to your death."

Clint nodded, his eyes dropping down, head following suit.

"You know," I continued, "I think maybe Jesus is asking us the same question. Do you love me, Clint? Do you love me, Peter Daniel Young?"

Clint's head rose again. "He's asking *you*?"

I smiled. "Sure is. Hearing you talk about your journey the past several months has made me realize I haven't been all that faithful, either. I may not have walked away, like you said you did. But I'm not sure the way I've gone about figuring out my faith in new ways has pleased Christ all that much. So I need to confess as much as you."

Clint sat up at the edge of his chair with urgency. "Will you confess with me?"

"Sure thing, friend. But only if you do the same with me."

CHAPTER 31

CLINT and I left Saxbys and hustled to my hatchback across the street as the slushy onslaught picked up its pace.

Since the passenger door was busted, he climbed in through my side. I felt a little silly, the pair of us sitting in my car, wondering about the heads turning in curiosity seeing two dudes sitting together side-by-side in an aging, sagging Honda. But whatever. I didn't care. We shoved aside the empty Saxbys cups and bags of fast food to the back, and then we stuffed ourselves inside to rededicate ourselves to our Savior, our Lord.

"Maybe we should keep our eyes open," Clint said as we closed the doors. "Just so people don't get the wrong idea."

"I think people are gonna get lots of ideas whether our eyes are open or closed!"

We both laughed and looked outside for potential passersby.

"So, how do we do this thing?" Clint said looking out the window, our breaths steaming up the inside.

"Maybe we can do what we both did as kids. Confess our rebellion and need for continued rescue. Ask God to forgive the things we've done against him and our neighbor. Receive Jesus anew as our King, and reaffirm our trust in Jesus's death and resurrection for new life."

"I like that. That sounds good. Can I go first?"

I smiled at Clint's eagerness. "For sure, bro. Go for it."

"OK." He grew silent. He stared forward, his lanky legs bunched up in my front passenger seat. Then he closed his eyes and bowed his head.

"God," he started in a hushed, reverent tone. "I've been a real jerk to you lately. Have totally treated you like crap." He stopped and turned to me. "Do you think it's alright if I say that?"

I wanted to laugh and weep all at once. Instead, I smiled. "I think God can handle your honesty."

"OK, good," he said before continuing. "So, yeah, I've been a total ass—err...I've totally turned my back on you, God. And that's a pretty crappy thing to do. I know that now. Thanks for not giving up on me—even with all my questions and doubt, especially with all my disbelief. No, my *rejection* of beliefs. I'm sorry that in rejecting certain beliefs I rejected you along the way, Jesus. I know you came to rescue me from all the crappy things I do to people—to you, too. Thanks for that. I know I *needed* you to rescue me from all the crappy things I do. I don't quite know what to make of that rescue anymore and what it means to be a Christian and all—but I know I need it. I need you, to be my Savior and Lord again. So...I guess what I want to say is, will you? Will you be who you were for me before I turned my back on you?"

His voice began to strain under the weight of his confession. I glanced over to him, and I saw a trickle of tears making its way down his left cheek. He smiled and turned to me.

"I feel like it's happened again. Like he's my Savior and Lord again. Like we're good!"

I squeezed his shoulder in celebrating his renewal. I felt my own trickle coming on as the weight of the moment settled deep in my bones. There was no greater joy than helping a fellow believer find their way back to relationship with Jesus. Perhaps the only thing better was helping someone explore and find Jesus for the first time, but still. And I got to experience that after I was fired! I said a silent prayer of thanks to Christ for giving me that moment.

"What about you?" Clint said, turning to me. "You said you needed to confess yourself."

I smiled and nodded. "Sure do. Will you sit with me here in our little confessional booth a few more minutes?"

"Absolutely!"

I bowed my head and closed my eyes. I felt awkward praying out loud, but felt I owed it to Clint—as much as I felt I needed to do it for my own soul.

"God, I echo my brother's own prayer, about being a jerk to you lately. In my rush to figure out my faith, I realize I haven't let you into that process all that much. I've just set out on my own, trying to chart my own path. That was wrong. Sorry about that, God. And then the way I've gone about it with the people in my life...I've been a jerk to them, too."

I paused, considering my ministry and my parents—how I'd treated them the past few months.

"I confess I haven't loved the people around me very well. I haven't loved you with my whole heart, mind, and strength, either. I am truly sorry and I humbly repent. For the sake of Jesus Christ have mercy on me, Father, and forgive me. So I might delight in your will and walk in your ways. To the glory of your name I pray Jesus, my Lord and Savior. Amen."

Clint echoed in agreement with his own *Amen.*

When I lifted my head I saw the trickle had returned.

"What's up, bro?" I said as I pointed to my cheek.

"Oh, that," he said, wiping his cheeks on his sleeve. "I don't know. I've never sat with someone who's done something like this. It was moving. Thrilling, really! Is that what it's like? Your job?"

"Not always. But when it is—when it *was*...Yes, it's thrilling."

"Cool..."

We crawled out of my car just as a couple walked past. The guy turned around and smirked before continuing on toward Georgetown with his girlfriend. The snowy slush had stopped its onslaught, and the sky began to open up, the clouds parting to reveal a blue sky and sun shining down.

It was like some sort of confirmation from the good Lord above.

"Thanks, Pete." Clint said. We clasped hands and embraced.

"For sure, bro."

We stood outside my car, leaning on its hood as the clouds continued parting, sun beaming down upon us, offering its warmth and comfort.

"So what's next for you, now that you're, like, unemployed?" Clint said.

"Honestly, no idea."

"You know what I think? I think I'll kick your ass if you give up on ministering to people."

I laughed. "Oh, yeah?"

"Yeah. You're too good at it. You should go be a pastor or something. Can you study for something like that?"

I was stopped by his encouragement and remembered again that word I felt back in Roger's office. *Seminary.*

"They do, actually. It's called seminary. It's like graduate school for ministers."

"Then do that. Go to cemetery!" We both laughed at his mess-up. "I mean, *seminary.*"

"Alright, little buddy. I'll think about it."

We embraced for one final goodbye. I hoped we would reunite someday, because Clint had become more of a brother than my own family. I silently prayed for Clint, that he would continue to grow in the knowledge and goodness of Christ.

I prayed the same for myself.

CHAPTER 32

"THAT'S what this has been about!" I shouted, braking hard as I rounded Dupont Circle on my way back home.

I was positively riding high on adrenaline from the elixir of our conversation. I cranked the volume to U2's "I Still Haven't Found What I'm Looking For," thanking God for the sweet victory. Not only for Clint and his spiritual journey, but for myself and my own journey. I felt vindicated from my ministry firing. I also felt lighter for having confessed my part in it all.

"Sweet, sweet victory!"

As I wound my way back home, I replayed the past few months in my head—from the first conversation with Clint to the *Everyday Evangelism* experience in Dallas, from the Alfred Morris and Bryan McLaughlin debate to the recap with my guys, and to my first sit-down with Roger and then to my firing through to the moment a few steps back when Clint rededicated his life to Jesus.

I realized this whole blasted experience the past year hadn't been about me and my story. It had been about other people's stories. Specifically Clint's.

If the Lord's taking away the surety and solidness of my faith, if his taking away even my *ministry* was what led to that moment outside Saxbys and a thousand other ones along the way to bring Clint to the point of returning to the Christian faith and transcending the fundamentalism that made him flee it in the first place—if that's what it took, then it was totally worth it.

"It *was* worth it," I affirmed, sliding into an empty spot in front of my row house.

And yet, what does one do next who's been kicked out of ministry?

I sat in my idling car, considering the question. *What is next for my life? For my ministry?*

The answer came as quickly as it came the first time I thought I heard it, and Clint encouraged it:

Seminary.

I shook my head and laughed. Twice now in the span of an hour.

God, is this from you? You really expect me to train to be a pastor—after all this?

I didn't know what I expected to hear. Sirens in the distance caught my attention, as did the bass of some pimped-out car rolling up the street behind me with oversized wheels and spinning chrome hubcaps.

I sighed and finally got out of my car, isolation and confusion stealing my joy. On my way to my apartment I checked the mail. There was a large manila envelope addressed from Coopersville.

"Mom and Dad?"

I tore open the envelope as I ascended the stairs to my apartment. Inside was a catalogue and application to Grand River Theological Seminary, one of a few ministry graduate schools back home.

A sticky note was attached to the cover of the catalogue. I was blown away by what it said:

Hi Petey,

The other day this came for you in the mail to our address by accident. Did you send for it? I thought I would send it your way. Who knows? Maybe it's a sign :)

Love,

Mom

"For real, God?" I said as I opened my apartment door.

I looked at the catalogue's cover filled with smiling, eager Midwest Christians and scoffed. "Maybe seminary is in my future, but definitely not this one. Definitely not going back home again!"

I threw it on my couch and began preparing a spaghetti dinner. I opened a bottle of wine from Trader Joe's, a Two Buck Chuck Cabernet Sauvignon. About all I could afford without going totally dry. I took a long sip, savoring the semi-heavy notes of blackberries, as cheap-tasting as it was, while stewing over the idea of leaving DC to prepare for some sort of pastoral ministry through seminary.

I made a mental list of the schools I wanted to apply to. Fuller Theological Seminary, in California, was at the top of my list. I jumped on my laptop as my sauce began to bubble, linking over to Fuller's website.

The site gleamed with California sun, matching the more progressive atmosphere and reputation it had garnered. I recognized several professors, who several Prosurgent thinkers and Darren Thomas had referenced. I filled out an online catalogue and application request form and hit *Send*, eager to apply and head to the West Coast for what I hoped was the next leg of my journey.

I closed my laptop and noticed the GRTS catalog on the

couch. I took another sip of wine, considering the school as I stirred my sauce. I took out a noodle with a fork to check its tenderness and begrudgingly shuffled back over to the couch to pick up the catalogue. I figured I might as well take a look, considering it could very well have been an act of God that brought it my way in the first place. Definitely didn't want to jinx myself by tossing it in the trash after all I'd been through.

I sauntered back to the kitchen as I read some of the history of the school, about its Baptist roots and shedding that cloak a decade ago to become a nondenominational school. Their aim was to train the next generation of Church leaders, even going so far as to offer a church planting track for Master of Divinity students. Which I found interesting as I read more about how they prepared students to engage with their changing post-Christian, postmodern world by making the Christian faith relevant to the twenty-first-century world.

Sounds right up my alley...

I read some of the bios of the professors: there was an Anglican historical theologian; an Old Testament scholar famed for his archaeological work; a New Testament professor who had written a well-received commentary on the Gospel of Matthew; and a younger theologian who had already written several books and was part of the conservative Reformed movement.

"Definitely won't get along with that guy."

I continued flipping through the catalogue and then threw it on the couch.

"Who am I kidding. Doubt my progressive, Prosurgent views will be welcomed at a school rooted in my conservative, backwater town!"

Pride, Peter. Pride.

There was that voice again. As sharp, clear—and convicting— as the one that breathed the word *Seminary* into my soul back in Roger's office.

And it was right. That ugly head of pride, once again.

I leaned against my kitchen counter and took another sip of wine. I stirred my noodles and considered that still, small voice. It returned again, telling me my pride would be the only thing driving my decision to choose a seminary like Fuller over Grand River.

It was true. I couldn't stomach the idea of going home to a place I vowed I would never again return, to a place from where I had changed so sharply.

A place I believe I'm better than, I admitted in a moment of honest self-reflection.

Yet, maybe that was exactly where I needed to be.

God, are you calling me back home?

I read the sticky note Mom had sent me. I wasn't one to look for signs and all, but I couldn't shake the fact that GRTS had sent me their catalogue. Then my mom sent it on to me. On the very day I was contemplating my next moves.

God, what are you up to?

A shiver ran up my spine thinking about the possible providential connections.

"OK, you win, Lord. I'll apply. But to both!"

JUNE FELT as cold as winter after my guys left for summer break. I tried to busy myself in both their absence and the absence of any job to go to after my temp work dried up. I filled the void by reading lots of Prosurgent writers, their books and blogs—and waiting for my acceptance or rejection from Fuller and Grand River seminaries.

One day, nearly a month after applying, two envelopes arrived. There they were, sitting side-by-side on my coffee table. One postmarked from Pasadena, California; the other from

Grand Rapids, Michigan. I tried divining their contents, too nervous to open them to see their verdicts for myself.

Finally, my nerve failed and I ripped open the envelope from California.

Dear Mr. Young,

We are pleased to inform you the admissions staff of Fuller Theological Seminary would like to invite you to the Master of Divinity program this fall...

"Score!" I yelled. I took a deep breath, relieved for some clear direction. I said a prayer of thanksgiving to the good Lord for helping direct my steps.

The rest of the letter read like a standard acceptance letter. It also outlined the second most important thing: the financial aid package.

I was surprised and disappointed how small it was, given the financial commitment to moving, living, and schooling in California. Had no idea how I could afford it, but in the moment it didn't matter. I had a future, and its name was California!

I almost forgot about the second envelope still sitting on my coffee table, an ugly duckling at that point compared to the swan I was still holding in my hand. I set down the Fuller letter and opened the one from Grand River.

Dear Mr. Young,

Thank you for applying to the Master of Divinity program at Grand River Theological Seminary. Each year we get hundreds of applicants and take great care to select the ones who have the highest potential for vocational ministry.

We are thrilled to inform you that your application was well-received and you have been selected into the program for this fall...

I smirked. Nice letter, but there went the clarity. I sighed and threw it on the coffee table. Now I had a choice between two schools.

But is it really a choice? Fuller Theological or Grand River Theological? California or Michigan? Pasadena or Grand Rapids? Progressive or traditional?

No contest!

I walked to my kitchen to open a more expensive bottle of Malbec wine from Argentina to celebrate, taking the Fuller letter with me. I re-read it before pouring a generous glass and toasting to myself.

Ahh! A good Malbec, a fantastic acceptance letter—things were looking fabulous.

From across my apartment I could see the Grand River Theological letter. It held my attention, a tractor beam tugging my attention toward it.

Is that where I need to be? Is that where you're calling me, God?

I picked up my glass and took a longer sip, trying to suppress any doubts with the oaky, peppery nectar.

Pride, Peter. Pride.

I remembered the inkling of direction I felt a month ago when I applied—the feeling that my pride would keep me from going back home again, which compelled me to apply to GRTS in the first place.

And now that feeling was racing back. And no amount of

oaky, peppery nectar would suppress it.

I felt a tinge of frustration, if not *anger* at the growing sense that God was calling me back home again.

"Why Grand Rapids, God?" I moaned. I took another long swig of my wine and let it linger in my mouth before swallowing. Then I asked again, "What's there for me?"

I didn't receive an answer. Not the way I heard and felt *Seminary*.

And yet...I just knew. Deep down I knew that God was taking me back home. I couldn't explain it. Didn't even want to try.

I walked over to my coffee table, Fuller letter and glass of Malbec in tow. I sat down and opened the GRTS letter again and set it on the table. I placed the Fuller letter next to it and stared at the choice in front of me.

A poem from Robert Frost came rushing to mind, the one about two roads diverging in a yellow wood. I had memorized it back in college, taken by its poetic metaphor for life. I wondered about it's final stanza, whether the truth of it would be true for me and my own life:

> *I shall be telling this with a sigh*
> *Somewhere ages and ages hence:*
> *Two roads diverged in a wood, and I—*
> *I took the one less traveled by,*
> *And that has made all the difference.*

But that was the question: Would taking the road less traveled—the road back home—make all the difference?

"Only one way to find out," I said with a sigh.

I crumpled up the letter postmarked "Pasadena, CA," tossed it in my trash, downed my wine, and headed to bed.

Grand River Theology Seminary, here I come!

CHAPTER 33

IT TOOK me three tries and three days to mail my positive response and deposit to Grand River Theological Seminary.

The first time I got all the way up to the USPS counter before giving some excuse about forgetting my money and quickly exiting back home. The second time, I just flat out turned back half-way to the post office. Each time I wanted to make sure —*certain!*—that I had heard God right, that I was making the right decision.

After another sleepless night, and no change in direction from the good Lord above, I went back to the neighborhood post office and shoved my envelope bound for Grand Rapids across the counter to the postal worker before I could change my mind.

I did it. I accepted my fate. Or, rather, God's providential movement in my life. And I actually felt at peace about it. *Excited* even!

For the long weeks of summer, I took it easy, knowing the next three years of my life studying to be a pastor were going to be intense. I hiked the Billy Goat Trail along the Potomac, enjoyed my final Fourth of July fireworks show on the National

Mall, dreamed and schemed with my Prosurgent DC friends about a new kind of Christian and Christianity every chance I got. I even snuck in a hike to my favorite cabin, Jones Mountain Cabin, in the Shenandoah mountains.

It was a good summer after a bad winter and spring. But now it was time to pack and say goodbye to the life I had built the last three years. By now, Mom and Dad were somewhere in Pennsylvania. Dad was driving his Chevy Silverado. Mom was driving him crazy, pestering and heckling him about his driving. I was surrounded by a scattering of my earthly possessions, trying to decide which ones to keep and which ones to pack away in the boxes piled next to my bed.

As I stuffed some long-sleeved shirts into a box, my phone rang.

"Hello?"

"So you were just gonna up and leave without sayin' goodbye?" It was Bernie, with all of his Brooklyn-accented glory.

I smiled, happy he called and feeling slightly bad I hadn't let him know about my move. But after everything went down with Campus Ministry six months ago, I didn't know where we stood.

"Hey, Bernie. Yeah, I'm moving. Back home, actually. Sorry I didn't reach out to say goodbye. But, well, with the firing and all it was a little awkward."

"I understand. I'm just glad I ran into Clint the other day. Said you're going back to Grand Rapids, something about seminary?"

"Yeah, seminary. Going to train to be a pastor. At least, I hope so."

"Sounds perfect, Pete. Always knew there was a pastor in there waiting to burst out!"

I chuckled. "Well, we'll see what happens. They might kick me out of seminary like you all—" I stopped, realizing what I was about to say.

There was silence on the other end. I hoped I hadn't hurt his feelings. But if I did, part of me was like, whatever.

"Yeah, about that, Pete...Sorry."

"No, it's fine, Bernie. I was only joking."

"Naw, I felt horrible about what happened. You know Roger. Once he jumped on the idea of cannin' ya, there was no stoppin' him."

"I understand. But, hey, make sure you give him hell for me while I'm gone."

He laughed. So did I.

"You're a good troop, Pete, a good troop. I'm just sorry things turned out the way they did. Sorry I couldn't have helped you more."

"No, you helped me more than enough," I corrected. "You're the one that supported me when I wanted to begin doing ministry a different way. You're the one who came alongside me when Roger demanded *immediate and sustained improvement with consequences up to and including termination.*" I gave my best Roger impersonation, to which we both laughed again.

Bernie said, "You're a special guy, and I wanted only the best for you. I'm gonna miss you."

"Me, too, Bernie. But we'll stay in touch, alright?"

"You better, or else I'm gonna track down your skinny little heinie!"

We said our goodbyes and ended the call. I was glad he rang me, glad I could close the door to a place that closed the door on me.

The rest of the afternoon I methodically packed my books, taking care to keep them in thematic and alphabetical order by author. The packing was slow, but cathartic. Closing up and sealing the boxes strewn about my apartment felt like a surgeon stitching together a gaping wound in order to bring the healing I so desperately desired—no, desperately *needed* from the trauma from the last year.

After taping shut the last of my boxes a little after seven, I ordered take-out Chinese from Wok and Roll a few blocks south. Thirty minutes later it arrived. I devoured my egg roll after not having eaten since the afternoon. Half-way through my Moo Goo Gai Pan my mobile rang again. I answered it.

"Pete!"

I smiled. It was Clint. I had planned on calling him the next morning before my parents arrived. I'm glad he had the same idea.

"Bro Clint! Nice to hear from you, man. How's the summer treating you?"

"Horrible. Dad thought I should start to learn what it means to be a working man. So he hooked me up with a job at a lawn care service one of his buddies owns. Have spent all summer mowing lawns and trimming rose bushes with barely any down-time. On the plus side, I've got a pretty sweet tan."

"That's definitely a plus."

"I'd rather be doing this in person, but I'm calling because I wanted to say goodbye. Well, maybe goodbye is a bad word. So long, or maybe farewell is more like it."

"Thanks, buddy. I guess I should say the same thing to you. Farewell, though we'll totally keep in touch."

"For sure. I wish I could have been there to do it in person. Actually, I had tried to make it happen, but this blasted mowing job foiled my plans."

"Yeah, you know, work. It's so overrated."

"Seriously!"

"Thanks for trying just the same."

"Of course! I mean, you're like one of the single greatest influences on my life."

I scoffed.

"I'm serious! If it wasn't for you, I'd be in a very different place. Probably fixing to be the next Richard Dawkins or something. So I just wanted to call to say thanks. For everything. For not saying anything when I just needed someone to listen to me. For not writing me off as some backslidden liberal atheist, or whatever. But then also for saying some things I needed to hear when I needed to hear them, and for kicking my butt when you needed to."

I laughed. "No problem, buddy. My pleasure."

"And, who knows. Maybe I'll join you at seminary after I graduate next year."

"Dude, that'd be awesome! You'd make a great pastor."

"You think?" Clint asked.

"Sure do. Especially since you've been through what so many other people are going through right now, the whole doubting and crisis of faith thing."

"Hmm, I'll have to think about that. Speaking of which, you excited?"

"Excited, nervous, scared. All of the above!"

"What are you scared about?"

I paused, considering my words. "Honestly, and this probably sounds lame, but I'm scared most about going back there again. Back home, I mean. About how I'll fit in at a place I've changed so much from, you know?"

"I hear that. It's been a bit daunting coming back home for the summer myself with how much I've changed. I mean, it could have been way worse had you not brought me back to my senses. But then again, I'm not where I was before. How could I be after traveling the distance I've gone. *We've* gone, together."

I nodded. "Exactly. So, yeah, I'm just nervous what it'll be like walking into seminary as a committed Prosurgent Christian— let alone walking back into my childhood home again as a committed Prosurgent Christian!"

"I hear you. But, hey, God is with you, man. And as Paul says, *'If God is for us, who can be against us,'* right?"

I smiled. I said a quick prayer thanking the Lord for not only the privilege of walking alongside Clint as his spiritual mentor, and for where he had come through his spiritual journey. But I also thanked God for his friendship.

"Right you are, brother. Right you are."

Before we hung up, we vowed to stay in touch and wished each other success and blessing for our school year in the months to come.

After ending the call, I finished my meal and crawled into bed, hoping for a good last night sleep in what had been home for the last few years.

CHAPTER 34

A HONKING CAR snapped me awake. It honked twice, then three more long, angry times.

I looked over at my alarm clock. It was blinking blue 12:00 numerals.

Crap! I had overslept.

I rolled out of bed, put on a t-shirt, and shuffled over to the window. I looked outside to see Dad's blue Silverado parked on the street out front, illegally blocking two cars against the curb.

Adrenaline surged through my belly in response to this beginning-of-the-end moment. I slipped on some jeans and went downstairs to let them in.

"Sorry," I said, voice still gravelly with sleep. "Just heard you down here. How was the drive?"

"Pleasant enough, dear," Mom said, hugging me.

"You look like you just woke up!" Dad complained as he gave me a pat on the back.

"I did. Alarm didn't go off. Had some sort of power outage last night. Sorry about that. I was planning on finishing up the packing this morning, so we've got some work to do until we can head out."

Mom said, "Come on, dear. Let's get you moved back home!"

I took my parents up to my apartment and showed them what was left to pack. Since I hadn't had breakfast yet, I headed to a bakery up the road to grab some coffee and bagels for me and the parents. On my way, I strolled past the Adam's Morgan Metro stop that was my portal into much of the city.

I passed Chet, the homeless man I befriended panhandling in front of the subway entrance. I said goodbye to him, explaining that I was leaving to study to be a pastor. He gave me a hug and thanked me for my kindness. He gave me a stick of gum, a gift for my friendship. I opened my wallet and gave him a twenty. He gave me another stick of gum before I went on my way to the bakery.

After ordering, I informed my bakery friends who had served me coffee and bagels for the past two years that I was leaving. I thanked them for their service, and they comped my order. I headed back to the apartment, trying to soak up as much of the neighborhood as I could. I was thankful it was a sunny, warm day, the kind of day that would beckon me to the Potomac to hike the Billy Goat Trail and climb the cliffs down to the waters beneath.

I tore into a bagel as I walked. "Man, I'm gonna miss this place," I said between bites. "Gonna miss my *home.*"

It was odd for me to voice that—that DC had become a home to me. Given my past, I had built up defenses to wall myself off from becoming too close to places—too close to the *people* in those places. But the people of DC were what made this place home to me. I thought about my old co-workers from Campus Ministry: Tabitha, Peggy, Ainsley, Bernie, even Roger—they all had helped make this place home. Then of course Logan, Deon, Thomás, Samuel, and Clint. They definitely made this place home. And my more recent friends from Prosurgent DC, particularly Darren.

As I rounded the corner on my street, I wondered if Grand Rapids would become home to me again. Yes, I was from there and all—my childhood home was there. But I wondered if it would *be* home once more for my young adult self. Would I feel welcomed there? Would I *be* welcomed there? Would there be people waiting to welcome me into their lives? Would I make an impact on people, like I did at Georgetown University—like I did with Clint? Would there be a good place to get a good beer? Because Lord knew I needed a good place to get good beer! Or what about a coffeeshop to make my nesting place?

I walked through the door to my row house, a sense of dread beginning to wind its way up my spine. I realized I had been disconnected from my old home for nearly seven years, between college and my time in DC. I was scared to go back, I secretly admitted to myself.

I stopped and sat on the stairwell. Setting my bag of bagels on the steps, I took a sip of coffee. I heard my parents arguing about something up above, and realized I had left them alone for too long. Questions continued to swirl, but I couldn't do anything about them. I had little control about what would unfold in my new future. But if I could make DC my home, then I could make my old home work too, I resolved.

"I got breakfast for you two," I said as I entered my soon-to-be-abandoned homestead. "Whoa! Am I all packed up?"

I set the pack of bagels and my coffee down on my bare countertop. The apartment and my former life was completely packed away, its walls a bare white with dusty hardwood floors piled with boxes.

"Yup! All packed up," Mom said, smoothing the last piece of tape on the top of one of them.

Dad said, "All set to go, Son. Got any coffee?"

I looked over at the bagels, realizing I hadn't gotten any brew for them. "I've got a coffee pot packed away somewhere."

Dad looked annoyed. "It's alright. No sense unpacking everything for a coffeepot!"

We munched on bagels as we hauled my life into the truck and trailer waiting below. Soon my apartment was empty, but for dust and corner cobwebs.

"Go ahead and head downstairs," I told Mom and Dad as I looked around my empty former life. "I'll meet you in a few minutes."

"Come on, dear," Mom said to Dad. "Let's leave Petey to say his goodbye." She patted my shoulder on her way out of the door.

I stood in the center, dust dancing in the noonday light streaming through my curtainless windows. I turned around slowly, mentally mapping the space into a permanent memory before I left.

I folded my arms, bowed my head, and closed my eyes. I put myself back at the National Cathedral, standing at the start of another labyrinth service. The harpist was playing her siren song, beckoning me to begin. As I traced the route to the center, the past year's events came flooding back: the conversations with my guys; their questions about faith, life, and everything in between; the personal doubts and crisis of faith; the talking to—make that *talkings* to by Roger; the misunderstandings and accusations and the finger pointing; the discoveries and growth and movement in my faith; the new friendships and companions along the way. I traced it all as I moved toward the center. Then I knelt in the middle of my bare apartment floor in prayer.

I prayed aloud, "Lord, you know how crazy the year has been. The questions and doubts, the struggles, the fear. But through it all, I know you've been with me, guiding and directing my path as much as caring for me while walking it. As I look back I can see how true that is."

I paused, mentally looking up at the aged neo-Gothic ceiling, imagining the throne of God hovering in that holy place.

I continued as I looked skyward. "But, Lord, as I look forward to the path ahead, I'm struggling to believe you are with me still. I mean, I feel like you are bringing me back home again. As crazy as that feels, I do know it to be true. But I guess I'm struggling to trust it. To trust *you*, that you will carry me through and provide what I need for the journey ahead. So I guess I come praying that you'll do just that. Provide the strength I need for what's ahead. Provide the people I need to encourage and support me. And please continue to provide all that I need to continue growing and changing and shifting in my relationship with you. I do trust you, God. If this year has taught me anything, it's that you really can be trusted. You've proven yourself to me over and over again! Now, Jesus, can you do it again?"

I stopped, searching my heart for more. Finding nothing else to voice, I ended with a simple "Amen."

I mentally rose and made my way out of the labyrinth, knowing that over the next three years God would lay, brick by brick, a fresh path that would look nothing like before, yet one that would be all too familiar.

When I opened my eyes, I realized that tears had flowed. In grief as much as in joy—for the past, the present, the future.

I wiped my eyes and nose on my sleeve. I took one more parting look around my barren apartment before heading out the door. I closed it with purpose without looking back, sealing shut that chapter of my life in its empty vault.

Mom and Dad were already sitting inside their Silverado. It was running and ready to journey back to Coopersville.

"You ready, Petey?" Dad asked.

"Ready as I'll ever be." I hit the hood of Dad's truck and walked around to my car. Before I got in, I took one more parting look at the window to the room that had witnessed so much change, so much pain, so much growth.

I smiled and nodded before climbing into my hatchback.

"Alright," I said through my open car window. "Let's roll."

I led the Young caravan down Lanier Place on to Columbia Road, which took us to 16th Avenue, the artery that would lead us straight to the Capital Beltway.

The Lord giveth and the Lord taketh away, they say.

After the past year of deconstruction, I prayed God was in a more generous mood for the year ahead. Because I was hoping that what I had been searching for the past year was waiting for me at the place I was from, yet vowed never again to return to.

"There's only one way to find out," I mumbled as I cranked my stereo.

I punched the accelerator at the onramp to I-495, the road that would take me back home again.

Where I would continue reimagining my faith.

ENJOY A REIMAGINED FAITH?

A big thanks for joining Peter Daniel Young and friends on their journey to reimagining out how faith connects to their world!

Here's what you can do next:
If you loved the book and have a moment to spare, **a short review is much appreciated.** Nothing fancy, just your honest take. Spreading the word is probably the #1 way you can help authors like me and help others enjoy the story.

Ready to continue Peter's quest to reimagine his faith? Grab the next book in the series. *A Rediscovered Faith* picks right up where Peter left off in his story.

You can also join another adventure by getting a full-length novel in my religious conspiracy thriller series for free! All you have to do is join the insider group to be notified of specials and new releases by going to this link:
www.jabouma.com/thriller

Continue the journey exploring a faith reimagined with your free course! Details on the next page or at www. faithreimagined.org.

Join Peter Daniel Young's own journey of exploration reimagining faith today.

Discover more at faithreimagined.org

Use discount code **RIF1FREE** at checkout

Are you interested in exploring the essence of the Christian faith but don't know where to start?

You're invited to an online learning experience designed for readers of this series to extend the reading experience and offer a way to explore the major elements of Christianity—reimagining your faith along the way.

Get free access to your course at www.faithreimagined.org and continue the journey beyond the book that Peter himself embarked on and continues through the series.

Simply apply the above discount code at checkout when you join the basic course at www.faithreimagined.org/join.

The story in these pages is a work of fiction. Yet it is more true to life than I could have imagined on my own as it follows many of the same contours of the real lives of real people.

Including my own.

You see, this story is loosely based on my own spiritual journey. It follows the major plot points during a season of my life that followed a personal crisis of faith I experienced fifteen years ago as a Christian twentysomething. So I wrote the book I wished I had and my parents had during this season of questioning and doubt. A book that would help me wade through my questions and confusion, a book that would offer some insights and direction—all so I could more authentically follow the One who died and gave himself up for me and passionately join his mission of rescue and re-creation in my world.

I chose to tell my own spiritual coming of age story through a fictional lens to hopefully provoke a conversation about faith, life, and everything in between. It could very well have been a nonfiction memoir-style book, but I hope this way of sharing my own journey through fiction rang true, and there is resonance with it for those similarly wrestling with the essence of Christianity and its connection to life.

Much of what Peter experienced I myself experienced. Like him, I grew up in what could be called Christian fundamentalism. While I appreciate the fundamentals of the faith I learned and its deep commitment to the Bible that was instilled in me, I eventually pushed back against it, particularly when it no longer seemed to be able to inform my own faith and ministry. Because like Peter, I was also trained to give answers to questions no one is really asking, like how to get saved and how to get to heaven without much concern for faith's impact on life before life after death. Unfortunately, this faith experience didn't equip me all that well to engage the world around me in meaningful ways, and it didn't help me answer people's truly visceral questions. So when I couldn't answer my friends' questions about faith and life, the weight and confusion of it all sent me on this journey to reimagine faith for our modern day.

Which brings me to a few aspects to this story that connect to real life. The ministry I worked for used a method for sharing the gospel called *Evangelism Explosion*, and both my training experience and its gospel message found in chapters 6 and 7 mirror it fairly closely. While I fully appreciate how God has used that method to bring people to faith in Jesus, that method and training provoked in me a whole host of questions about the essence of the gospel, the point of Christianity, and the nature of faith that led to my exploration of a more progressive version of evangelical Christianity. In chapters 3, 4, 5, 18, 23, and 29, I borrowed from much of that experience and the books by leaders within that movement. I also borrowed aspects of the debate between Alfred Morris and Bryan McLaughlin in chapters 14 through 16 from one held between Bill Nye and Ken Ham on February 2014, taking creative license with much of Ham's speech and debate points as a counter to McLaughlin's own points. Given the barriers that often exist for believers and nonbelievers alike surrounding the perceived conflict between science and Christianity, I thought it a good way to work through those perceptions given my own battles. Finally, I myself was also fired from ministry for many of the same reasons Peter himself was: pride and a haughty spirit, a theological and doctrinal direction that seemed to conflict with my ministry. I also distinctly remember the call to being a minister that sent me back home again to seminary—which is right where book two picks up the story.

When I set out to write the *Faith Reimagined* series, I made a few assumptions about you, the reader. I'm guessing you are currently or are on the verge of experiencing your own crisis of faith. Or maybe it's not a full-fledged crisis, but you're asking questions you haven't asked before and the creepy, crawly claws of doubt are beginning to prickle the back of your brain. Regardless, you're wondering if the Christianity of your childhood or past still connects to your modern world.

Maybe you're scared or empowered or thrilled or confused or any number of other emotions because of this crisis and period of questioning. And so you've come looking, not so much for answers, but for direction. Maybe you've read some other books looking for that direction—books that have inspired and encouraged you to explore and embrace a new kind of Christianity and to be a new kind of Christian. Maybe you're taken by those ideas or maybe you're skeptical—either way, you've come to this book to get another perspective in your quest to own your faith, maybe for the first time in your life.

Please know that I respect your journey and understand shades of it, and I'm deeply honored you've invited me along for the ride. Because I empathize with that journey, I wanted to write a set of books that offer my own story as a way to guide you along your own path of faith and life, offering what I hope are a few insights along the way. Perhaps the lessons I've learned will help.

I hope the faith journey of Peter Daniel Young is a helpful one, a journey you'll discover is less about him and more about the people he encounters along the way, and the Savior who is big enough to wade alongside us through our sea of questions and carry our boulder-sized doubts upon his shoulders. My hope is that you would learn what Peter begins to learn, and what I myself learned a decade ago: That it's only in going backward that we can truly move forward in our spiritual journey.

ALSO BY J. A. BOUMA

J. A. Bouma believes nobody should have to read bad religious fiction—whether its cheesy plots with pat answers or misrepresentations of the Christian faith and the Bible. So he wants to do something about it by telling compelling, propulsive stories that thrill as much as inspire, while offering a dose of insight along the way.

Order of Thaddeus Action-Adventure Thriller Series

Holy Shroud • Book 1

The Thirteenth Apostle • Book 2

Hidden Covenant • Book 3

American God • Book 4

Grail of Power • Book 5

Templars Rising • Book 6

Faith Reimagined Spiritual Coming-of-Age Series

A Reimagined Faith • Book 1

A Rediscovered Faith • Book 2

A Ruined Faith • Book 3 (Fall 2019)

A Resurrected Faith • Book 4 (Early 2020)

ABOUT THE AUTHOR

J. A. Bouma believes nobody should have to read bad religious fiction--whether its cheesy plots with pat answers or misrepresentations of the Christian faith and the Bible. So he wants to do something about it by telling compelling, propulsive stories that thrill as much as inspire, while offering a dose of insight along the way.

As a former congressional staffer and pastor, and bestselling author of over thirty religious fiction and nonfiction books, he blends a love for ideas and adventure, exploration and discovery, thrill and thought. With graduate degrees in Christian thought and the Bible, and armed with a voracious appetite for most mainstream genres, he tells stories you'll read with abandon and recommend with pride -- exploring the tension of faith and doubt, spirituality and culture, belief and practice, and the gritty drama that is our collective pilgrim story.

When not putting fingers to keyboard, he loves vintage jazz vinyl, a glass of Malbec, and an epic read -- preferably together. He lives in Grand Rapids with his wife, two kiddos, and rambunctious boxer-pug-terrier.

facebook.com/jaboumabooks

twitter.com/bouma

amazon.com/author/jabouma